Deadl

An Inspector Mowgley Mystery

George East

A La Puce Publications
www.la-puce.co.uk

LA PUCE PUBLICATIONS
www.la-puce.co.uk

Deadly Tide
Published by La Puce Publications

© George East 2013
This paperback edition 2018
website: www.george-east-france.com

Typesetting and design by Nigel Rice
and Francesca Brooks

This paperback edition ISBN 978-1908747-082
e-pub book version ISBN 978-1-908747-129
mobi-kindle version ISBN 978-1-908747-112

About the Author

Whilst seeking a vocation to suit his talents, George East occupied himself as a pipe fitter, welder and plumber, private detective, film and TV extra, club bouncer and DJ, demolition engineer, labourer, bread and lemonade rounds man, brewer's drayman, magazine editor, pickled onion manufacturer, snooker club and hotel manager, publican, failed rock god, TV and radio presenter, PR and marketing honcho, seamstress... and the world's first and probably only professional bed tester. He gained his early knowledge of police procedure and attitudes as a result of a number of arrests in his extreme youth. In the 1980s, he gained more of an understanding of and a definite affinity for plain clothes policemen while running an inner-city pub which acted as a local (and once as a murder room) for a whole police station's-worth of CID officers.

The world stands at the dawn of a new Millennium, but the future holds little promise for Detective Inspector Jack Mowgley. The Special Branch officer nominally in command of a major continental ferry port is a casualty of a costly divorce and rapidly-changing attitudes in the police force. The start of the new year finds the antediluvian detective seriously hung over, broke and dossing above an Indian restaurant. Worst of all, Mowgley has a new boss, and she is a woman. Then a series of grisly events occur on his patch, and the maverick police officer finds his life as well as his job at risk.

"Deliciously non-PC."

"Jack's the Lad for me."

"Deceptively clever, funny and eminently readable."

"At last, a hero for our times - if you are fed up with political correctness gone mad."

Deadly Tide main characters

(roughly in order of appearance)

Detective Inspector Jack Mowgley:
Officer supposedly in charge of police affairs and interests at the City's continental ferry port.

Sgt. Catherine 'Melons' McCarthy:
Mowgley's fierce defender, conscience, confidante and drinking companion.

Sgt. Dickie Quayle:
Capable but generally unloved member of Team Mowgley.

D.C. Stephen Mundy:
Son of Mowgley's former boss and junior member of the Fun Factory team.

Two-Shits Tanner:
Local pub landlord who earned his sobriquet by claiming to have done everything bigger, better and more times than anyone else.

Detective Chief Superintendent Cressida Hartley-Whitley:
Mowgley's new boss and feminist fast-tracker.

DCI. Jane Stanton:
Very special Special Projects Unit Officer.

Capitaine Guy Varennes:
French police officer, *amour* of Melons and friend and admirer of Mowgley and his attitude to police procedures.

Yann Cornec: Former Breton *Gendarmerie* officer and now private investigator.

Offender Profile

Name: John ('Jack') Mowgley

Rank: Detective Inspector (just)

Height: 5ft. 11inches

Weight: 16 – 17 stones (depending)

Body shape: Muscular, mostly gone to fat

Distinguishing feature: ACAB tattooed on fingers of left hand. Scar on right temple. Frequently broken nose. Right earlobe missing.

Eyes: Two

Teeth: Mostly

Hair: Dark, copious and untended

Facial type: Lived in (as if by squatters)

Favourite Haunt: Proper pubs

Favourite activity: Drinking in proper pubs

Favourite drink: Any cheap lager

Favourite smoke: Any duty free rolling tobacco

Favourite food: Indian and fry-ups

Favourite film/s star/s:
Alan Ladd in *Shane*, John Wayne in *True Grit* and *The Shootist*, Clint Eastwood in *Dirty Harry*, Paul Newman in *Hombre* and *Cool Hand Luke*, Marlon Brandon in *The Chase* and Johnny Cash in *Murder in Coweta County*.

Favourite film music themes:
Amongst others, 'The Trap', 'The Magnificent Seven', '633 Squadron' and 'The Great Escape'.

Favourite music:
Proper Rock 'n' Roll and Country & Western.

Favourite songs:
'Mystery Train', 'Ring of Fire' 'Nessun Dorma' and 'Twenty Flight Rock'.

Favourite singers:
Elvis, Johnny Cash, Ricky Nelson and many more.

Heroes:
Father and Mother, William Tyndale, Winston Churchill, Margaret Thatcher, Dennis Skinner MP, Cassius Clay/Mohammad Ali.

Politics:
Right, left and centre (depending).

Ideal woman:
Modest, demure, caring and companionable, with really big tits.

Fact

Police officers with Special Branch accreditation are based at all UK continental ferry ports. Their brief is to investigate criminal matters taking place within or involving passage through the ports.

Fiction

Although based in part on real people, places and events, the characters and events and places featuring in this story are all works of complete fiction.

Further disclaimer

The police procedures and principles followed in this book are based on fact, but may have been amended or completely abandoned in the interest of the needs of the plot, or because I got it wrong. The point is that this book, just like *Gulliver's Travels*, is fiction so don't come whingeing to me with your petty, anal cavils. If you don't like or disagree with what I have written, why not write a bloody book yourself? Everyone else is nowadays.

Dedication

Thanks are due to the Portsmouth CID's finest during the 1970s, 80s and 90s. Special thanks are due to old and sometimes arresting friends Trevor, Dougie, Floodie, Hoppy, Nick-Nick, Bingabong, Ace, Jock and most of all my hero 'Mad-Eye' Big John M. If you haven't already gone, mind how you go, lads.

Talking in tongues

Portsmouth is a treasure trove for anyone wanting to sample a whole range of dialects, slang and other alternative uses and abuses of the Queen's English. We Pomponians talk so funny for a number of reasons. To start with, the city has been a premier naval port for many centuries and the Royal Navy has a language of its own. Also, generations of naval ratings arriving in Portsmouth from all parts of the British Isles have left their regional linguistic mark. Then there is the picaresque linkage with London, and Portsmouth has long been a popular stop-off point for travelling folk. All these elements have combined to create an often impenetrable argot (even to some locals) which blends rhyming slang, Romany, naval patois and all manner of regional dialects.

I have steered clear of giving full rein to my extensive repertoire of traditional Pompey street-talk in this book, but have included the odd word or expression which might give someone not of my area and upbringing a problem of interpretation. To that end I have included a brief glossary of some of the more esoteric examples of Portsmouth *lingua franca* at the end of the book.

Part One

One

The sound of the shot echoed flatly across the open waters.

With no more than a surprised grunt, the body rolled over and slipped beneath the surface, leaving only a spreading stain of red to mark its passing.

On shore, the man straightened up, took off his head-phones and looked out to where a fishing boat chugged towards a reluctantly rising winter sun. He had heard that some professional fishermen shot any seals they spotted. There was a colony on the other side of the harbour entrance, and he had read that each one could eat up to ten percent of its body weight in fish every day. It didn't seem a lot, but an adult seal can weigh in at more than five hundred pounds. Whichever way you did the sums, that was a lot of fish. You couldn't blame the fishermen for protecting their livelihoods, but the animal rights brigade would be up in arms if they found out.

He reached down and patted Alfie's head and thought how sentimental humans could be. It was fine for the boat's crew to catch and kill thousands of fish every day because people liked to eat them. But even quite logical people would be horrified at the idea of shooting an inedible - unless you were an Eskimo - seal. He put the phones back on and started the next sweep. He'd been over this stretch of the beach every day for the past week and this would be his last trawl. It was unlikely at this time of year that he would find any recently mislaid money or valuables, but more historic shallow-buried and detectable coins, jewellery and other items worth picking up might lie in wait. This was because these hidden treasures were constantly on the move as a result of heavy seas or even modest tidal changes. The incoming tide also brought small and non-floating objects lost at sea in to the shore.

So far he had not won enough from sand, sea or stones to do more than cover the cost of his detector, petrol for journeys to and from the beach and the odd pint at the Legion. But he had convinced himself that there was some really good stuff down there, and it would make all his efforts a waste of time if he chucked it in and stopped looking. He had been hunting on this beach and coastline for more than a decade, and knew something really worthwhile was waiting for him to turn it up. Of course, all beachcombers and metal hunters thought that, or they would not do what they did in all weathers and times of day and tide. But it was undeniable that there were some very rich pickings for the lucky ones.

Finds along this part of the coast over the years included ancient coins and rings and other ornamental pieces which were sometimes made of gold. Once, a guy with a detector had literally stumbled upon what the papers described as a priceless Celtic figurine. When it had been declared treasure trove, the finder had made nearly fifty grand and something along those lines would do him nicely. If, or rather when it happened, he would buy a state-of-the-art machine and take a long break in some suitably exotic location where pirates had done their best business. The experts said that there never had been any such thing as buried treasure, but the odd mislaid doubloon or piece of booty would be quite enough to keep him going. Somewhere in the Caribbean would be nice, but until then, life was a beach on the rarely sunny and often shitty south coast.

The man half-smiled at his bad pun, then frowned as a middle-aged woman walked past with her cocker spaniel on a lead. She was not a problem, but the annoying thing for any hunter was that most of the really good stuff was found by people walking their dogs or taking an early-morning stroll. But it was about time his luck changed, and the start of a new century was a very suitable time for him to strike gold. Or anything else worth a good few bob.

He breathed deeply and set his shoulders like a warrior preparing for the fray, checked his settings and switched on the finder.

Almost immediately, a strong signal came through his headphones.

He took them off, pulled the mini-trowel from his belt, sank to his knees and began to probe the shingle.

Unsurprisingly, his search turned up nothing more exciting than a strip of metal foil and half a dozen ring-pulls. Beer or soft drink can ring-pulls were the most common cause of a signal, but if you set the machine to discriminate against them, you were also discriminating against what could be much more valuable items, including gold. He shrugged resignedly, put the handful of junk into his gash bag so he would not find it again, and stood up. Perhaps now the tide was right, he would try a bit of wet sand sounding. It looked really strange, but people did not understand that you could use a metal detector in water as long as it did not reach up to the box, and shallow waters could be the happiest of hunting grounds.

After lighting a cigarette and having a good cough, he was on his way down the beach when he saw something floating in the water. It was black and bulky and seemed about the right size, so at first he thought it was the body of the seal. Then he put on his distance glasses and felt his heart quicken. It was not a dead seal, but some sort of bag. Not a bin liner, but a proper bag. It was floating high on the gently moving surface, but showed no sign of coming in to shore.

He looked round to where Alfie was worrying a strand of seaweed encrusted with slipper limpets, and whistled. When the brindle Staffie arrived at his side, he pointed at the bag, threw a stone at it and made encouraging noises. As he had suspected, Alfie regarded the bag coolly, then put his head on one side and looked at his master as if doubting his reason. Some dogs loved the water; others like Alfie did not. In fact he clearly thought it undignified to go chasing off anywhere after something uninteresting and inedible just because his master thought it was a good idea.

Keeping his eye on the bag, the man switched the detector off and laid it carefully down on the sand well beyond the reach of the incoming tide. He thought for a moment about taking his shoes and socks off and rolling his trousers up, then saw that the bag appeared to be moving slowly away from the shore in spite of the tidal movement. Its height and square shape was probably giving it the properties of a sail, with the action of the wind helped by the slight undertow. Without bothering about his state of dress, he splashed into the shallows.

As he got closer, his heart rate upped again and his heavy breathing was caused by more than the effort of wading through the icy water. From this distance, he could see that it was no ordinary bag. It was black and roughly the shape and size of a small cricket bag, with large, looped handles. The flap was secured by two strips of leather, their stylised brass ends held in place by an ostentatiously ornate brass padlock. The bag had a crocodile skin texture, and given its overall quality, he would bet it was the real thing and not a knock-off. He was no follower of fashion, but knew that this sort of designer handbag cost a fortune. They were a very upfront way of showing other women that you or your man could afford to spend more on a handbag than a lot of people paid for their cars. Also, the sort of women who owned bags like this one did not usually use them to keep their sandwiches in. If genuine and empty it could be the best find for many a month. If not empty, it might contain something worth even more than what it would make at the weekly boot sale.

He stopped, took a last draw on his roll-up, dropped it in the water and breathed deeply to try and calm his racing pulse. The reason his heart was trying to get out of his chest was that he had fantasised about a situation like this for years. Some people dreamed of winning the lottery or having sex with a supermodel. He dreamed of being presented with a valuable gift from the gods of the sea.

He was waist deep now and within arm's length of the bag. Reaching down and taking hold of the handles, he realised it was not empty, and that whatever was in it was quite heavy. Rather than try and heft it from the sea, he turned and waded back to the shore, towing the bag by one handle.

Onshore and completely unaware of the effect of the icy wind on his wet legs, the man pulled the bag from the sea. He looked at the small golden lock, then reached for his belt and the screwdriver he used to fine tune his detector.

A little more than a mile away and on the other side of the harbour entrance, a yacht was heading for the shore. Enthusiasts would have recognised it as a Westerly Centaur, and real yachting anoraks would have known it was a little over twenty-one feet in length and eight foot five inches in the beam. The Centaur was a popular and enduring model which had been designed and launched with a suitable fanfare at the 1969 London Boat Show, and this one had obviously been well looked after. The sails were furled neatly and it was running under the power of its MD2B 25HP Volvo diesel engine at a cruising rate of around five knots. In the cockpit, the large chromed wheel was unattended and moved slightly from side to side as the vessel came in at almost a right angle to the shoreline of the deserted beach.

The keel hit bottom as the water depth dropped to less than half a fathom, but the impetus of the boat and the continuing thrust of its propeller pushed it on for another yard before the *Daydream* juddered to a stop. It sat upright in the shallows for a few moments, then slowly toppled over to one side. The engine laboured on for a little while, then coughed and stalled. Then, the lapping of the small waves against the hull was the only sound breaking the calm of the day and place.

* * *

The elegant padlock was obviously more for show than protection, and surrendered meekly to the screwdriver. Turning the swivel catch, the man separated the strips of leather and lifted the flap. It was full light now, and he could see a layer of rectangular, plastic-wrapped packages close to the top of the bag. The plastic was opaque, so he could not see what it was covering, but when he took one out it seemed solid and quite heavy. Unfortunately, it was clearly not as heavy as a gold ingot would be. He put it down and gently lifted another block out, and then another and another until there were nineteen packets ranged neatly on the sand. Their removal revealed another layer of packages. These were narrower than those in the top layer, and the shape and size was immediately familiar.

The plastic was also fairly translucent, and what he saw

through it caused his heart to beat even more strongly.

He had never owned a Euro note, but he had seen them featured on the wall of his local post office since it had become a Bureau de Change as well as issuer of stamps and tax discs. The sandwich board outside showed a selection of notes, and one of them had the same size, shape and stylised number 50 that he could see through the plastic wrapping. At a very rough guess, there would be around a hundred more notes in the packet, and there was a whole layer of packets.

As he began removing them, he realised that Alfie seemed as interested as he was in the bag's contents. The dog had begun to scrabble at the side of the bag, and was making a low, keening sound his owner had not heard before.

As he continued to empty the bag, the man became aware of a slight but distinctive odour. He thought for a moment what it reminded him of, then remembered. His regular drinking partner at the working man's club was a butcher, and though apparently quite fastidious in his dress and matters of personal hygiene he gave off the same faint, almost sweet smell.

The odour grew stronger as he removed the last of the packets and the layer of plastic sheeting he found beneath them. Alfie was now so anxious to get his nose into the bag that the man had to grab and hold his collar.

Leaning closer, he felt what he accepted to be a completely unjustifiable flutter of disappointment as he saw there appeared to be no more money in the bag. All that remained was another plastic-wrapped package, this time almost as long as the bag and roughly oval in shape. He pulled it out and, holding it up clear of Alfie's frantic scrabbling, peeled off a length of brown duct tape.

As he did so, the sickly smell increased and he instinctively turned his head away. Removing the final strips of tape, he opened the packet and saw what was inside. Then he gasped, stumbled backwards and felt a rising warm tide in his throat as he dropped the object on to the sand.

Alfie showed no such signs of aversion, and with a somehow triumphant growl he opened his jaws wide, took a firm hold on his prize and scampered away up the beach. He was a mostly obedient dog, but nobody was going to deprive him of several pounds of slightly decaying but still fairly fresh meat.

As the log book would confirm, the triple-nine call from the beach hunter was made at 8.49 a.m. As per procedure and after being taken at Netley Control Room, it was transferred to area control for Havant. As a result, the nearest patrol car to the beach was despatched on Priority One to locate the caller, detain him and tape off the immediate area of the beach where the bag had been found.

The nearest senior CID officer had been about to enjoy his first breakfast of the new century in the canteen at Cosham, but felt duty-bound to abandon it and was at the scene not long after the patrol car officers had cordoned off the beach at Sandy Point.

The Scene of Crime Officers - a middle aged male and a younger female civilian specialist - had also come from Cosham, and the man was finishing a bacon sandwich as their car pulled up by the narrow concrete strip leading to the beach. In the next hour, the white-suited pair would carefully examine the bag and its contents, and take a number of photographs of the items where they lay. Using her dual credentials as a forensic officer and fashion-conscious woman, the female half of the SOCO team declared the bag to be a genuine Hermes Birkin, valued new at around £6,000. Had it been the version with its handles studded with diamonds, she informed her bemused colleague, it would have been priced at around £30,000.

Regardless of its value, the bag would be labelled and packaged and sent for more detailed forensic examination at a central laboratory in Aldermaston. Before a sweep team was called in to conduct a fingertip search of the beach, the packets of banknotes and those containing an unknown substance would also be examined, photographed, tagged and bagged ready for despatch. The same treatment would be given to the human arm which Alfie had been persuaded to release, and also the one still in the bag. Both would be taken with all speed to the Pathology laboratory at the Queen Alexandra hospital, some five miles and fourteen minutes away, with the driver of the patrol car relishing the opportunity to use his siren and flashing lights to good effect.

TWO

The woman parked on yellow lines and walked across the road towards an alleyway which ran alongside an Indian restaurant. All was quiet, she noted, in spite of the advanced morning hour. It seemed almost as if the city had woken up, taken a look at what the new Millennium had to offer, then decided to have a lie- in.

Sidestepping a brownish, lumpy pool of what could be curry sauce, vomit or worse, she shuddered slightly, pushed the unlocked back door open and walked up the stairs, her heels clacking on the uncovered staircase. One of the doors leading off the landing was ajar, and looking through she saw a young Asian man standing by the foot of a bed. He was naked, and their eyes met before she moved on. As she climbed the steep stairs to the attic, she reflected that he had not looked embarrassed, angry or lustful; rather, his expression had been apprehensive, even fearful. Perhaps, she thought, he was not supposed to be in the building, or perhaps not in the country.

The smell of curry farts, stale rolling tobacco and unwashed socks welcomed her as she opened the door to the attic room. The curtains on the small dormer window were open but the glass was so filthy that she could only just make out the mound on the bed. But she could hear a rhythmic creaking and panting, so coughed loudly.

"Happy New Year. If you're busy I can come back."

The creaking stopped abruptly and a bedside lamp was switched on, revealing a figure sitting up in bed with a blanket around its shoulders. Detective Inspector Jack Mowgley held a spoon in one hand, and a large foil container in the other.

"It's alright, I was just trying to soften up this lamb bhoona. It's set solid."

Of all people, Sergeant Catherine McCarthy should know of and be inured to her immediate superior's little ways, but she still winced when confronted with some of his grosser excesses. He saw her expression and paused mid-spoonful.

"What's up? Lots of people have breakfast in bed."

"Yes, but not cold curry."

"Are you not being a teeny-bit racist, Sergeant? Millions of people around the world eat curry for breakfast. Anyway, for some reason I was not in a state to eat it last night and it would have been a waste and an insult to Bombay Billy to chuck it away. He left it on the stairs after closing as a New Year's present. At least that's what I hope it was left there for..."

Mowgley laid the container down, stretched, yawned, sucked thoughtfully on and then scratched himself with the spoon in an area thankfully hidden by the blanket, then asked in his best hopeful little boy manner: "Have you come to take me down the pub for a recovery session?"

"Maybe later. I'm afraid I've come to take you to work first. I did try to phone, but a strange man answered."

Mowgley ran a finger around the inside of the foil container, licked it clean, then nodded as he remembered. "Ah yes. That would be King Dong. We had a bet in the khazi at the Leopard and I lost."

Melons shook her head, reached in to her handbag and took out Mowgley's phone. "I know, I stopped off at the docks to pick it up on the way here. You owe me twenty quid. I won't even ask what the bet was."

"Good Idea. Not to ask, I mean. Put the money on my account, will you, Sergeant?" He reached out and took the phone, looking at it resentfully. "So why have you come to take me to work on a national holiday?"

"Crime never sleeps. They've found something nasty on the overnight boat from Caen."

"Well, it's a French boat, isn't it? What do you expect? Have they started putting snails and that tripe stuff on the menu again?"

"Not as far as I know. But I don't think Senora Maria Assumpta Sanchez expected to find what she did in the cabin she was about to clean."

"What, a couple having it away? Someone having a poo with the curtain not drawn?"

"No, a man's body."

"Oh." Mowgley swung his legs over the side of the bed and got down on all fours to begin a fingertip search of the floor for his smaller items of clothing. "Well, it happens, doesn't it? I read somewhere that a statistically disproportionate number of men die of a heart attack when they're on holiday. Was he getting on a bit?"

"Don't know, there was no passport or any means of identification in the cabin."

Mowgley gave an unconcerned shrug. "So what? Surely a detective of your years and training can tell from a bloke's face roughly what age he is."

Melons reached down, picked up a sock and handed it to her boss. "Not if he doesn't have a face."

"You mean someone had bashed it in?"

"No, like I said, he didn't have a face, or rather he didn't have a head. Nor any arms or legs."

* * *

Mowgley continued dressing in the car on the way to the ferry port. Although the grisly find was interfering with his plans for a leisurely day at his local, it was, he conceded, an interesting start to the new Millennium. A handful of people died on cross-Channel ferries each year, and there were procedures in place to deal with such an event in a dignified and unobtrusive way. Normally, it was someone expiring from age or with a chronic medical problem.

Much less commonly, a death on board was the result of an accident. Even more rarely it was manslaughter brought about by a fracas, and murder on board only happened in Agatha Christie whodunnits. There was the occasional death- related event of interest, as when a woman tried to smuggle the body of her elderly husband on to a ferry bound for England. He had conked out in Cherbourg the day before the couple were due to return, and she had left him in the car overnight. At the check-in she had claimed he was sleeping, but she had neglected to close his eyes. When questioned by the French police, she had said they had not taken out insurance cover for the mini-break, and she knew it would have been a lot of red tape and expense to ship him back or bury him on the wrong side of the Channel. Besides, she said candidly, he hated the French and it would have been unthinkable for him to spend eternity in their country rather than his own.

"Bugger."

Melons glanced at where he was struggling with his shirt. "What's the matter?"

"The bloody thing's shrunk in the wash. I can't do the buttons up."

She gave a scornful grunt. "Shrunk in the wash? You have to wash clothes for them to shrink. Unless you were laying about in the rain outside the pub last night, perhaps? Otherwise I have to tell you that the reason your shirt will not do up is because you have got quite porky since moving home from the scrap yard to The Midnight Tindaloo. And it can't be good for you to live on curry."

"You're verging on being racist again, Sergeant. If you don't mend your ways I might report you to our Gender Equality and Diversity Awareness Officer."

"Erm, that's me, actually."

"Who says so?"

"You did when that journo from the local rag asked if we had one."

"Oh. Okay then. Make a note to have a word with yourself."
He gave up the struggle with his shirt collar as they reached the entrance to the ferry port. Melons drove under the giant goalpost and took the lane alongside a long line of cars waiting at one of the check-in booths. An illuminated screen on top of the booth was repeatedly apologising for the delay but, Mowgley noted, did not explain that the reason the punters were being held up was because a major body part was occupying one of the cabins.

He gave a regal wave and smug smile as they sped past the row of glum and fractious faces, then sighed reflectively.

"Why oh why do they do it?"

"What?" asked his colleague.

"Spend a fortune to be banged up in a car for hours with the kids screaming and the dog being sick, then be herded on to a rusty old tub and fleeced for hours, before having two miserable weeks being ripped off in a place where the natives can't even be bothered to pretend they appreciate the billions the Brits bring over the Channel and leave in their country."

Melons shrugged. "Having rows and being ripped off is what going on holiday is all about."

"That's my point. They could have had twice as much fun and saved shed-loads of dosh by having their rows in the comfort of their own homes."

* * *

Having shown their warrant cards to an over-fussy uniform guarding the gangplank, they made their way to the main deck and its information bureau.

Being a modern French ferry, this part of the ship looked like a cross between a set in a 1970s science-fiction film and the stage area of a Eurovision song contest hosted by a minor country determined to make up for what it lacked in status and Gross National Product with a total overkill of bad taste. For not the first time, Mowgley looked around and wondered how the French were generally acknowledged as being such good designers when they were clearly so crap at it.

It was difficult to appreciate the true awfulness of the area, he thought, as it was a throng with people in various stages of frustration, irritation and bubbling rage. All the banquette seating having been taken, some passengers were sitting on their suitcases, while other mostly younger travellers sat or lay stretched out on the floor. Some of the seasoned voyagers who were more accustomed to unexplained delays browsed in the shops, while dozens of clearly unhappy passengers were milling around the information point as if looking for someone to blame.

"That's another thing I can't understand," said Mowgley as they approached the spot where Detective Sergeant Quayle was clearly failing to ignite a spark of interest in the aloof young blonde woman on the other side of the counter.

"You mean why Dickie Quayle works so hard to pull women that are obviously not interested in him?"

"No. Why they call it an Information Point when the one thing you can guarantee you won't get there is information."

"Yes," said Melons, "I suppose that's an oxymoron."

Mowgley looked across at a huge abstract sculpture in stainless steel at the foot of the heavily chromed winding staircase. "Is it? I thought it might be a rearing horse or a French fireman climbing a ladder."

"No, I mean calling it an information bureau is an oxymoron. It's a contradiction of terms, like 'sensitive man'. And talking of insensitive men..."

Quayle straightened up as they arrived. "Ah, you've arrived, then...Sir. As you can see, it's a right faux pas here."

Mowgley noted the fractional but significant pause before Quayle had tacked the 'Sir' on, and that the least popular officer in the Fun Factory had deliberately pronounced the French words as if they were English. That would be meant as a bit of revenge on the bored blonde. Nothing Quayle said or did lacked a purpose.

Clearly picking up his superior officer's irritation and almost showing his pleasure at it, Quayle went on to explain the situation. All commercial drivers and more than half the car owners had driven over the link-span and quit the port before the alarm had been raised and disembarkment stopped. The foot passengers and coach parties were, as he could see, still on board and would be held until they had been interviewed. The Spanish cleaner had serviced all the cabins which had been officially in use and were on her list, and had only looked into the Gauguin Suite to check it was all in order.

"The what?" asked Mowgley.

"The Gauguin Suite, Sir. As well as the two and four-berth cabins, there's a handful of fancy ones. They're much bigger and there's a proper bed and a telly...and a complimentary set of bath stuff and chocolates. They cost about the same as a room in a four-star hotel so aren't that popular - unless someone can afford it or has pulled on the crossing and doesn't want his style cramped by a single bunk."

Quayle smirked as if to indicate he himself had taken advantage of the facilities, and drew a scowl from his superior.

"So how did the body - and whoever put it in there - get into this 'suite'?"

"It's quite usual for people to take a cabin although they

haven't booked one, and they often turn up at the desk at some time during the crossing and pay cash. The experienced travellers know that they can get a spare cabin cheap just by waiting."

"But there's a list?"

Quayle made a wry face. "Sort of. The person behind the counter just takes the money, hands over a card key and makes a note of the cabin number."

"But not of who took it?"

"Yes, Sir."

"Yes they do make a note of the name of the booker, or yes they don't make a note?"

"Yes they don't, Sir."

Quayle went on to explain that the member of the crew who had given out the key to the cabin where the body was found was waiting in the purser's office; the cleaner who had found the unexpected occupant was also there, and in a bit of a state.

"Fancy that," said Mowgley with what he knew was wasted irony, then asked for directions to the cabin.

Leading the way through the crowd, he looked over his shoulder and asked his sergeant to be sure to put Quayle's name in the Punishment Book.

"I would if we had one," she said, "but what's his offence?"

"Being himself will do for starters. You can't get much more offensive than that."

"Fair enough. I'll get a book tomorrow."

* * *

It was not hard to locate the Gauguin Suite as there was a large uniformed constable guarding the door. In a way that implied he was suggesting the Inspector did not enter, he said that the Scenes of Crime team were inside.

"Team?" responded Mowgley with no small degree of irritation, "having a game of cricket, are they?"

As he reached for the handle, Melons' phone rang once then stopped. She moved around the corridor, then shook her head and said "Rotten signal. It's from Stephen and he never calls unless it's important. I'd better go up on deck."

Mowgley grunted. "Any bloody excuse to avoid looking at a

body." He turned away so that his sergeant would not see him take a deep breath, then pushed the handle down and opened the door.

* * *

"So what was it like?" Melons asked.

"Quite comfortable, really. The bed was well-sprung and the free chocolates were okay if you like the poncy dark kind. There was one of his crappy paintings on the wall. I think it was *Still Life with Flowers*. As I'm sure you know, after his marriage broke up, Gauguin joined a collective of American painters at Pont-Aven in Central Brittany. They got up to all sorts of naughtiness in the woods between splashing stuff on canvas, and Gauguin invented Synthetism. The idea was that the artist should paint what he saw and not what 'was'. Just an excuse for not being able to paint very well, I reckon."

"But I thought you were a big fan of Van Gogh and Impressionism?"

"I am. But Vincent was genuinely trying to break new boundaries in art and capture the moment by painting what he saw. Besides, he died in absolute poverty like an artist should. And he was really potty. Gauguin just pretended to be."

"I see." Melons exhaled a feathery stream of smoke. They were leaning on the rail of the main deck and looking out across the ferry port towards their office and local pub. "Actually, I meant what was the body like?"

"Oh, you know," said Mowgley with studied nonchalance, "once you've seen one headless and limbless torso, you've see 'em all."

"So how many have you seen before?"

"Well, none, now I think of it. I was speaking figuratively. Boom-Boom. Funny enough, it was sort of not as bad as seeing a proper body which has been messed about with. Having no arms and legs and head, it looked more like something in the back of a butcher's shop. It was just a big lump of meat and had no real...humanity."

"I bet you still honked."

"Only a bit," said her boss defensively," and I got to the toilet bowl in time. But I think SOCO were not happy with my contaminating the scene."

Melons aimed the butt of her small cigar at the narrow gap of water between the ship's side and the jetty. "Any other clues?"

"Not that I could see. The scratch 'n' sniff pair were a couple of foreigners from Southampton and not at all helpful. But they did say they'd had a good look and there was nothing in the room but the torso. No bag, no clothes, no nothing. There was a load of blood though, so they reckon he was cut up in situ."

"So it was male, then?"

"Yep. At least they'd left that little appendage. Well, not so little, really."

"At least we know where his arms are - I think."

"How do you mean?"

Melons held up her mobile. "The call from Stephen. He said that a bag has been found on the beach at Hayling Island. Looks like it had some Class 'A' stuff in it, and a load of euro notes. Oh, and a pair of arms."

Three

The Fun Factory occupied the top floor of a generally dilapidated office block in the commercial area of the ferry port. It was of the classic cubist, no-frills office block design of the 1970s. Although unimpressive in appearance and facilities and alongside the busy elevated dual carriageway leading in to the city, the Team Mowgley offices would have offered panoramic views of the port and open sea beyond had a new multi-storey car park not been put in the way.

After giving up on the lift, Mowgley and his colleague took the stairs and arrived at the door bearing the information for visitors that the whole floor had been designated a compulsory smoking area.

Being a public holiday, the civilian members of Team Mowgley were absent, but Detective Constable Stephen Mundy was working at his neatly organised desk. Lacking sufficient breath to speak as well as walk, Mowgley silently summoned the young DC to join them in the glass and partition box that served as the Inspector's office.

Inside, Mowgley draped his overcoat over a filing cabinet and collapsed into the chair behind his desk. Melons cleared away a stack of papers and perched on its edge, while DC Mundy stood almost at attention in front of it.

Stephen Mundy was tall and thin with a full head of dark, straight hair. His height and demeanour inclined him to a stoop and what Mowgley called his obliging face and generally apologetic air was claimed by some officers to be worn because of who his father was, or had been.

Chief Superintendent Sidney Mundy had until recently been the city's senior officer, and it was alleged in some quarters that he had engineered his son's attachment to Team Mowgley. If that were so, his plan to have a spy in Mowgley's camp had not worked. The young man had proved to be loyal to his new boss, and Mundy senior had been unable to glean any damaging information about his most maverick officer. Having retired in the closing months of the previous century, the former head of the City Force was now plain Mr Sidney Cyril Mundy, and spent his days working on his golf handicap and status ranking in the local Masonic lodge. Given the lack of regard between the two officers, it had initially been thought that Mundy's retirement would be a real result from Mowgley's perspective. Then came the news that the Chief Superintendent's replacement would be a woman. A book had already been started by the police club steward, and the odds on Mowgley surviving a whole year were approximate to those on Elvis Presley taking over the burger van which sat alongside the port gates. As the appointment had been so recent and Mowgley and the lady had not yet met, some punters had placed a wager against him lasting beyond their first encounter.

* * *

"So," said Mowgley a little later, "we're all happy that the arms in the bag belong to the body on the boat?"

Melons lit a cigarette. "I think all we're agreed on is that the bag was most likely dropped or chucked from a boat, whoever the arms belong to."

Mowgley frowned. "We've got a body with no arms in a cabin on an overnight cross-Channel ferry, and a pair turn up in the sea a few miles away from the port. Young Mundy says he's checked out that the tide was right, so what's your problem?"

"To start with, given the amount of drugs and cash that was in the bag with the arms, it's hardly likely to have been put over the side on purpose."

Mowgley groaned theatrically. "Why do you always have to come up with objections to the bleedin' obvious? Perhaps the cutter-upper used the bag to carry the arms up on deck to chuck them over the side and was disturbed. Or lost his grip and let the bag go."

"You may be right," said Melons in a way which indicated she did not think he was. "But there is another possibility."

Mowgley looked resigned and reached for his baccy tin.

"Go on, then, Sergeant."

"It could be that the arms don't belong to the body, and the bag could have floated away when the boat carrying it sank or was sunk."

Mowgley thoughtfully plucked a tiny bouquet of hairs from his nose and examined it with interest. "Isn't it strange," he observed, "that as you get older you grow more and more hair where you don't want it, and less and less where you do." Wiping his finger on the edge of the desk, he sighed and continued: "And what about you young Mundy; have you got any pebbles of disruption to throw into the pool of unanimity?"

DC Mundy looked nervously at Melons, who smiled encouragement. He adjusted the large knot in his tie, then said: "I've been thinking about that, Sir. The head and legs and belongings of the victim could have been weighted and ditched over the side in mid-Channel when nobody was on deck. Or they could still be on board. The arms could have been put in another bag for some specific reason."

Mowgley leaned back and looked doubtfully at the ceiling. "Hmmm. You can be sure that, at this very moment, smart-arse Quayle will be having all vehicles and baggage searched as well as all nooks and crannies on the ferry. But riddle me this. With all the attendant risks, why would the killers keep the appendages? For souvenirs?"

Mundy cleared his throat and tweaked his tie again. "It could be that it was a contract killing, and that the arms or other body parts were taken as proof that the job had been done."

"Hmmmm again." Mowgley re-commenced his nasal investigation, then said: "'Contract killing'? I hope you've not been watching too much telly. Anyway, if that were so, why would the bag end up in the water?"

"As Sergeant McCarthy said, Sir, it could have been lost

overboard from the ferry. Or it could have been transferred to another boat from the ferry. Or..."

"Go on lad. Spit it out."

"It could be that the arms don't belong to the body in the cabin, Sir."

Mowgley puffed his cheeks out. "So in other words, we don't really have a clue. So let's get back to basics. Were there any distinguishing marks on the arms?"

"There was a tattoo on the left forearm, Sir."

Mowgley looked unimpressed. "Well that narrows it down to about thirty million males in Europe."

"It was a special tattoo, Sir."

"What, you mean it had the owner's name and address on it?"

"No Sir." Mundy handed a piece of paper across the desk. "I got a description of the tattoo from someone I know who works with the SOCO team at Cosham. This is it."

Mowgley patted his shirt pocket, then the top of his head, looked perplexed and then held out a hand to Melons. Without speaking, she opened her handbag, took out a pair of reading glasses and handed them to him. He put them on and moved the paper back and forward to get the best focus. The print-out showed a shield. In the centre was a cross and a sword with its blade pointing vertically upwards. Beneath the hilt was a double- headed eagle. Under the shield were the letters SDG, and above it a depiction of a snarling tiger.

Mowgley looked over the top of his glasses at Mundy: "I take it from your smug expression that you know what it means?"

"Yes, Sir. It was quite easy to find on the Internet."

"And what did you discover?"

"It's the badge of the Serbian Volunteer Guard."

"And who might they be - some former Yugoslavian equivalent of Dad's Army?"

"No Sir. The Guard did not exist till 1990, when it was formed by twenty Red Star Belgrade football club supporters."

"You don't say? Bet they wouldn't stand much of a chance against a few members of the Provisional Millwall FC Defence League."

Mundy persisted: "The group was said to have ten thousand members at its peak. The most feared section was known as Arkan's Tigers, and they identified themselves with tattoos of the shield and a tiger on their left arms."

"And is or was there an Arkan?"

Mundy nodded. "He was the leader of the paramilitary force which was said to be equipped with arms and even tanks and helicopters by the Serbian police. They fought in Serbia and Croatia, and were alleged to have taken part in massacres involving thousands of victims."

Mowgley stopped extracting nose hair, sat back and puffed out his cheeks. "Blimey, not quite like the Home Guard, then?"

"Not really, Sir."

DC Mundy went on to explain that as well as a murderous militia leader, Arkan was a Serbian career criminal, and in the 1970s and 80s was on Interpol's Most Wanted list. He was known to have been involved in robberies, murders and drug-trafficking on a grand scale, and was now being held for crimes against humanity. If all went to plan, he would stand trial later in the year.

After Mundy had finished his report, Mowgley looked at Melons and rubbed his chin thoughtfully.

"What are you thinking?" she asked. "Do you reckon there's a link between this Tiger lot and the killing and a smuggling operation?"

Mowgley scratched his cheek thoughtfully. "What I am actually thinking is what a wonderful thing this Internet thingy is. Or not." He stood up. "Apart from that, I'm mostly thinking that I haven't had a drink since last year." Turning to Mundy the Younger, he patted him on the shoulder. "Well done, Stephen. I think we should celebrate your achievements so far by going down the pub. Have you got any money on you?"

Mundy instinctively patted his back trouser pocket, then said: "About fifty pounds, I think, Sir."

"That'll do for starters, lad. I'm sure Sergeant McCarthy will be able to set up a slate for you at the Leopard."

Four

The unmarked police car left the ferry port and joined the steady flow of traffic heading out of town. As it drew level with a black sports utility vehicle with huge chromed bumpers, Mowgley saw why the young woman at the wheel was travelling at such a modest speed. One improbably long-nailed hand was on the steering wheel, while the other was holding a mobile phone. At the same time, its owner was regarding her hair in the vanity mirror on the back of the sunshield while using a little finger of the phone- bearing hand to make minor adjustments to the outline of her lip-gloss.

Mowgley shook his head in honest admiration. "So that's what they mean by multi-tasking."

"Do what?" Melons looked across at the car as Mowgley gave the driver a mock-approving look while making an extravagant clapping display. "If it was a bloke," Melons continued, "he would have been eating a pie or doing something even worse with his spare hand."

The driver of the 4X4 looked blankly at Mowgley as he took out his warrant card and waved it at her while mouthing 'Happy New Year'.

Melons shook her head and drew away from the 4x4. As she picked up speed, she looked across at Mowgley and asked: "What was that all about?"

"What?"

"All that performance and flashing your card."

"Just wanted to throw a scare into her so perhaps she'll only do one or two things at the same time as driving in future. Did you know that 14 percent of all car accidents are caused by women looking at themselves in the rear-view mirror instead of at the road?"

"No I did not know that. What's the source? *Misogynist Monthly*?"

"Neither. I just made it up. Good though, weren't it?"

The detective turned his attention to the gaunt blocks of low-rise flats lining the dual-carriageway, the rows of washing spanning a hundred balconies making a downmarket salute to the ceaseless parade of vehicles.

"I wonder if it's true," he mused. "What?"

"That they built the flats back to front, and they were supposed to be facing and not backing on to the road. Is it possible the council could get it so wrong?"

Receiving no more response than an unconcerned shrug, Mowgley looked across from their position at the top of the flyover to the site of his former accommodations. Although the muddy acreage between the greyhound track and the creek was still littered with a selection of former military vessels and vehicles, the lightship which had formed the detective's grace-and-favour residence was no longer moored at the quayside. Neither was the WWII German submarine which had once floated alongside.

The clean-up deal between Mowgley's former school friend and proprietor of the scrap yard and the council was the result of the local authority's ongoing efforts to improve the aesthetics of the approach to what they hoped would one day become, in PR speak, 'a major honeypot maritime heritage destination'. As well as the general clear-up and a number of initiatives making use of the abandoned areas of the naval dockyard, the main project which would take the city into the next thousand years and which the authorities were most excited about was the Millennium Tower. Plans for its shape and size and exact location had not yet been made public, but it was said that the futuristic erection would prove such an attraction to paying visitors from across Europe that its design, construction and maintenance would not cost ratepayers a single penny. In Mowgley's experience, that specific claim made about any publicly-funded project usually guaranteed it would not look at all like the artist's impression, would not do what it was supposed to, and would come in wildly over time and budget.

Sitting back and trying to relax after reminding Melons that she was not in pursuit of fleeing terrorists, Mowgley closed the window she had opened and rolled a cigarette.

"Now then," he said, "you need to remind me of where we're going, and we need to discuss the important issue of what we shall call this case. Personally, I lean towards the Trunk Murder. I know the body was not found in a trunk, but 'torso' doesn't have such a nice old-fashioned ring to it."

"I agree," said Melons, "and you know it's strictly forbidden to smoke in a company car. I shall have to report you unless you light one up for me."

Taking the cigar tin from her handbag, Mowgley did so as Melons reminded him of the action plan agreed the previous evening in The Ship Leopard.

"Firstly, we're on our way to speak to the metal detectorist about his find on the beach at Hayling Island."

"Are you sure?"

"Well, I hope so. This is the A27."

"No, I mean are you sure he's a metal *detectorist*? It's a funny word, '*detectorist*' isn't it? Perhaps it should be 'metal detector operator' or 'metal detector hobbyist', though granted they both sound a bit cumbersome."

"Whatever." DS McCarthy made a dick-head sign at the driver of a BMW which had offended her. "Anyway, Mr metal detector is known as Christopher John Slape."

"Anything known, apart from his address and penchant for beachcombing?"

"It's beach-hunting if you are a metal detecting person, apparently. Beach combing is just looking for stuff that the tide has brought in and might be useful to you."

"How do you know?"

"I looked it up on the Internet. Anyway, Mr Slape lives above one of those pawn-shops-by-another-name in the shopping centre at Leigh Park. According to my enquiries, he's got no previous, is retired, never married and spends his time on the beaches of Hayling Island or in his local British Legion."

"When you say your enquiries, how do you know all that if

he's got nothing known?"

"We had a nice chat on the phone when I arranged for us to call."

"Of course. He sounds a nice enough chap, anyway. And what about Quayle and Young Mundy? What are they up to?"

"You put them both on to tracking down all the escapees from the ferry boat. The operating company has got the contact details of the passengers who got off before the torso - sorry trunk - was discovered, so now it's just the slog of tracking down all male travellers who weren't detained. Quayle has got a surprisingly large team from City CID to talk to everyone who was on board for that crossing. Stephen is calling all the passenger contact numbers as supplied to the ferry company."

"And remind me again. What are we going to be talking to Mr Slape about?"

"About finding a lot of drugs and cash as well as a pair of arms in a Hermes bag, and to ask him if he left all the contents - apart from the arms - where he found them."

* * *

"Shit."

Melons paused and turned to look at him. "What's the matter?"

"I forgot the shotgun."

"Why did you want to bring a shotgun?"

"We're in Injun territory, aren't we?"

"Oh ha ha. It's not half as bad as it used to be. Lots of people have bought their homes and made a lovely job of doing them up. And the crime rate is no worse than in most places in the city."

"And that's supposed to be a reassuring statement?"

They had arrived at what was said to be, according to who said it, the biggest or second biggest council estate in Europe. On the outskirts of the city, work had started after World War II with the intention of housing families made homeless by bombing. Over the years, the estate had become a convenient repository and overspill, and now had a population of a fair-sized town. It had also become the target for countless jokes, scary statistics and urban myths, only some of which it deserved.

Leaving the unmarked Volvo in a car park outside a downmarket supermarket, they crossed the road to the parade of shops above one of which their interviewee lived.

At the time of its conception, design and building in the early 1970s, the Parade had been a genuinely thoughtful construct. The idea was to re-create a typical neighbourhood shopping street, providing for all the daily needs of the estate. When it opened for business, the small grocery stores, butchery and bakery outlets, post office, newsagents and fish and chips shop within the precinct had thrived. Then a ring of out-of-town supermarkets had gradually encircled the vast estate and enticed the residents through their welcoming doors. Not content with that, the same supermarkets had opened smaller versions adjacent to the Parade, and the only sole traders remaining were two cafés specialising in all-day English breakfast, a unisex hairdressing salon specialising in nipple piercing, the original fish and chip shop, two Indian takeaways, a valiantly surviving newsagent and convenience store and no less than nine charity shops.

When they reached the premises above which the metal detectorist lived, Mowgley looked up and gave a small groan of disappointment.

"What's the matter?"

"When you said he lived above a pawn shop, I thought you meant a dirty book shop, not a place that sells stuff that the previous owners shouldn't have bought in the first place."

"They don't have dirty book shops anymore. It's all films now, and anyway, you can get it free on the Internet."

"Good God, is there no limit to its usefulness? And how does one gain access to this font of all knowledge?"

"You have to have a computer and be able to type."

"Ah," said Mowgley as he pressed the bell on the door beside the shop, "there's usually a catch with these things."

"He might be out," said Melons, "we're not due for another half-hour."

"I know," said Mowgley, "but I like to be early."

* * *

"Excuse the mess, I'm just sorting a few things out."

"So I see. Are you moving?"

Squeezing past an elderly television, two battered suitcases and a collapsible wheel chair, Mowgley paused at the bottom of the stairs and looked enquiringly at the man who had opened the door.

"No, just having a clear out for the charity shops. The wheelchair belongs to a lady over the road. I take her out for a walk to the park most days."

Christopher Slape appeared to be in his mid-70s, but was probably younger. Life appeared to weigh heavily on his shoulders, which were stooped. What remained of his hair was scraped uncompromisingly across a scrofulous pate, and his nose and ears looked as if they had been made for a bigger man. He wore badly-repaired half-rimmed glasses attached to a length of pink ribbon looped around his neck, and his rheumy eyes were clearly troubled. He led the way, moving with an agile but crab-like motion; as they followed him up the stairs, Mowgley saw that he was wearing a surgical boot.

Apologising again for the untidiness, Slape led the way into a room dominated by the huge television which had clearly replaced the one at the bottom of the stairs.

"Ah." Mowgley pointed at a corner. "Is that the famous detector?"

The little man nodded.

"But it looks brand new," said Mowgley admiringly, "you must look after it really well."

"Yes, I... like to keep my things nice."

Accepting the invitation to take tea, Mowgley and Melons exchanged glances as their host left the room, then the Inspector crossed to the mantelpiece, picked up a handful of brochures and began to leaf through them. As china rattled in the kitchen, he pulled one from the bundle and held it up. The cover showed a kindly-looking pirate with a peg leg. He was waving a cutlass above his head with one hand, while the other held a glass garnished with fruit and a cocktail umbrella.

Above the cutlass was an invitation to join Pirate Pete and his crew at the world-famous Caribbean fun 'n' sun 'n' sea resort of Treasure Island.

* * *

"How much do you reckon he took?"

"What do you mean? How much stuff did Brian Jones take before going for a dip in the pool? Or Jim Morrison over a lifetime?"

They were on their way back to the City, taking what Mowgley called the scenic route which avoided the motorway. He was not a good driver, was a bad passenger, and one who got worse the faster the speed.

"You know what I mean. How many packets of euros did he nick from the bag?"

"We don't know he took any."

His sergeant snorted, then pointed through the windscreen. "Oh look, there's a squadron of pigs doing a fly-past. A brand new wall-to-wall telly, and the metal detector was obviously box-fresh. *And* a load of brochures for exotic holidays in the sun. I can't see him managing all that on his state pension. The flat is rented and he's probably on top-up benefits."

"He might have won the Euromillions," said Mowgley mildly, gesturing for Melons to replace her hand on the steering wheel. "And I think it was a really nice idea for him to take the lady over the road for a holiday."

His sergeant looked across at him and shook her head. "What a strange man you are."

"That's funny coming from someone who sees squadrons of pigs in the sky."

"You know what I mean. There was 85,000 euros with the bag when SOCO arrived."

"So?"

"Well, it's an odd sort of number, isn't it?"

"'An odd sort of number'? What, you mean it's the sort of number that collects sets of false teeth or dresses in women's clothes at the weekend?"

Melons snorted again. "I mean I bet it was 100k before he lifted a few packets."

"Mind that lorry, Sergeant and stop waving your arms around, please. Since when did drug smugglers pack their bags only with round numbers in multiples of a hundred? 'It's an odd sort of number' is hardly the basis for an investigation, and besides, we have other much bigger fishes on our plate. And if he did help himself, I bet he didn't put it in the bank."

"No, but we could get a search warrant and the tax

people could ask him to explain where the money for the telly and metal detector came from."

Mowgley took his eyes off the road and turned to look at her. "Why would we want to do that?"

"Why? Because that's what we do isn't it? Or what we're supposed to do. Detect crime and prosecute criminals. Or have I got it wrong?"

"No, but there is such a thing as relative morality. Would you agree Mr Slape has probably had a shit life? He certainly wasn't at the front of the queue when they were handing out looks and physical ability. He lives in that shitty little flat and his idea of a good time is to have a cheap pint at the Legion. And in between ritzing it up there, he spends his waking hours trying to find something of value on the beach and taking an old lady out for walks. And did you see his foot?"

"So having a club foot makes it alright for him to steal money that wasn't his?"

Mowgley paused before replying, then said: "Yep, Sergeant, do you know I kinda reckon it does, in the circumstances. The money in that bag came from scumbags who made it from other scumbags. If the original owners hadn't mislaid it, it would have been spent on buying more drugs and, without being overly dramatic, causing more misery, pain and death. This way and if Mr Slape did help himself to a free sample, it gets spread around a bit by a decent man who's probably never had a bit of luck in his long life. If he was another sort of bloke, he would have whizzed the lot and been really comfy for the rest of his life. If he did nick some, it's truly what they call, usually wrongly, a victimless crime. He just got lucky for probably the first and maybe the last time in his life. And finally, if you'd been in his position, wouldn't you have had a skim off the top?"

"No I bloody wouldn't. Would you?"

Mowgley nodded: "Like a bloody shot. And mind that petrol tanker *if* you please, Sergeant..."

Five

The new Millennium was several days older.

At the Fun Factory, Mowgley was gratified to hear that progress had been made with the Trunk Murder case. Other news was not so heartening.

DS Quayle and DC Mundy had verbal reports to make, and Team Mowgley's civilian administrator had a number of messages and calls to pass on. As she informed him, the most in number and urgency had come from a senior director of the French company which owned the ferry boat in which the butchered body had been found.

After complimenting her on her new purple-tinged hair-do, Mowgley asked the eternally patient and indulgent Jo what the fuss was about.

"Basically, they want their boat back."

"Sorry pardon?"

"In accordance with your instructions, the *Kenavo* has been refused permission to sail since the discovery of the body on board and while Douglas and co have been interviewing the passengers and crew."

"But that's only been a couple of days."

"More than three, actually, and in which time, says Monsieur Davide Boulance, the company has had to cancel seven crossings and compensate or reschedule the journeys of six hundred and ninety-eight prospective passengers and their vehicles. The loss of revenue and extra costs will run into tens of thousands, says Mister B, and he is threatening to send a bill for the final tally made out to you personally."

"Oh." Mowgley looked around for inspiration. "Well, this is clearly all Quayle's fault, and if anyone should pay, it's him."

"He says it's actually your fault as he told you yesterday morning his team had finished with the passengers and the boat."

"That's a load of crap."

"He says he has the call logged and verified."

Mowgley thought about the situation for a moment, then said: "Okay, well, can you give Mr Frog a bell and be really nice to him and say he can have his boat back, and we're sorry it took so long but we are not of course as effective and efficient as our French equivalents. And, could you say how lovely I thought the Gauguin suite is, and that it might help with my investigations if I could take a trip overnight in it to sort of put myself in the victim's place and see if I can get any intuitive responses from the crossing? And, if it's no trouble could he change the complimentary chocolates to milk rather than dark? It might soften him up a bit if you sent him a sample from my forensic chocolate cupboard."

"I can ask the question, but can you really see a French line putting Curly-Wurly's in their poshest cabins?"

"I suppose not." Mowgley looked at his glum reflection in the office window, then reached for his baccy tin. "Is that it, then?"

"I'm afraid not. We had a call on the dot of opening time - and that's opening time for the office not the Ship Leopard. It was from BCU and the office of - and the snotty and very camp caller actually said 'the office of' - your new boss."

"You mean the dreaded Cressida double-barrel? What does she want?"

"You, basically. She wants you at her desk, and again the 'at her desk' bit is a direct quote from her aide-de-camp, at precisely noon tomorrow."

"Ah," said Mowgley like a vegan threatened with an undercooked steak. "is that finally it, then?"

"Isn't it enough?"

"Yes thanks."

There was better news from DS Quayle and DC Mundy.

According to Quayle, every passenger and member of crew on the *Kenavo* had been interviewed and, where relevant, their statements, contact details and interviewing officer's comments added to the murder file. He had personally interviewed the cleaner and the member of crew who had dealt with the mid- Channel booking of the Gauguin Suite.

"And what did they have to say?"

"Not much. The woman on the desk said the guy turned up while she was doing some work on the computer. He asked if he could take a cabin for the rest of the journey and she gave him the choices. She was surprised when he took the suite, especially as the journey was half over and it was the most expensive option. She said he seemed amused by the idea of taking a suite, and she assumed he wanted to impress his partner."

"How did he pay?"

"Cash, Sir." Quayle looked as patronising as he dared, then said: "I don't suppose even the dumbest murderer would leave his credit details before chopping up a body."

Mowgley restrained the urge to give his sergeant a smack and settled for fantasising what it would be like. Then he said: "And what makes you so sure that the guy who booked the cabin is the murderer and not the victim? Sloppy thinking, Sergeant."

Quayle flushed and looked for a moment as if he were thinking about responding, but obviously thought better of it and kept silent.

Mowgley smiled at having got through to the sergeant: "And what about a description of your victim-stroke-killer?"

"Piss poor...Sir. Average height and build, anywhere between late twenties and thirties. Balding with dark, short hair, swarthy and with no distinguishing features or characteristics she noticed. Dressed in an orange overall of some sort with no company name or logo she could remember. She thought he might be a lorry driver. He spoke in English."

"With an accent?"

"Not one that she could be specific about. But she was sure he wasn't Italian or Spanish or the like. If anything, she said he sounded like a Russian."

"Well, that's something, I suppose."

"Yes, I suppose so, Sir."

Assuming their intercourse was over, Quayle stood and got as far as the office door before Mowgley called after him. "Better get on to the face book, then, Douglas."

Quayle frowned. "Why would I do that, Sir? I didn't see the bloke."

"No but you took his description. Should be a piece of piss to check out if there's many swarthy, balding Slavic shortarses in the book."

Quayle looked unenthusiastic. "I was just going for lunch, Sir. Perhaps this after-"

"No," said Mowgley, smiling pleasantly, "I think you should get started straight away. It has been nearly three days since I impounded the ship, as you know; and there's not, as they liked to say in Nelson's Navy, a fucking minute to be lost..."

Quayle looked at him for a moment, then nodded silently and left the office. Mowgley crossed to the forensic cupboard and took out a bumper-sized Curly Wurly. Since its updating at the end of the year, the face book now contained more than three hundred mug shots and descriptions of terrorists, major criminals and generally nasty people who might have reason to use the ferry port. It would take Quayle at least half a day to go through it, and Mowgley would make sure he did go through it by asking for a short list of all swarthy, dark men in the book. A small victory, but it was some recompense for Quayle's stuffing him with the responsibility for the extended impounding of the ferry boat. And for his smartarse dumb insolence.

To rub it in further, he summoned DC Mundy to his office and loudly suggested that the young detective make his report over lunch at the Ship Leopard.

* * *

To naval historians, His Majesty's Ship *Leopard* was a 50-gun fourth-rated warship which saw action in the French Revolutionary, Napoleonic and 1812 Wars. In 1807, she boarded the USS *Chesapeake* in search of deserters from the Royal Navy, and nearly set off a war with what were the relatively recently United States of America. To its regulars, The Ship Leopard was the last surviving proper pub in the docklands.

If asked what they meant by proper, most of the locals would probably say it looked and smelled like a proper pub. The overarching bouquet greeting the customer was of stale cigarettes and beer, and proof of the Leopard's popularity was that the carpets stuck to one's feet while progressing to the bar. Another important factor was that food came low down on the menu of priorities, and the beer was reasonably priced. Had the Leopard stocked cask-conditioned ale there would have been little call for it, and anyway all Campaign For Real Ale members and their fellow travellers or indeed anyone with a beard and in possession of his own pewter mug was automatically barred for life and beyond.

Undoubtedly, a core reason for the success of The Ship Leopard was its location, although not in respect of passing trade. Several million passengers passed through the ferry port each way every year, but a miniscule percentage used the pub. Sited as it was behind a row of decrepit warehouses, ferry users would not know of its existence; if they did, they would probably think twice about crossing the threshold when looking through the door and seeing the decor and general customer profile.

The great bulk of the clientele of the Ship Leopard was made up by those with a variety of reasons to be in its vicinity. Virtually all made their living from the port or the boats and travellers using it. The car park of the Leopard had a higher proportion of unmarked white panel vans than outside a Dagenham factory, and the Ford Transit was clearly the vehicle of choice for those who ran a modest import or export service. Some did both, taking shipping orders of cheddar cheese, Marmite and sliced white bread on their outward journey, and stocking up on rolling tobacco, cigarettes and cases of bottled beer for their return.

Other habitués of the Ship Leopard would include fishermen, ferry company staff and crew between crossings, those who worked in the office blocks or marshalling yards, various officials and even Customs officers turning a Nelson eye to minor import offences. Together with those officially and unofficially earning a living from the docks, there would be those who made their way to the Ship Leopard just for the pleasure of so doing. Such was the pull of a characterful pub in a world of ever increasing bland conformity and chain outlets with names that were more interesting than their interiors, regulars would travel many a mile to visit the pub they were pleased to call their local.

A probable point of contention amongst all these regular and irregular regulars would be how much the Leopard's success was because of or in spite of the man whose name was above the entry door.

Some customers do not know or care who the landlord of their favourite pub is. Some use a pub because they like and respect the landlord. A surprising number use a pub regularly because, however perverse it may seem, they dislike the landlord.

For many of the regulars, the Ship Leopard was known as either the Shit Leopard or Two Shits' place. The nickname of the landlord of the Leopard had come about not because of the regularity or incidence of his bowel movements, but because of his penchant for topping any personal achievement or situation or past occupation mentioned in the pub. If a customer told of an adventure in exotic climes while in the Royal Navy, Two-Shits would have a story about his more adventurous adventures in even more exotic parts of the world while serving at a senior level or even as captain of a warship. It would be the same if the tale teller was a former soldier or airman, and Two-Shits had been known to have claimed membership of all three services and the elite Special Boat Service and Special Air Services in the same session.

Because of the ceaseless activity at the port, the Ship Leopard set its hours by custom and convenience rather than regulatory requirements, so was open more often than it was closed. A quiet session was rare, and shoulder-jostling was the norm. It is a curiosity of the British pub that customers usually prefer those that are uncomfortably busy. Perversely they like it when it is hard to find a space at the bar. This happy state was seen as normal at the Ship Leopard.

Being a weekday session, Mowgley and Melons expected to find the Ship comfortably full and their reserved seats and route to the bar kept clear. But on entry, they found a scene which would have inspired Hieronymus Bosch when stuck for a theme or subjects and situation.

Some sort of function was under way, and the flashing

lights struggling to pierce the dense fug of tobacco smoke imbued the scene with an almost other-worldly sheen. Many of the faces and bodies sporadically illuminated were unfamiliar, but it was reassuring to see that the usual suspects were out in force.

Struggling towards the bar, Mowgley noted that Billy Woolworths was still trying to convince Twiggy the barmaid that his inheritance would be through soon. Even though he knew that she knew he had earned his nickname by contriving to get himself locked in the store of that name over a long-past Christmas and that his actual name was Rafferty and his father had died deeply in debt, the comforting ritual was observed by both sides.

Further along the bar, the latest incarnation of Pompey Lil was discussing terms with a diminutive long-distance lorry driver who could have taken shelter under her prodigious, shelf-like bosom. Alongside her, Oscar Ebenezer Green was telling a small group of admirers about his exploits far above the battlefields of France in World War I.

Originally from the East End of London, Oscar had thought it wise to relocate when he had fallen out with one half of the twin brothers running the underbelly of his part of the capital in the 1960s.

Arriving in Portsmouth with a new identity and no means of income, he had set up a business making and delivering liquid concrete. The affair had prospered because of the quality of his products, and it was said he had learned to make concrete so well in his days working as a disposal agent for the murderous twins.

What made Oscar especially interesting to his regular audience was that, like Pompey Lil, he had had many former incarnations. One of them, he believed, had been the Bloody Baron Von Richthofen.

Another familiar figure and fixture of the Leopard was the aged potman WingCo. As ever, he was scurrying adroitly through the crowd collecting glasses, some of which were empty. WingCo was the little man's chosen sobriquet, and he was distinguished by being the only person in the pub who claimed to have served in more armed forces and seen more action than the landlord.

Finally reaching his destination, Mowgley braced his back

against the bar, looked around with a deep and abiding affection, breathed of the heady mix of smoke, cheap perfume, beer and more noxious fumes. Then after a brief coughing fit, he made their drinks order and asked Twiggy for a list of the full range of lunchtime specials.

"Chef has informed me," she said, joining in their regular game and leaning forward to give him a better view of her impressively deep and fulsome cleavage, "that today's choices are pasty and chips and beans, chips, beans and pasty...or-"

"Let me guess. Beans, pasty and chips?" Mowgley made a little bow and handed the imaginary menu back across the counter. "You choose for me, beloved, and my companions will have the same. And please take note that the tall weedy one will be settling our tab."

"Actually, I reckon he's rather cute."

"Well," rejoined Mowgley picking the glasses and packets of pork scratchings up from the bar with practised ease, "that's you and his mum won over, then."

Before he left the bar, he learned that the reason for the crush was a wake to mark the passing of one of the city's best-known if not always most-loved characters. Terry Trader had spent more than half a century selling goods at well below list price (if there had been lists) in the pubs and clubs of the city. His Unique Selling Point was the insinuation that the goods he sold were stolen. In fact they rarely were, but as a student of human nature he knew that the belief they were hooky would explain the apparently low price and make them seem even more attractive. The actual reason for the low price was invariably that the items were factory rejects or otherwise inferior and would rarely last more than a few outings or usages. But almost astonishingly, Terry's victims kept coming back for more, perhaps in the hope that this time their cut-price bargain would actually work and last. In some cases and highlighting another curious aspect of human nature, some of his clientele actually enjoyed being taken for a ride, as long as the journey was not too expensive or made too obvious.

Another reason for the big turnout today was that his regular customers were shocked as well as saddened to hear of his demise. Like Pompey Lil, Tel had been a constant factor in the pubs of the city for many decades, and an unchanging constancy in a constantly changing world. He had also been complaining of a severe heart condition for at least forty years, and so even his youngest friends and customers had naturally assumed he would outlive them.

As he reached the table normally reserved for his exclusive use, Mowgley saw that it had become a temporary shrine to the deceased. It had been covered with an almost clean tablecloth, at the centre of which stood a plain urn containing Terry's ashes. Around it, as a warrior would lie in state surrounded by shield, spear and helmet, a display had been made of his most memorable if not successful lines. An open box revealed a layer of chocolates which were white with age and not by design, yet bore a stick-on sell-by date of the following year. Alongside was a complete set of ornate and allegedly gold-plated cutlery with what the box promised as a lifetime guarantee, but which had already lost much of the glister and all the handles from the knives. Thus would Terry Trader be remembered. But he had had, as most of his past victims would agree and say, not an ounce of harm in him, and that was why his wake was so well attended. It was also, of course, a good excuse for a piss-up.

* * *

"Very nice," said Inspector Mowgley, pushing his plate away and raising his voice over the repetitive bass beat of the disco, "so off we go, Stevie boy. Have you got a name and a face for the body?"

"I'm pretty sure I have, Sir."

DC Mundy reached into an inside pocket and produced a folded piece of paper.

As Mowgley took it, Mundy explained: "There were over a hundred commercial drivers and car owners who disembarked and left the port before the body was discovered. It was no problem tracing the commercial drivers, as we just went through their offices and depots. Of course, we knew the victim was probably not a commercial driver as there were no abandoned lorries on board. Though if he were, the killer may have taken his rig. Anyway, we know that not to be the case, as all drivers turned out to be bona fide. The owners of the thirty cars, seven motorbikes and four bicycles were also fairly easy to trace and check, though we had to call in the help of a couple of regional forces to do the leg work. They all turned out to have arrived safely home, except one female driver who was unfortunately killed in a road accident just outside Rotherham."

"So are you telling us that every passenger is accounted for, and the body belongs to someone who was not officially on board?"

"No Sir. There was one male who was booked on the crossing and who definitely boarded the boat but is still unaccounted for."

Melons lit a small cigar, then leaned forward. "How do you know he definitely caught the ferry, Stephen? There's a record of all passengers who have passed through check-in at the kiosks, but nothing between then and actually boarding the ship."

"That's right, Sergeant. There were in fact two cars and one van which passed through check-in but did not board. One of the cars broke down before reaching the linkspan. The van was seized by French Customs because of its contents, and the other car because its driver was Known and Wanted."

"Okay." Mowgley looked meaningfully at his empty glass, then held up the piece of paper. "All tickety-boo so far, young Mundy. But can you cut to the chase? How do you know or reckon you know that-" he paused to refer to the sheet of paper "-David Christopher Burgess is the owner of the body on the boat?"

"Erm, I don't, Sir. What we can be sure of is that Mr Burgess checked in at Caen, embarked, and was on board during the crossing."

"Before we go any further, is anything known about Mr B?" Mundy shook his head. "Afraid not, Sir. Clean sheet except for a few points on his driving licence, so no fingerprints or DNA on record."

"And how can you be so sure he was on board?" asked Melons.

"He was or is a boat trader," said Mundy. "He buys launches and sailing boats on this side of the Channel and sells them in France, where they can fetch almost twice as much as in Britain. Sometimes he delivers boats for people living in France, and sometimes he brings boats back to Britain. The smaller ones are taken across on a trailer on board a ferry. The bigger ones he will take over by sea."

"And how come you know all this?" asked Mowgley.

"Mr Burgess is very well-known by the crew, Sir. He travels frequently with the company, and has an arrangement with the deck hands so his van and trailer will be in pole position for disembarkation. He gets to be first on and off, and they get a regular little sign of appreciation in cash or goods."

"So what makes you think he's the victim?" asked Melons. "I don't remember any mention of a boat and a trailer being left on board."

"No, Sergeant, and that's the point," said Mundy. "His van and the boat he was bringing over left the ferry and the port okay, but he has been uncontactable since then. He's not answering the mobile he uses for all his contacts with the ferry company, nor is he responding to messages to his e-mail address."

"So what?" Mowgley interjected testily. "He could be in mid-Channel delivering a boat. It's what he does, for God's sake."

"Yes Sir, but..."

"But what?"

"One of the deckhands who knows him well saw the van and trailer off the boat. He said that Mr Burgess always flashes his lights in thanks when he's going over the linkspan, but this time he didn't."

"Big deal. Perhaps he was in a bad mood or had something on his mind."

"Not according to the deckhand, Sir. He said he got a good look through the windscreen when the van passed him, and he's sure the driver wasn't Mr Burgess."

"Ah." Jack stood and reached down for the empty glasses. "Now you're talking, lad. I am so impressed, I am going to break the habit and rule of my pub career and not only buy the drinks, but go and get them."

"And there's more," said Melons, laying a hand on his arm.

"More what? Pork scratchings?"

"Nope. Don't look now but there's a bloke playing pool and he's got a tattoo on his arm."

"I don't believe it. A man playing pool with a tattoo on his arm. Surely not, Batwoman?"

"Not any old tattoo, boss. It's the same as the one on the arm in the Hermes bag."

Six

"So do you reckon it's him?"

Mowgley sat up and looked sharply at the man at the wheel of a blue Jaguar which was streaking past.

"What, him?"

She sighed. "No. You know who I mean. The body. You reckon it's Burgess?"

"I bloody hope so, or we've got a right mystery on our hands."

Melons touched the brakes to give a bad moment to the driver of the white van too close behind, then took the turn-off signposted to Hayling Island.

"Well, at least we know about the swarthy little bloke who booked the cabin. If he's the one who drove Burgess's van off the boat, it sounds like he's our man."

"Sure does."

"What I want to know is, if it was him, why would he want to kill a small-time boat trader and then dismember his body?"

"Perhaps he was a dissatisfied customer."

"No, seriously. Why go to all that bother and mess?"

Mowgley gave a medium-strength shrug and took the lid off his baccy tin. "Dunno. Why do so many people cut their victims up?"

It was Melons' turn to shrug.

"Unless they enjoy the odd bit of butchery and cannibalism like Jeff Dahmer, I would say it's nearly always to try and stop identification of the body."

"Correct," agreed Mowgley. "But the best way would have been to have dumped the torso over the side as well. Then everyone would have assumed Mr B had left the boat in good order and one piece."

Melons sighed. "But we've been all through that. It could have been that the torso was too big to get up to the deck, or he ran out of time or was disturbed."

"Perhaps. But just let your mind run free, Sergeant, and imagine that he wasn't too bothered about identification. If not, why then go to all that trouble, and clean out the cabin and take the victim's bags and passport?"

"I dunno. You tell me."

Mowgley inspected his roll-up, nodding in satisfaction at its near-perfection.

"Maybe just to slow things down for a while. Remember, the body was found in the suite and not the cabin which Burgess was booked in to. And the van and trailer had been driven off, which would indicate that Burgess was alive and well. If the deckhand hadn't spotted the driver of the van was not Mr B, it could have been weeks before we cottoned on."

"So you reckon he was happy for us to find out it was Burgess, but not for a while?"

Mowgley looked out of the window, let a stream of smoke dribble from the corner of his mouth, then shook his head. "I reckon he may have actually *wanted* us to find out it was Burgess."

"Okay, I'm with you so far, I think. But there's another tricksy little question."

"Where we're going to have lunch?"

Melons pressed on: "If it is Burgess's arms in the bag, why would a British subject have the badge of the Serbian Defence League tattooed on himself?"

"Why do stroppy kids with not a drop of Irish blood in them have IRA tattoos? Why do people living in Calcutta have the Manchester United badge done on their arms? Why does anyone have tattoos?"

"You did." Melons looked pointedly at the letters A.C.A.B. emblazoned on the fingers of his left hand.

"Yes, but not voluntarily. And don't forget that bloke in the pub had the same badge on his arm."

"But he turned out to be a Polish truck driver and a former supporter of Red Star Belgrade. Or so he said."

"That's not really the point, Sergeant. I don't pay you to come up with objections to my hypotheses, if hypotheses is the plural of hypothesis."

Melons frowned. "It's a bit like consortium or consortia isn't it? Plurals can be tricky."

"Pass again. It's all Greek to me. Boom-Boom."

* * *

As the name implies, Hayling Island is detached from the rest of the United Kingdom. Unlike some so-called islands, it is a true claimant to the title and joined to the south coast only by a sturdy bridge. The bridge needs to be strong and resilient, as up to 20,000 vehicles pass across it every day.

Hayling is roughly the size of its neighbour, but less populated by a factor of ten than Portsea Island, on which lies the city of Portsmouth. In the years when Britons took their holidays on home ground and were grateful for what they got, Hayling Island was a popular working-class resort. Those who liked to be organised would take an all-in week at one of the three holiday camps. More independently-minded or less well-breeched families would take a caravan or wooden chalet about the same size, and sometimes not much better-appointed than a garden shed. At peak demand, some residents were known to let out their sheds or garages. Once embedded, the holidaymakers' days would be spent on the beaches in anything but really inclement weather, or visiting the funfair and amusement arcades. At other times they would just walk up and down the narrow strip of concrete which passed as a promenade. Evenings would be spent sitting in one of the handful of pubs while nursing a watery pint or port and lemon. On nice evenings there might be a game of French cricket outside their chalet. A welcome visitor was the night soil man, who would arrive in his lorry at some time after dusk to pick up the contents of the chemical toilets.

In its heyday, Hayling Island offered an affordable break from work and familiar surroundings for millions during the first half of the 20th century. Then, as ordinary working people began to splash out on package holidays in exotic locations abroad, the glory days were but memories. The chalets, crazy golf course and most of the amusement arcades disappeared to be replaced by neat bungalows lining the seafront road. The remaining holiday camps worked at changing their image and facilities as the island became ever more residential. Elderly people with false memories of endless sunny childhood holidays retired to die where they had spent such happy times, and it was said that there were more disability scooters per head of population on Hayling Island than anywhere else on the planet. In recent years, the scooters had become so common on the Island that they became known as Hayling cabriolets. Nowadays, the population was an uneasy mix of the elderly, middle-aged and terminally bored youngsters.

Although the other holiday accommodations had suffered with the decline of the holiday trade, the handful of caravan parks had adapted to survive. Some had bars and swimming pools and offered for sale, as the brochure said, affordable holiday homes. Others contained a mixture of old and new caravans belonging to owners or renters who lived in them year round. Bay Tree Park was one of these communities, and, according to the ferry company's contact details, where David Burgess spent his time between voyages.

* * *

"Mind that chicken, Sergeant."

Had they been houses, the location and view from the shoreline across the mud flats and bay to the distant rolling downs of Sussex would have bestowed a value beyond rubies upon the caravans at Bay Tree Park. As it was, the going rate for a no-longer mobile home with a picket fence marking the garden boundaries was no more than the price of a one-bedroom flat in a not-so-salubrious part of Portsmouth.

Melons having avoided the chickens and parked near the five-barred gate leading on to the park, Mowgley levered himself out of the car.

"Are you looking for someone?"

He had noted a twitch of the net curtains in the caravan nearest to the gate, which was why he had instructed his sergeant to park there. Because of where she lived, the elderly lady standing in the doorway of the small grey caravan would be familiar with the comings and goings of residents and visitors; with luck, she would probably also know more about the residents than they could have guessed or would like.

"Morning." Mowgley nodded and smiled ingratiatingly, then turned to his sergeant. "Did I see a little shop on the way down the lane?"

"You did, and it was open."

"Good. I'll stroll up there while you have a word with the dragon at the gate. I bet she'll know what colour underpants Mr B wears as well as where his caravan is - and where he is or is supposed to be right now."

"But don't you want to be there when he answers the door if he's at home?"

"If he is, I don't want to spook him and I bet he'd rather find you on the doorstep than me. But I have a funny feeling you'll find the place locked up. If he is on the premises, have a nice little chat with him and then give me a bell so I can turn up and play the heavy."

"But why the shop - are you low on baccy or fag papers?"

"No, just want to find out what the person behind the counter knows about our boaty man."

"So if he's not at home I'll meet you back here?"

Mowgley looked at where his watch would be had he worn one, stroked an imaginary beard and shook his head: "I did notice there's a friendly-looking pub back along the lane a bit before the shop. And according to the sign it sells home-made pastys. I feel it my duty to drop in and see if our man used the premises at all. I'll meet you there when you've made your enquiries. I'll be the bloke with the Daily Mail and a pie and pint..."

* * *

A half hour later, Melons found Mowgley in commune with a large pig.

"What's his name?"

Mowgley looked up. "This is Patsy. Patsy, this is Melons, or Sergeant McCarthy if she's got a strop on."

Fumbling in her bag for her cigar tin, Melons took a seat at the bench table next to the sty and reached for the smaller of the two glasses.

"Why have you put a beer mat on top?" she asked as she lit up. "There's not many wasps about at this time of year."

"To keep it warm, of course." He turned back to Patsy and ran a hand down her bristly spine, then sighed. "Why can't all females be like you? Amicable, non-confrontational and not obsessed with personal hygiene and being a tad overweight. And I bet you'd always buy your round."

"Are you talking to me or the pig?"

"Touché, Sergeant."

"Do you think it's a good idea to be feeding her with that pie?"

"Like me, I am sure she would have preferred a pasty, but they're not ready yet. This was just a stopgap."

"I meant that it's a *pork* pie."

"I don't think she's a Jewish pig."

Melons gave up the struggle and took a sip of cider. "Mmmm, very good. Do my eyes deceive me, or are you drinking beer without a single bubble in it?"

Mowgley looked defensively at his glass.

"I'd hate to be thought of as predictable. It's brewed here in that barn, and in spite of its silly name it tastes quite good. What with Patsy and the home-made pies and all this pastoral stuff and the tranquillity, I thought ..." He paused and took a reflective swallow, then said: "Do you know, I reckon I could be happy here."

"What, in this pub?"

"No, I mean living here, on the island. I could rent one of those caravans near the water, sort out a veg patch, keep a few chickens and get a little boat and go out fishing on a long sunny summer day, then stroll up the lane for a pie and a pint with Patsy until she and the pies became one."

"Yeah, right." Melons scratched her chin in an exaggerated manner. "I bet you'd go mad in a week without all the traffic and people to get fed up with and have a rant about. You'd be sure to set fire to the caravan through smoking in bed, and get stuck in the mud in your boat, and be barred from the pub for upsetting the staff and customers as well as the landlord. Anyway, you've already got a country seat."

"A what?"

"*La Cour* - The Yard. Your stately home in Normandy. Or rather your home in a state in Normandy. Don't you fancy retiring there when you've had enough of this stuff or get caught?"

Mowgley looked over her shoulder into the future and its possibilities. "I dunno. It would be nice to be Mowgley of the Yard, but I can't live in it till it's habitable, and can't afford to do that while I'm working, let alone when I've jacked it in and trying to live on what's left of my pension after Madge the Cow has had her whack. Anyway, France is nice to visit, but I don't think I'd like to live there. There's no real pubs or proper English curry shops, the *Telegraph* and *Mail* cost a fortune and hardly any of the locals can speak English. Anyway, a man can change and Hayling isn't as dead as you might think. There's a tidy few Class 'A' transactions going on at any time, what with the island being nicely placed next door to Pompey and up the road from London. Then there's a handy stretch of shoreline only a couple of hours in a fast boat from Holland. *And* there's a bit of a scene going on here. One of the local uniforms was telling me the other day that there's a lot of swinging action amongst the over-Sixties."

"Geddaway?" Melons knew what was coming but obliged with his cue.

"Yep. He said he went to a wife-swapping party and got a nice flat-screen TV for her. Boom-Boom."

"And I bet you didn't know they give the male residents in the old folks' homes here a shot of Viagra every night."

"No, surely not?" Melons yawned. "So they can have sex with the old ladies?"

"No, to stop them falling out of bed."

"Boom-Boom again."

Melons reached for Mowgley's glass. "Do you want me to tell you what I found out now, or after I get a refill?"

"Are you serious? And check if the pastys are ready yet. If so, one for me and one for Patsy, if you please."

* * *

When lunch had been taken, Melons told Mowgley of her investigations at the caravan site and conversation with the unofficial warden.

"You were right. Mr Burgess was not at home, and according to the guardian at the gate, he hasn't been home for the best part of three weeks. Well, two weeks and four days exactly. Mrs Tallock has got a very precise recall facility."

"You mean she's got a good memory for her age?"

"No, I mean she's got a log book and makes a note when any of the residents come and go."

"You are kidding."

"Nope. It's what she does to fill her day, the poor old soul. Anyway, her records show that the date Mr B last passed through the gate coincides nicely with his outward bound booking with the ferry company. He must have gone straight to the ferry port from here, and we know he started his return journey according to schedule."

"So you're betting he's the owner of the body on board? Is that what you're putting your twenty quid on?"

"Not yet," said Melons, giving Patsy the last of her pasty. "He could have delivered the boat to some distant place and not got back here yet."

"And put a swarthy, bald mask on before he got into the van?"

She shook her head. "The loader may have been mistaken; or he might have confused Mr B's van with another one."

"Which was also towing a seventeen foot day boat with a blue cuddy cabin?"

"Well no," Melons conceded. "Anyway, that's my report. What about you? Do you know something I don't as a result of speaking to the shopkeeper?"

"A bit. She said Burgess came in now and then for top-up stuff. Usually instant meals and snacks like bars of chocolate and biscuits. He didn't have much to say for himself, and never took a paper or bought cigarettes or booze."

"Well, he wouldn't need to with all his back-and-forwarding across the Channel, would he?" Melons looked contemplatively at Patsy.

"So that's it, then? All we can do is wait and see if he shows up here, or someone finds any more of his bits."

"There is something we can do."

"What, have another drink?"

"Well, that as well, yes, but I'm thinking of a trip across the Channel when I've had my first meeting with our new boss."

"It might be your last if you get on her wrong side. Best not to take a return ticket, perhaps. But why the trip? Are we short of supplies?"

"No, but across the water is where Mr Burgess has his second home."

"Do what?"

"The lady in the shop said when he was last in he bought a shipping order of Pot Noodles, jars of Marmite, treacle, Penguins and biscuits. When she said it was a lot, he said the grub wasn't for the caravan. He said you couldn't get proper food like that in France. When she asked if he was going to smuggle it into his hotel room, he said he had a little boat that he lived on when he was that side of the Channel."

"Blimey. That could be of interest. And did he say what the boat was called and where it's parked?"

"It's 'berthed', not parked, Sergeant. That is if it's in the water, of course, and not on legs in a car park somewhere. In which case, then I suppose you could be right with the terminology. No, all he said was that it was in Normandy."

"Well, that narrows it down a bit. So you reckon on going over and calling in at all the marinas and boatyards in Normandy to ask if any Brits live on board?"

"I think we can do better than that. With a bit of luck and as he's a professional and would want to keep his nose clean with the authorities, Mr Burgess has hopefully had his liveaboard boat registered in his name in the UK or France. Young Mundy will know how to find that sort of thing out. All we have to do is think of someone in Normandy who can make the necessary enquiries over there."

"Ah!" Melons' face lit up and it was her turn to look beyond the pub garden and think of future possibilities. "Are you thinking what I am thinking, Sir?"

Mowgley shuddered. "I certainly hope not, Sergeant McCarthy. What you get up to off-duty is literally your own affair, but I don't even want to think about it. I am just interested in you using your influence on your *Gendarmerie* bit on the side."

"I'll call Guy tomorrow." She got up and collected their glasses. "I'll also ask for SOCO to give the caravan a good going-over. They should get something to compare with the body in the cabin. Time for another drink?"

"Indubitably. And pastys all round again, if you please.

They are only tiny, and Patsy looks peckish. Blimey, I think I've got it!"

Melons paused and looked back. "What, you've solved the Trunk Murder Mystery already?"

"No. I just worked out why she's called Patsy. It's an anagram of what she is going to become. A pasty..."

Seven

Detective Inspector Mowgley shifted uneasily on the unyielding bench and looked glumly at the row of posters on the opposite wall.

As he transferred his weight on to the other buttock, he thought about when Central had been a proper station and the centre of police activity in the city. Then, the CID and Traffic had each had their own floors with the top one devoted to the police club. More booze was consumed there than in a busy pub, and the regulars would only have to stagger down the stairs and back to work.

In those days there would also have been a real uniform on the front desk, not some civilian with a fancy costume to try and reassure the public she would or could do anything about their problems. If they could get in to ask for help when they needed it. Unlike crime, the building now kept office hours. It had also taken him several minutes to gain the attention of the woman on the desk and get her to press the button to release the lock. He'd only managed that by banging heavily and repeatedly on the expensively smoked glass door and starting to unzip his fly.

Now he sat waiting for his first meeting with his new superior officer, reflecting on how it was not just the building and what went on in it that had changed. According to Dickie Quayle's contacts at what they now had to call BCU HQ,

Cressida Hartley-Whitley was from exactly the sort of background her name suggested. After acquiring a double First at Cambridge in subjects completely unrelated to police work, she had been fast-tracked at Bramshill and had been appointed amidst much self-congratulatory PR trumpeting as the first female Chief Superintendent in Hampshire.

The smart money was on her becoming the first female Chief Constable for the county. In spite of himself, Mowgley conceded that she might be a capable woman, and her name and privileged breeding was not her fault. She was clearly clever enough to decide to follow a career in police work at the best of all times for an ambitious woman with a good education and understanding of how to use her gender as a playing card.

It had taken years to overcome covert and sometimes overt opposition to women holding virtually any rank. Now it had become fashionable, the feminisation of the Force was going ahead at full tilt. But that was how it was, and there was no point in trying to oppose the inevitable. The thing about pissing into the wind was that it got you wet. He was just glad that he was coming up for the end of his time in the job. It wasn't that he thought women at the top would make any worse a fist of it than a lot of the male officers he had worked under. It was just that, in his experience, taking a female-skewed view of crime and suitable punishments did not result in much natural justice being done.

While he waited, he passed the time judging and awarding points based on the level of banality of the posters on the wall of the reception area. He had just given top prize to one warning of the dangers of drink-driving when the Chief Superintendent's personal assistant arrived to lead him to her domain. He had read somewhere that people make up their minds as to what they think of and how they are going to work with new colleagues within five seconds of meeting. Somehow, he did not think it would take either he or his new boss that long.

* * *

The road between Central and the nearest pub was busy. In a bad mood, Mowgley took a sour pleasure in walking very slowly across it, staggering slightly to give the impression he had been drinking. As he knew, it was a fact that far fewer drunks than sober people were injured while crossing roads. This might be because more people who were sober than drunk crossed roads on any given day, but that would be too prosaic a reason for him.

Directly opposite the entrance to the station was the CID's former local, used when they wanted to do some ferreting or had a reason not to be seen in the police club. It was also handy to have somewhere to drink when the club was shut, as the owner of The Labour In Vain valued liberty and self-determination above the strict terms of his licence. 'Lock-in' had taken on a new meaning when the going got really serious, and several of the CID officers had found the cells beneath the station accommodating when home was too far away to walk and too risky to drive to. Even in the old days, uniforms showed no clemency to plain clothes officers who were over the limit; some actually took pleasure in pinching them.

Now the pub had become an estate agency, and the one further down the road was now a building society. The nearest place to get a drink was in a cut-rate hotel which had sprung up on the site of an old laundry.

Mowgley thought about how life and places changed, mostly for ill, shivered against the cold and the future and headed for the bar.

* * *

"Fancy meeting you here."

Mowgley looked up from his crossword. "Are you working undercover or should I address you by your rank, Ma'am?"

It was the second police officer he had met that day with a higher rank than he, and that both had been female was in harmony with the changing times.

When ushered in to her office Mowgley had found his new boss at her desk. Although bigger than Mowgley's by a factor of three, it was completely free of paper except for the sheet she was studying. It probably bore no more than the canteen menu for the day, Mowgley conjectured. Although new to the job, she was obviously *au fait* with the old trick of keeping your inferiors waiting and in their place by pretending to be busy.

And of course, letting them know that you were only pretending.

As he stood schoolboy-like in front of the flight-deck desk, his eyes had met those of another woman, sitting in the bay window behind Ms Hartley-Whitley. At first he had thought she might be his new boss's permanent assistant or PR woman, but she did not look the sort who would find bag-carrying or making up stories for a living an enjoyable or even bearable activity. She had looked at him coolly for a moment, then given a smile which showed she knew that he knew what was going on in the room. She was also a real corker.

Although she had been seated, it was obvious she was tall, nearly as tall as Mowgley. She was also, he reckoned, about seven stone lighter, and much younger. Her dark hair was cut raggedly short and streaked with blonde highlights. It was not, though, as short as the savage crop affected by the new head of the city force. Cressida Hartley-Whitley went for the I'm too-busy-and-self-confident-to-be-bothered-about-my-hair look, which, Mowgley reckoned, would take a fair bit of time and attention to make it look that way.

Unlike the DCS, the mystery woman was clearly not afraid of using make-up. Some of it accentuated her large eyes, and some her wide, full lips. He noted that her neatly symmetrical ears were tiny and lay flat back against her head; they also had no lobes. In spite of that situation, she had found somewhere to hang long, dangly earrings which, as she nodded to him, moved in a way Mowgley found somehow disturbing.

Now she was standing over him, and he found her proximity even more disturbing. Without looking too overtly, he saw that her fitted skirt finished well above her knees, and that the matching jacket was also fitted to emphasise the narrowness of her waist when compared to the flare of her hips and generosity of her breasts. Had he not known, he would never have suspected she was a police officer, and especially a ranking police officer.

Detective Chief Inspector Jane Stanton was clearly at ease with her looks, and did not think that displaying them to their best advantage would be likely to damage her career. Given the level of her rank at a relatively early age, her appearance had clearly done her prospects no harm so far.

"Well," she said in a very un-Detective Chief Inspectorly way, "What's a girl got to do to get a drink around here?"

* * *

An hour had passed, and Mowgley felt almost as much at ease as when drinking with Melons McCarthy. He had almost forgotten that Jane Stanton was a superior officer, but certainly not that she was a very attractive woman. As Melons had more than once observed, he liked his women on the big side, strong and intelligent, but not too intelligent. Now Mowgley knew who she was, he was looking forward to seeing more of her in the coming months. Especially as he now knew she had not been brought in to take his place at the ferry port.

As well as being well up the ladder for her age, DCI Stanton was also a member of a very select part of the Metropolitan Police Force. The Special Projects Unit was limited to thirty officers, all tasked with stopping professional assassins carrying out their contracts, and the bringing to justice of major drug and firearm traffickers operating within the United Kingdom.

None of this had been explained to Mowgley when DCI Stanton was introduced at the meeting. DCS Hartley-Whitley had merely given her rank and said she was down from London on a specific investigation which would involve the ferry port, and should be given all assistance as she made her enquiries.

His new boss was obviously a woman who disliked giving information away, but he still had some conduits of communication within the force. After he left the office, a phone call to a former Special Branch drinking companion with almost as many contacts at New Scotland Yard as a tabloid journalist had assured Mowgley that Stanton was not a threat. Given her job, pay scale and prospects, being appointed to his role would be a significant demotion.

Mowgley watched contentedly as she arrived with the next round of drinks. He found her readiness to pay for and bring drinks to the table a huge marker in her favour.

He raised his drink, watched approvingly as she took the head off hers and then asked: "So am I allowed to ask what you're doing down here ...Ma'am?"

As he waited for a reply, he could not help sneaking a look at where the tailored jacket fitted snugly around her sizeable breasts. He doubted she was carrying, as there were no lumps or bumps which were not entirely natural, and wondered if she ever kept her gun in her handbag. All members of SPU were trained to the very highest level in the use of firearms, and it gave him quite a stir to think of her with Glock in hand, especially if clothed only in stockings and suspenders.

"No, it's all me. There's nothing artificial underneath unless you count a wired bra."

Mowgley flushed as for a moment he thought he may have spoken his thoughts aloud. Then he realised she had been watching him watching her walk back from the bar, and, being a good detective, had worked out at least one of the things he was thinking.

* * *

"Where have you been? Why didn't you answer my calls? Why didn't you call me for a lift? I was just coming to look for you."

Melons had been waiting in the car park alongside the fun factory, and had the same sort of anxious, angry look his mother used to wear when he was late back from school.

"Steady on." Mowgley borrowed a five pound note to pay the taxi-driver, then asked his sergeant what she was doing in the car park.

"I needed a cigarette."

"But the whole of our floor is a compulsory smoking area."

She looked away. "That's not the point. I was coming to look for you anyway. Why didn't you get me to pick you up?"

Mowgley held up both hands, palms vertical in the recommended manner to defuse a situation. "I left my phone at the flat this morning."

"Liar. It's in your bloody pocket, or was when I dropped you off at Central."

"Erm, what I meant was that the battery's flat. I couldn't be bothered to find a payphone and there was a cab outside the hotel."

"What hotel? How did you get on? Are you still my boss, or do you need a hand to clear your desk?"

"I'm touched you're so concerned," said Mowgley, leading the way to the entrance to the building.

"It's not just you I'm worried about. Don't forget, if you go, I'll have to break a new boss in."

* * *

The lift still not working, they took the stairs. When they arrived, Melons led the way into his office, and shut the door.

"So how did it go?"

Mowgley threw his overcoat at the filing cabinet and missed. "Okay, really. I'll tell you about it in the pub."

"Smells to me as if you've been drinking already."

"Hang on." He made a square of his thumbs and fingers and peered through it at her in the way film directors are said to line up a shot. "No. It's still you. I thought for a moment you had become my wife. We had a swift drink in the pub after the meeting, if you must know."

"What, you and the new Super? That sounds promising."

"No, me and the new Chief Inspector."

"What new Chief Inspector? And what's he doing wearing perfume?"

"I didn't say it was a him. She's from SPU and has got some business down here. I had a drink with her to try and find out what she was up to, but she stayed shtum. And how do women do that?"

"What?"

"Pick up the slightest hint of perfume on a bloke."

"In your case it's not hard. So what's she like and what's she doing down here?"

"Who, Cressida Double-Barrel?"

"No, this new DCI?"

"Oh, you know." Mowgley scratched his chin and leant back in his chair: "On the large and lumpy side. Nothing much to look at. More than a tad bossy, likes a smoke and a drink. Bit like you, really." He stood up, then leaned over to pick up his overcoat, failed to make it and indicated for his sergeant to help. "Come on then, I'll tell you all about it in the pub. Anything happened here in my absence?"

"A couple of messages. Do you want them in ascending or descending order of importance?"

"Erm, ascending, please."

"Okay. You remember that report about a yacht running ashore at Selsey with the engine going but nobody at the wheel or on board?"

"Vaguely. Why, what's afoot?"

"Nothing. Your mate from West Sussex CID called to let you know that they hadn't found the skipper yet in whole or in part. Buster said he'd keep you in the loop."

"Good, we might be able to find an excuse to nip along the coast for a skimmish with him. He likes a pint. And...?"

"He likes a pint and what?"

"No, I mean what else did you have to tell me?"

"Oh, right. We got a call from your mate at SOCO yesterday - I told her you were out drinking with another woman, and it turns out that you were."

"Gee thanks, Sergeant. What did she want?"

"She called to say they won't be able to have a dig around in Mr Burgess's pied-a-terre on Hayling Island."

"And why not, prithee? Are they under-resourced or got something better to do?"

"Neither. The caravan was torched in the early hours of yesterday morning. It is now no more than a pile of twisted metal and melted plastic."

Mowgley left off the struggle to button his overcoat.

"That's interesting. So somebody didn't want us to go nosing around for bits of pubic hair in the shower."

"Maybe, or maybe not. There's been a fair bit of vandalism on the island in recent times. Bored kids and no youth clubs and all that. And there's a home for runaway youth offenders just down the road. So far this month they've set fire to three beach huts, two cars and nearly an old lady putting her bins out."

"Hmm." Mowgley reached for the door handle. "As you say, maybe it was a coincidence, but to paraphrase the great Sherlock: 'Coincidences are very rarely a coincidence in this game, Watson.'" He looked at his imaginary watch. "Come now - I see it is opening time at the Leopard."

"It's always opening time at the Leopard."

"True, so we had better go and check Two-Shits is abiding by the other terms and conditions of his licence."

Eight

"As the new head of the Basic Command Unit, Detective Chief Superintendent Cressida Hartley-Whitley is the first woman to be appointed to the area's top police job. But she does not consider her gender should be an issue. 'I believe any appointment should be made on the basis of finding the right person for the job,' says DCS Hartley-Whitley. 'Going forward and as we stand at the beginning of a new century and Millennium, I think we need to recognise the way society is changing. And so should our perceptions of how modern police procedures can best serve all the people of this vibrant and multicultured city and surrounding areas. I intend to make a priority of bringing this force well and truly into the 21st Century.' And she adds, Chief Superintendent Hartley-Whitley has a number of particular targets and priorities for the coming year: 'We must stamp out any trace of institutionalised racism and sexism and prejudice against sexual orientation. I shall also be tasking my officers to do all they can to significantly reduce the rate of rape and sexual assault offences, and increase the prosecution rate. A study last year revealed that this city has the highest figures for sexual crimes in the country. That has got to change, and all my officers have got to understand the need for an immediate and significant change of attitudes.' More information on the appointment of CS Hartley-Whitley from Jaki Chambers, head of public information and bullshit dispensing."

Mowgley made a retching noise, then crumpled the press release into a ball and threw it on their table in the airport coffee shop.

"Does it really say that?" asked Melons.

"About the bullshit dispensing? Believe it or not, I made it up."

"No, I meant the bullshit about the vibrant and multi-cultured city?"

"Yep, it surely did."

"Ugh." Melons shrugged: "But, what's your problem? It's just the usual sort of PR crap."

"But it's just all so...crappy. Make a note to add 'vibrant' and 'multicultured' to the list of proscribed words and expressions in the Punishment Book - and put them in the Maximum Penalty section. *And* take the name of anyone at work who starts spelling their first name funny just to be different. 'Jaki' in-bloody-deed."

Melons shrugged again and picked up her cup of coffee.

"I think 'multicultural' is already in the book, and I'm not sure that 'multicultured' is a real word."

"Never mind. Put it in anyway."

If it had existed, The Punishment Book would have been a thick tome. Top of the list in the Behavioural Misconduct section was not buying DI Mowgley a pint when encountered on licensed premises. Included in the Offensive Gestures and Movements section was punching the air in triumph, wearing an Offensive Item of Clothing and Walking in a Generally Lairy Way. The longest section was devoted to taboo words and expressions, one of which was 'taboo'.

Although the book had no physical shape or substance, punishments for transgression were real, nearly always of a fiscal nature, liable to amendment at any time and invariably required the guilty party to buy his or her senior superior officer (i.e. Detective Inspector Mowgley) a drink, or contribute a fixed sum to the Christmas office party.

Having blown his nose into the press release, Mowgley looked around the airport departure area for something else to complain about. Used to travelling with him, Melons knew he was also looking to take his mind off the flight ahead. Seeing no obvious targets, her boss nodded at a young businesswoman who had made her purchase and was working her way along the counter in the coffee shop area. Mowgley watched with a heavily exaggerated expression of bemusement as she squirted cream, then some sort of other flavouring into her oversized mug and finally sprinkled the surface with what looked like the little balls normally used to decorate the top of cakes. Finally satisfied with her creation, she frothed the mixture up, licked the spoon and walked to a table holding the mug high in front of her like a prized trophy. Mowgley shook his head, curled a lip and puffed out his cheeks. "That's what Costa Plenty is all about, isn't it? Bullshit. And it was nearly a fiver for two cardboard cups of coffee and a couple of doughnuts. And the coffee really is crap."

"It was six doughnuts, actually. And the coffee tastes crap because you're drinking it black," said Melons mildly. "You're supposed to have lots of whizzed-up milk and stuff on top to mask the taste. You saw that woman. She's probably never tasted neat coffee."

"That's my bloody point. It's like everything else nowadays. All bloody bullshit. People will pay anything for a load of crap if it's trendy to be seen buying it. I'm not surprised these places have to have their own lawyers on site in case anyone wants to sue them for the criminal prices."

"What do you mean?" asked Melons, then followed his pointing finger to a sign above the counter.

"There you go," said Mowgley. "It says they're looking for barristers to work here."

She sighed and looked at her wrist watch, "You know very well that it's not barristers they want. 'Barista' is a trendy word for bar staff."

She looked around for something else to keep Mowgley occupied, in the way that parents seek out distractions for bored children when on a long car journey.

But it was not that Mowgley was bored. As the time for their flight came closer, he was becoming noticeably more agitated. The truth was that he disliked flying even more than he disliked car journeys. Melons was one of the few people allowed to drive him, but could expect a constant stream of cautions and alerts and reprimands. She knew that his take on the subject was, as with most things, quite complex whilst appearing straightforward. As with other situations, he liked to be in control when on the road. If he or those with him were going to be injured, he would prefer it to be his fault. If he was going to die in an accident, he would rather be the pilot than the passenger. As he could not fly a plane, he had no choice but to put his wellbeing into the hands of a total stranger when it became necessary to take a flight rather than a ferry. Perversely, he had no qualms about someone else being in charge on the ship's bridge when he was crossing the Channel. This was because there were plenty of lifeboats and he could swim quite strongly. When a plane fell out of the sky, there was not much that passengers could do to survive. He had, as he had pointed out several times on the way to the airport, only agreed to crossing the Channel by air because of the urgency of the situation.

DC Mundy having located the boat which was David Burgess's base when doing business in France, Mowgley was under pressure from the new Chief Superintendent to make progress on the case. So the plan was to make the visit to Normandy a daytrip. A further reason for not spending too much time away was that he had asked Jo to propose a working lunch with DCI Jane Stanton at the end of the week. Melons was not happy that it would literally only be a flying visit to Normandy because it would limit her time with Capitaine Guy Varennes, but had covert plans for extending their time in France.

Finding David Burgess's boat had been surprisingly easy - or DC Mundy had made it appear so. As he had explained at some length, while registration of non-commercial craft is not compulsory in the UK, the owner's details and proof of purchase must be available if a boat is taken into international waters. It is also possible to trace a boat through a radio licence, but in the case of David Burgess, none of this was necessary. Mooring a boat permanently in a French marina can be surprisingly good value when compared with Britain, but, as Mundy had learned from Guy Varennes, there is a yearly levy on any French- registered vessel, calculated on its size and value. Whatever the size of the bill, settlement is pursued with the rigour and enthusiasm for which Gallic tax-collectors are renowned, and Varennes had heard of luxury yachts being stormed by water-borne Customs officials when the yearly *impot* had not been paid on time.

The good news for Team Mowgley was that Burgess had bought the *Belle Amie* in Brittany and registered the change of ownership. Guy's information was that the cabin cruiser was now moored permanently in a small *port de plaisance* not seventy kilometres from Cherbourg.

"I do like a man in uniform."

Melons' comment brought Mowgley back to his present surroundings, and he looked across the busy floor to where a slim, tall man in an immaculately well-cut uniform was striding with an easy, long-legged gait towards the Air France desk. He was swinging a slim metal briefcase with casual nonchalance, and carried a carefully folded and very expensive-looking overcoat in the crook of his other arm. His peaked hat was set at what was obviously a carefully contrived angle, and in spite of being indoors, he wore a pair of Aviator sunglasses which Melons knew would cost more than her boss had spent on his entire wardrobe in the last year.

"Typical," she continued. "They get a gorgeous Alain Delon lookalike to wing them to Paris. On Flymaybe, we'll probably get someone in a uniform a bus driver would be ashamed of and with his sandwiches and flask in a knock-off Nike bag."

Mowgley shrugged philosophically. "The passengers will be paying three times what we are for the pleasure of having him as the driver, and they'll be no better off for it. Anyway, how can you fancy a bloke who's obviously batting for the other side?"

"What do you mean?"

"It's obvious isn't it? He's a shirt-lifter."

There was a pause as Melons shook her head wearily, then said: "That's typical as well."

"What is?"

"You claiming that any man who keeps his fingernails clean and doesn't walk like the Missing Link must be gay."

"Not at all," said Mowgley defensively. "It's just that we ...normal men can tell these things."

"Oh no, not that old acorn. Next you'll be telling me you have to be on your guard in case you get propositioned. Why do so many not exactly attractive men think that every gay wants to sleep with them?" She looked at her boss, then said "Anyway, what is it with you? I know you're not a bigot. You just like to wind people up by pretending to be, don't you?"

"I wouldn't say that, some of my best mates are irons," said Mowgley, "but I used to know and like a lot of poofs, and still do with the more...traditional ones. What really pisses me off nowadays is that instead of just getting on with it, they're out for a fight all the time. It's like being bent is somehow special and better than being straight, and that's a counter-productive stance, if you'll excuse the expression. As soon as anyone starts telling me I'm prejudiced, I feel like living down to their expectations. I really don't care what they get up to in the privacy of their homes, pubs, clubs and bars. I just don't want them shoving it down my throat all the time."

Whether or not Sgt McCarthy would have been able to resist this opening she would never know, as their discussion was curtailed by an announcement that they should proceed through the security check to the departure lounge.

As they stood, Melons observed the faint sheen which had appeared on Mowgley's upper lip, and his dilated pupils and heavy breathing were even clearer indications of his state of mind.

"Come on," she said encouragingly, linking her arm through his, "and don't forget; whatever the nice security guard says to you, do not, repeat do *not* come up with your trembler switch gag."

Nine

As is customary with other French regions, Normandy is divided into *départements*, or administrative divisions. The Lower Normandy port of Cherbourg is in the department of Manche and sits at the top of the Cotentin Peninsula. This is a finger-like protrusion, pointing accusingly across the English Channel at the south coast of England some seventy miles due north.

The peninsula occupies most of the Manche department and is a place of varied landscape and shoreline. The western coast is known for its cliffs and sometimes wild seas, while the eastern shoreline was chosen as the landing point for the Allied D-Day invasion mostly because of its shallow tides and long, flat, sandy beaches.

Spanning the peninsula where it meets the rest of France is a vast area of marshland. The *marais* provides thousands of hectares of good grazing land in summertime, but is mostly under water in the winter months. Its lack of trees and features make it a brooding place of mists and legends. Three rivers travel lazily eastwards through the marshes, and their point of confluence is just outside the small town of Carentan. A long, straight canal was built to help the water find its way to the open sea, and a marina sits at its beginning. The *port de plaisance* offers moorings and berths to passing sailors, and the clubhouse offers hot showers and toilet facilities. Alongside is a bar and an excellent restaurant providing food and service to a standard expected by French patrons, and especially the French owners of million-euro vessels.

As well as catering for passing trade, the marina also offers mooring space to a flotilla of much humbler craft, some of which act as holiday or even permanent homes. For a modest sum, owners can buy access to the facilities and live in extremely pleasant surroundings.

According to the authorities, it was here that David Burgess's boat was to be found.

By the time they reached the car park next to the restaurant, Melons was more than ready for a drink. Not only had she had to nurse her boss through the security search at Southampton airport, but also through the hour-long flight.

Also to be taken into account was the disappointment of not finding her lover Guy Varennes waiting at the terminal, and the strain of accompanying Mowgley on a journey in a car driven not only by a Frenchman, but a French policeman with official dispensation to drive like a lunatic.

As the siren and engine died, Mowgley released his death-grip on the front seat head restraint and tottered from the back of the car, followed by his sergeant. Waiting at the door to the bar was the tall figure of Capitaine Guy Varennes, and all thoughts that she would appear piqued at his not being at the airport melted in the warmth of his white-toothed, full-lipped smile. Out of respect for Mowgley's feelings and inevitable comments, the couple had come to an arrangement not to embrace in his presence, but the eyes and body language of each made their pleasure of meeting more than clear.

Unlike so many sophisticated French women of a certain age, the *Belle Amie* was not wearing well.

Formerly a mid-size sailing boat, she had been converted into a cabin cruiser by the simple expedient of removing her mast and related rigging. Other amendments included a shaky- looking framework of blue plastic and wooden lathes at the stern, presumably knocked up to create a vaguely weatherproof cockpit. Elsewhere there were signs that improvement and maintenance works were not on the owner's list of priorities. The entire hull was covered by some form of virulently green growth which had spread to the deck and superstructure, and many years of exposure to salty air and water had pitted the metalwork beyond redemption. What looked like significant damage to one side of the bows had been patched with more of the blue plastic material and at least a roll of gaffer tape. Overall, the *Belle Amie* was not an attractive sight, and the expensive vessels on either side seemed to be straining at their moorings to prevent any contagious contact.

Slightly disappointed that Guy had acquired a set of keys from the Captain's office and thus prevented him from taking out his bad mood with a forced entry, Mowgley watched as the tall detective lowered his head to avoid the roof of plastic sheeting, stepped down into the cockpit and fiddled with the lock on the wooden panel giving access to the cabin. After a moment, the key turned and Guy pushed at the panel then turned his head sharply away.

"What's the matter, unwashed socks?" asked Melons.

"I don't think so," said Guy. "I think it is perhaps more likely that it may be the rest of your body."

* * *

Taking a torch from his inside pocket and using the other hand to pinch his nostrils, Guy Varennes led the way into the cabin.

The torch beam pierced the gloomy interior, resting momentarily on a bunk bed, a closed provision cupboard, the galley range and an open door which revealed a dirty wash basin and toilet bowl. Then the beam lighted and settled on something on the table in the bows.

As they moved towards it, Mowgley saw that the source of the stench was a brown paper carrier bag with the name of a major supermarket chain along its top edge. Surrounding the bottom of the bag was a congealed, rusty-red pool of liquid, which had obviously seeped from within. Surreally, it appeared that the bag was moving in a way which had nothing to do with the gentle undulation of the boat.

Taking his hand from his nose, Guy handed the torch to Melons, reached into his pocket for an expensive-looking pen and used it to delicately separate the top edges of the bag. He then retrieved the torch, pointed it into the bag, bent forward and looked in.

"Ah." As this was the French detective's only comment, Mowgley took his hand off his mouth and nose long enough to ask if the bag did contain some of the remains of the missing parts of David Burgess.

"I am not sure," replied Guy, stepping aside to give Mowgley access, "but I think it more likely a bit of an animal than a human."

Looking into the bag, Mowgley saw a writhing, wriggling mass of dirty white. The maggots were competing to get at what looked as if it might once have been a leg attached to a large pig. Given time the maggots would have stripped the meat completely from the bone, and he wondered what happened when they had eaten all of that which had bred and nurtured them. From pub conversations with his favourite SOCO girl, he knew that the date of death could be calculated by the stage of insect eggs, larvae or maggots. They were very efficient eating machines, she had told him over a pasty and chips at the Leopard. The front end of your typical maggot was mostly mouth hooks which shredded and then passed the decomposing flesh back to the tail end and anus.

The clever arrangement of their posterior spiracles meant they could eat non-stop for 24 hours a day without having to pause for breath. A bit like Mowgley when he was talking and smoking and drinking at the same time, she had added.

Guy stepped back and turned off the torch. "I think it best we leave things as they are and I will get our people in now to conduct a thorough and more scientific search of the boat. In the meantime, I have heard very good things about the restaurant here. Will you be my guests for dinner?"

* * *

Mowgley laid down his knife and fork and looked out of the restaurant window to where an elegantly-dressed woman was watching fondly as her miniature poodle defecated almost exactly in the middle of the tow path. For such a small dog it made a sizeable heap, which the woman carefully stepped over before carrying on along the path. It was another curiosity of French character and attitudes, he thought, that the area around the marina was so free of litter yet so infested with dog shit. For some reason, the French liked to take their rubbish home but leave their dog crap for others to enjoy. Thinking of the condition of many Gallic toilet bowls he had encountered, the custom held good for human excrement.

He sighed gloomily then returned his attention to the cause of his immediate despondency, which rested on the large, stylishly rectangular plate in front of him. It always upset him when he picked the wrong item from a French menu, and especially so when in an expensive restaurant where someone else was footing the bill. His mistake had not cost him or the British taxpayer, but he had missed out on a good feed. Because of what they thought they had found in the *Belle Amie*, he had not fancied the dish of the day, which Guy had said the waiter had said was a brace of pork chops, pan-fried after being left to marinade overnight in a solution of cider and herbs in the cauldron hanging in the restaurant's cavernous fireplace. Other customers seemed to be eating fish, which to Mowgley was not proper food. So, despite Guy's offer of help, he had run a finger down the list and asked for the *andoullettes* on the basis that they did not sound like any fish of which he had heard.

Although glowingly described in the menu and graced with the approval of the AAAAA (broadly translatable as the Association of Lovers of Authentic Andoullette), he had soon learned that the dish would have been known in England as stuffed chitterlings, which was the official name for the inner tubes of a pig. He found the sausages difficult to cut and chew and stomach, and thought they had an odour only marginally less unpleasant than the mystery remains aboard David Burgess's boat.

"How was your food?" Guy looked fondly at Melons, who had ordered crab.

"Delicious, thanks." She shot a warning glance at Mowgley and reached for her wine glass. "So, I suppose we're no closer to knowing if Mr Burgess is alive or dead?"

"I am sorry for that," said Guy, raising his glass to her, "but I cannot say I am sorry the search brought you here." Smiling at Mowgley's facial reaction to his gallantry, the French detective ordered coffee and a very expensive brandy made from apples, then said: "Although this may turn out to be a pointless journey in your search for Mr Burgess, I think I may have an offer which could be of interest to you, Jack."

Mowgley grunted dubiously. "Don't tell me you've found a buyer for *La Cour*?"

"No, but there could be some money for you."

As Mowgley sat up and showed much more interest, Varennes explained that he had been talking to a colleague who had recently retired from a *Gendarmerie* unit based in central Brittany. "Like you, I think, my friend Yann did not quite see eye-to-eye with his commanding officer. The officer could not get rid of him so easily, so they came to an arrangement."

"You mean your mate had something on his boss," said Mowgley.

"Yes, there were some matters concerning the past and my friend knew his commander had a..." he broke off and looked to Melons, "*un squelette dans le placard*?"

"Skeleton in the cupboard." Melons smiled encouragingly. "Yes, it's the same thing."

"Anyway," continued the French detective, "Yann left the *Gendarmerie* last summer. He had some capital and his pension thanks to the...arrangement, but felt he was too young to stop working."

"Can you be too young to stop working if you can afford it?" Mowgley mused.

"I beg your pardon?"

"Nothing. It was a rhetorical question."

"I am sorry...?"

"It's a question which is really a statement, like me saying 'I wonder whose round it is?' when I'm in the pub with Jack," said Melons.

"I see," said Guy in a way that implied he did not. "Anyway, now my friend Yann has set up an agency in Brittany and plans to have offices in other parts of France. It is an agency for helping people and companies with things they feel the police cannot or will not deal with."

Mowgley raised his eyebrows in interest. "You mean he's set up as a private dick? 'Down these mean streets a man must go' and all that?"

"What?" Guy looked at Melons again.

"*Un detective privé.*"

"Ah yes, of course. He called me the other day to say the

business is doing very well."

"Booming," interjected Mowgley.

"Yes, blooming like a big flower. I think you say he has lots of bread on his board-"

"Plenty on his plate."

"Of course," Guy said, "he has plenty on his plate. Naturally, he has many contacts with former colleagues which has led to work involving French people, but it is not so good when dealing with the English."

"If you're looking for a translator," said Mowgley, holding his glass up to a passing waiter and making an encompassing circle of the table with his other hand, "I think Mel - Catherine might be more up your street, mate. I can do the sign language stuff but I'm not so hot on the words."

As if to prove the fluency of his non-verbal communications, the waiter appeared with a cafetiere of coffee and three large glasses of Calvados brandy. He said something to which Mowgley responded with the usual neutral shrug which he hoped would be taken as a suitable reply. Guy politely intervened, spoke crisply to the waiter and then carried on. "No, no. Yann speaks much better English than me. What he needs is someone in your position to help him with his enquiries."

"Do you know," said Mowgley, holding his glass to his nose and inhaling the familiar sharp tang, "In all my years on the job, I have never asked anyone to help me with my enquiries. What does your mate mean, exactly?"

Guy gave a strength three Gallic shrug. "I think that is for him to tell you. But he says he will pay well for any help you can give him. Is it that you could be interested?"

"It certainly is that, my friend. So when can I meet him?"

"Tomorrow would be a good time, he says."

Mowgley turned the corners of his mouth down. "That's a bit tricky. We won't be here as…" he paused to look at his watch, "…we were on the plane to England an hour ago."

Guy and Melons exchanged glances and smiled, then Guy said: "Knowing you would miss your flight, I took the liberty of booking you and Catherine a one-way passage from Brest tomorrow afternoon. My driver can take us to Brittany in the morning and you can meet Yann for lunch, then we can go on to the airport. How does that sound?

"Like I've been stitched up like a kipper, if that is not too much of a metaphorical mix. And where are we going to kip tonight? Not on Mr Burgess's boat with a million or so maggots for sleeping partners, I trust?"

Guy smiled and shook his head. "There is a very nice family-run hotel in the town. I have been there before and I reserved some rooms yesterday in case you missed your flight from Maupertus."

"Hmmm. When you say 'some' rooms, may I hazard a guess that you actually mean two?"

Guy smiled again while Melons looked suitably coy. "How did you guess?"

Mowgley drained his glass and started to semaphore at the waiter for a refill. "Just everyday police detection work. A mixture of intuition, observation and cognition."

Guy looked puzzled.

"Cognition...?"

"Never mind. I'm sure Catherine will explain later when you find the time to talk."

* * *

The moon danced a jig on the dark waters as Mowgley strolled along the towpath, pulling contentedly on his roll-up.

The echoing roar from an unseen vehicle raced beneath his feet and he realised he was approaching the end of the towpath. The High Dick canal is unusual in that it passes over rather than under the nearest thing to a motorway that the Cotentin peninsula has to offer. Forty-odd miles north along the RN13 lies Cherbourg, and Mowgley's mostly ruined *manoir* was relatively just up the road. Again, he thought that *La Cour* and its surroundings would not be a bad place in which to live out the autumn of his days.

He stood for a moment looking at the lock gates separating canal from estuary, then threw his cigarette end into the basin, turned and walked back the way he had come. It would be interesting to see what tomorrow and his meeting with Guy's friend might bring. If he could earn a few bob this side of the Channel, it would be nice to build up a bit of a slush fund for the future, especially if circumstances meant he had to move across the Channel in a hurry. If there was enough in it, he might even be able to have some improvement work done on *La Cour*. Any work on the place would of course be an improvement.

Inside the restaurant, the waiter was setting the tables for the following day. The two men looked at each other through the glass door, then Mowgley lifted a cupped hand to his mouth and made the universal sign for having a drink. The waiter looked at him reflectively for a moment, then gave a perfect Gallic shrug and the slightest of nods.

Mowgley smiled ingratiatingly and made for the entrance, only narrowly failing to avoid the pile of still-warm poodle shit.

Ten

Brittany occupies the top left-hand corner of France and is about the same size as Wales. For historical reasons, the Bretons have the same general view of the French as some Welsh have of the English.

This may help explain the appeal of the region to Britons who wish to live abroad but somewhere not too foreign or far away. Once upon a time, only retired British schoolteachers or Welsh druids set up home in Brittany. Now all sorts of British expatriates can be found there. Another reason Brits feel so at home in Brittany is that the region has more independent breweries than the rest of France put together. It also rains even more in Brittany than in the wettest parts of the United Kingdom.

Much to Mowgley's distress, the police car broke all records for the three hundred kilometre drive from Normandy to Central Brittany. It was no more than two hours before they arrived at the town where Guy's former colleague had set up shop as a private detective.

Sitting at the bottom of an estuary opening on to the north-west coast, Morlaix is an ancient town best known for its inland port, soaring viaduct and the medieval beam-and-plaster-fronted buildings which surround the market square.

The residents first experienced how Brits abroad could behave in 1552, when an English raiding party sacked the town. According to legend, the raiders gained entry by dressing the most attractive of their number as women, who talked their way through the gates and let the rest in while the guards were admiring what they thought were the comparatively hairless legs and underarms sported by English females.

Obviously having heard about the alcoholic intake levels of British tourists, the surviving locals waited until the raiders drank themselves insensible, then killed them all.

The car having arrived in the market square in a cloud of blue smoke, flying gravel chips and irate stallholders, Guy pointed out the bar where Mowgley would be meeting his former colleague, then took Melons off for lunch at a restaurant where the size of the portions was in direct contrast to their price.

Walking through the square, Mowgley nodded consolingly to a morose-looking man tending a deserted English book stall. Further on, a van dispensing fish and chips was under siege from visiting Britons.

After making a mental note to return later to check out if the van sold pastys, he climbed a set of steps from the market square up to a pub in a terrace which could have been built as a set for a Hollywood movie about Robin Hood.

In its own way, the pub was as genuine yet fake-looking as the medieval beam and plaster fronted houses. The inside had been carefully tailored to look like people would think a Middle-Ages tavern would or should look like, from the uneven slate-slabbed floor to the cavernous smoke blackened fireplace and carefully mismatched chairs, benches and tables.

At the satisfyingly rustic wooden counter, a pretty barmaid served him an imperial pint of lager. This, together with a variety of crisps and a card of pork scratchings on display indicated that the pub was a favourite haunt of British settlers. A handful of them were sitting at a table next to where Mowgley found a place, and were obviously well into their lunchtime session.

However much they claimed to have found paradise abroad, most British expatriates Mowgley had met were unhappy. Unlike Tolstoy's unhappy families, the settlers were invariably unhappy in the same way. However much they pretended to have made the right choice in moving to live abroad, their unhappiness with how things were done differently in foreign countries was always near to the surface, and inevitably brought out by a surfeit of alcohol. The men at the next table had reached the stage of complaining of the shortage of proper sausages in the region, so were probably on their third pint.

His eavesdropping was interrupted as a man arrived at the table and held out a hand. Without thinking, Mowgley offered his empty glass, which the man took. As he smiled and shook his head in the bemused way French people often affect when confronted with a strange British custom or activity, Mowgley was put in mind of a Gallic version of his former boss. Like Chief Superintendent Mundy, the newcomer was completely hairless above the small forest erupting from his unbuttoned shirt collar, and this together with his puffy face gave him the look of a very prematurely aged baby. In this case, the flattened nose and pockmarked face gave him the look of a dangerous baby. The eyes were deep-set and surrounded by what looked like scar tissue, and the scar running diagonally from one corner of his mouth showed lividly against an almost brick-red complexion. It appeared, Mowgley reflected, that he either enjoyed a regular punch-up, or led with his face and was seriously bad at defending himself.

As if reading his thoughts, the man touched the damaged skin on one cheek. "Most of this came from a fire when I was a child. In those days they were not so good with plastic surgery - unless you had a lot of money."

Not sure if he were meant to comment, Mowgley smiled in what he hoped was a mildly sympathetic way, and stood up. The newcomer was several inches shorter than him, but much wider in the upper body. Like many short men, he had obviously worked on making up for lack of height with power of handshake, and Mowgley made a mental note not to challenge him to an arm wrestling contest if the drinking session advanced.

"It is good to meet you, Inspector Mowgley," the man said, becoming one of the few people of any nationality to have pronounced his name correctly.

Mowgley nodded and smiled. "You must be Yann?"

"Must I?" The man said mock-aggressively, then smiled. "It's okay. Yes, I am Yann Cornec."

Without asking what Mowgley was drinking, he crossed to the counter and returned with two pint glasses. "This is from a local brewery and made with wheat," he said, holding up one of the glasses. "I know it is cloudy and looks like horse piss, but it does not taste like it. Well, not that much."

As the expat table moved on to the deficiencies of the French postal system, the square-set Breton sat opposite Mowgley and took a long pull at his beer. "So, how are you liking it?"

Mowgley sampled the beer and nodded. "Fine. As you say, not like horse piss at all. More like cat's piss, I would say."

Cornec looked at him for a moment, then smiled. "Yes, I guess you are right." Taking another long pull, he put the glass on the table, turned and looked steadily at the circle of men on the next table. "Excuse me," he said to the largest of the men, "Can I ask you something?"

The man frowned, then Cornec leaned forward and asked in a somehow scarily pleasant tone "If you find everything here so bad, why don't you just fuck off back to your own country?"

Without waiting for a reply, he turned back and finished his beer. The group at the table fell silent, looked at each other then decided it was time to go.

* * *

Over the next two hours, Yann Cornec introduced Mowgley to the full range of Breton beer on tap at the *Ty Coz*, and in between rounds made his business proposal. As he knew Mowgley knew, he had taken an office just across the square from the *Gendarmerie*. It was also just down the road from the office of the town's leading *huissier*, or private bailiff. As well as sorting out debts and reclaiming items which had not been paid for, a *huissier* would act as witness in divorce proceedings. Often the act of being caught on the job was organised between husband and wife to speed proceedings.

With other related cases and his regular consultancy work with the police (which meant doing things and going places they could not officially encompass) business had been better than good since he established the Morlaix Detective Agency.

Mowgley expressed admiration and congratulations, then asked: "So why do you need a non-French speaking Brit copper?"

"Because I am getting more and more work concerning English people who have come to live here. Or, sometimes, escaped to here."

"Which is where I come in?"

Cornec frowned, looked over at the main entrance, then nodded as he understood what Mowgley had meant: "Exactly. Sometimes I am asked for a credit rating on an English person who has asked for a loan. Sometimes it is to look into the background of someone who has applied for a job in a sensitive area. In all cases, someone wants to know what the new settler got up to or left behind in England."

Mowgley looked at his empty glass. "So why not just get your mates across the road to make a few calls to the UK?"

Cornec smiled dryly. "As I am sure you can imagine, it is not as easy as that. Sometimes, believe it or not, former colleagues can be less than helpful, and at best it can take a long time to find out the answers to even simple questions."

"So, basically, you would give me a name to check it out and see if there was, as we say, anything known?"

"*D'accord.* Just to see if there was anything on record."

"And the remunerative package?"

"What? I am sorry?"

"I mean what's in it for me if I come up with the goods?"

"I would charge the client for the time spent by one of my imaginary investigators, including expenses if he would need to travel to England. You would receive a set fee or hourly rate, whichever worked best. We would obviously have to work things out, but today I just wished to establish an *entente* between us. And hopefully an *entente cordiale.*"

Mowgley stood, emptied his glass and held out a hand for Cornec's. "Well it all sounds very cordial to me. One for the road?"

"Of course. And don't you have any questions?"

"Only one at this stage. Does that fish and chip van sell pies or pastys?"

"Ah, the so-called Cornish pasty. *En fait*, there are some

Bretons who claim we invented the pasty. I know a place not far from here which sells the best in all Brittany, and they also sell *chouchen*."

"Chouchen?"

"Fermented honey with bee stings in it to give it some extra taste and power. The bar has coat hooks screwed to it so customers can use their belt buckles to stay upright. Are you interested?"

"Sounds right up my street, *mon ami*."

* * *

"By the left, I could muller a shant. There's nothing like a good pint of English lager - and mind that motorbike, Sergeant."

Melons sighed and made an exaggeratedly precise change of lane as they drove along the M27 from the airport at Southampton. "But it's the same lager in the Leopard as you've been getting down your neck in France for the past two days."

"Yes, but that's not the point, is it? It's where you drink it, not what you drink. And why do women always have to bloody do that?"

"What?"

"Look at the person they're speaking to when they're driving. Men never do."

"A lot of men don't look at you when they're *not* driving. That's 'cos they don't give a stuff if the person they're talking to is listening. Anyway, you still haven't told me what you thought of Guy's friend, and what he's offering you."

"That's because you haven't stopped rabbitting on about bloody Guy. I reckon he's a bit of a hard case, but I'm not sure I would trust him that far. He comes over as a right little bantam cock, but then a lot of small men are like that. It don't mean they can handle themselves. I'll reserve my judgement until we've done some business."

"And what business does he want to do with you?"

"Not sure," said Mowgley. "He says he gets asked for background stuff on Brit expats from time to time, and whether they've got any form or whatever. If I come up with any info from the national database or elsewhere, a nice lump of euros will appear in my French bank account."

"That sounds almost too good to be true."

"That's what I thought. I just got the feeling there was more to it than he said. We'll just have to play it by ear."

"Better be sure you use the one with the lobe still on it, then."

"Har de har, Sergeant, and watch that motor coming up on the outside."

"But it's one of ours."

"Exactly. You are dangerously close to exceeding the speed limit, and anyway, you know what crap drivers motorway cops are..."

* * *

Surprisingly for the time of day, the car park of the Ship Leopard contained only four vehicles. Two were anonymous saloons, one was an unmarked but official-looking white van, and the fourth was the patrol car that had overtaken them earlier.

While Melons parked, Mowgley became aware that a length of striped scene-of-crime tape was stretched across the main entrance. As they got out of the car, one of the double doors opened and a figure in a hooded white coverall emerged, ducked beneath the tape and walked towards one of the unmarked cars.

Hearing his call, the figure turned and looked in their direction, then stopped and lifted the face mask obscuring her features.

"Hello Jack," said the pretty and young Scenes of Crime Officer, "What are you doing here?"

"I was going to ask you the same thing. You lot don't usually wear your work clothes even when you go in the roughest of pubs, do you?"

The young woman smiled. "Only when we're on business."

"So what's to do, then? One of the old regulars collapsed after a price increase?"

"I don't think so. Don't say I said so, but there's a nasty smell in one of the cubicles in the Gents."

"That's nothing unusual."

"This one is. It's coming from a dead body."

Part Two

Eleven

Detective Inspector Mowgley looked glumly out of the Fun Factory window, then leaned back in his chair and directed a plume of smoke towards the nicotine-coloured ceiling.

"Do you realise," he said reflectively, "that the inside of your lungs probably looks the same as that?"

"What, all swirly plaster with cracks in and a broken neon tube and a cobweb?"

"No you dinlow. The colour."

"I think it's rather nice," said Melons. "It's better than the original shade of dirty white."

"True." Mowgley puffed his cheeks out. "I wonder if it's not raining in Japan?"

"Beg pardon?"

"*The Radio Ham.*"

"What?"

"Never mind." He sighed theatrically. "This thing with the Leopard is really upsetting."

Melons put her coffee cup on the edge of his desk, reached for her tin of baby cigars and nodded. "Yes, it must have been a shock for Two-Shits when he found the body."

"I didn't mean that." Mowgley paused in his attempts to blow a smoke ring worthy of the name. "My mate at SOCO reckons the Leopard will be shut for another day at least and that means we'll have to drink elsewhere. And why are you smoking those stupid little things?

"I told you. You don't inhale cigar smoke, so it must be better for me than fags. And because they're stronger, I'll be smoking fewer cigars than ciggies."

"Your logic is severely flawed, Sergeant." Mowgley gave her his Paddington Bear look. "For a start you do inhale them, *and* you're smoking as many as you used to do with fags, if not more. And anyway, why are you on a diet - it looks really odd to see you with a half pint glass in your hand down the pub?"

"Just trying to cut down a bit," said Melons defensively. "No harm in that."

Mowgley screwed his face up and gave an impish grin. "It's Guy isn't it?"

"What is?"

"All this health and fitness nonsense."

"You're imagining it - and you're just using the old attack-being-the-best-form-of-defence ploy, aren't you?"

"Rubbish."

"Not rubbish. Just look at you."

"I can't, there's no mirror in here."

"I bet there will be soon. For a start you're wearing a clean-ish shirt and your special bootlace tie, and you've clearly waved a comb in the general direction of your hair. And I reckon you've had a bath within the last week."

"Bloody cheek. You know I have a bath every week whether I need one or not."

"That's true. But you always get like this when there's a bit of crumpet on the horizon. Don't forget I know who you're having a 'working lunch' with."

It was Mowgley's turn to look uncomfortable. He fingered his fairly stubble-free chin, then stood up. Melons reached over and re-adjusted his tie, then said in a conciliatory tone: "Give me a minute and I'll run you to the meet."

Mowgley looked even more uncomfortable. "It's okay. It's a nice day so I think I'll walk."

Melons clutched her heart and staggered back in pantomime astonishment: "What? But it's more than a mile to the King and Queen."

"How do you know that's where I'm going? Are you spying on me?"

"No. Just using my deductive powers. The Leopard is shut

and you always go to the King and Queen when you want to be sure you won't be spotted. Besides, you're barred from most of the other pubs round here."

* * *

In the absence of a passing cab, Mowgley approached a low wall, sat on it and reached for his baccy tin. He was in need of a breather and realised the idea of walking from the Fun Factory to his luncheon appointment was perhaps over-ambitious.

Rolling a cigarette, he looked about him and reflected on how much this part of the city had changed and yet not changed. When he was a child and the pantomime arrived in town, the dame would ask a stage-hand for the name of the local red light district so he could drop it into one of his lines for the benefit of the mums and dads in the audience. In those days, Queen Street would be the location to guarantee a knowing laugh.

For centuries, the thoroughfare leading to the ancient dockyard had deserved its bawdy reputation. When a ship was in port and especially after a long voyage, Queen Street was where the pubs, working girls and tattoo artists did their best business. But in a relatively short time, one of the seediest areas of the city had become one of its most desirable. Some of the pubs were still there, but had generally smartened up their act. Most had carpets and all had separate toilets for men and women. In a marketing initiative almost beyond parody, the Blue Anchor had recently become the Anchor Bleu, but still staged at least one fight a week. The Salvation Army hostel, tattoo parlours and even a pawn shop were still open for business, and the tower blocks which tried to replace that which the Luftwaffe had taken away were still let to council tenants.

But the brewery which had since Medieval times been brewing beer for the fleet was earmarked to become a very desirable residential development. It was clear, though, that the old spirit was not giving up without a struggle, and the future owners of penthouse apartments and town houses with names like Harbour View would still have the denizens of the tower blocks for neighbours, and there were still more kebab shops than wine bars.

Mowgley resumed his walk, passing the gates to what used to be the Dockyard but must now be called the Naval Base. Once upon a time it had been the city's main employer, and the simultaneous exit of ten thousand dockyard mateys on their bikes was a sight which drew more spectators than the arrival of a new ship.

Nowadays the Naval Base was more of a tourist attraction than a place where ships were maintained and improved. Visitors arrived in increasing numbers to see Nelson's flagship HMS Victory and what was left of Henry VIII's Mary Rose. Soon, it was claimed, they would be queuing to visit the Millennium Spinnaker Tower. This grandiose concept was allegedly going to be in the shape of a giant sail in full bloom and would be within a day trip of millions of people living in Britain or across the Channel. Local cynics said it was already so far behind schedule that the project had been misnamed, though it might be ready for the next Millennium. Hardly a day went by without a new crisis or revelation of soaring costs, and the tower had become a symbol of council ineptitude. But as a recent Lord Mayor and drinking friend of Mowgley's had said, the punters would forget how long it was overdue and how much it cost them when it was up and running. Like the local football team, it would be theirs, and thus in a privileged domain and woe betide anyone from outside the city who criticised it.

Passing the dockyard gates, he turned the corner on to The Hard, where as a child he had watched mudlarks dive and fight for change thrown by drunken sailors. He had never been allowed to join in the franchise, but when a foreign ship was in, he and his mates would lay in wait at the gates to beg chewing gum from American sailors and hammer-and-sickle cap badges from Russians. Nowadays, young kids hanging around the gates were more likely to be pimping or dealing in dope. In spite of how almost unimaginably better life for ordinary people was now, not all the changes had been for the better.

Before entering the pub, he stopped to look out across the harbour and sighed heavily. He would have liked to have ended up in a nice flat overlooking the water. Had he known what lay ahead, he could have paid attention at school rather than playing hooky, and maybe made something more of his life. Or perhaps, as Nelson was said to have said as he lay dying on board the *Victory* after the Battle of Trafalgar, it was all down to Kismet. Whichever way we planned our lives, it would be Fate which decided our future or lack of it. Personally, he thought it was a bit of both. He sighed again, straightened his shoulders and string tie and entered the pub.

* * *

"Well, this is nice."

Mowgley looked at his companion to see if she were being ironic, then at the pub's fake wood-panelled walls. They were dressed with frames containing Indian ink drawings of the harbour area of the city as it never was, glass-fronted boxes containing carefully labelled knots, and brass portholes looking out to nowhere. In the middle of the floor on a raised platform was an empty and thus literally pointless but highly-polished brass compass binnacle. "To be honest," he said, "it's all a bit...poncy...for me."

Detective Chief Inspector Jane Stanton smiled agreement. "Me too. What I meant was it's nice having a few jars in the afternoon in reasonable company. And all on exes."

"Exes?"

She raised her glass and nodded."Yep. Believe it or not, you are about fifty but look seventy, have hair to your shoulders but none on top and are known as Cottage Grove Pete to your mates, and half the users in the city."

"Cottage Grove Pete? Blimey, I went to school with him. I haven't seen him for years. Surely he's not still on the scene?"

"Your mate on the local drug squad tells me he's semi-retired. He used to supply the whole of the city with Chinese Heroin scored in Soho in the old days. Mind you, that was only a relative handful of needle-users. Most of his contemporaries are no longer with us, but he still knows who's up to what. He's been handy and I slip him a fifty every now and then." She opened her bag (Mowgley was irrationally pleased to see she did not use a purse) and took out a thin wad of banknotes held by what looked like a gold clip. From the wad she extracted a fifty pound note and handed it across the table. "Today, Matthew, you are going to be Cottage Grove Pete." She returned the wad to her handbag, then said: "Don't think I'm patronising you; I just like to be the one who gets bought the drinks."

They were on their fifth round, and it was not just the effect of the alcohol or the hand-out warming Mowgley's feelings towards the Chief Inspector. The meeting had not only reassured him that she was not a spy visited upon him by his new boss, but that she was a police officer after his own heart. She also had a swallow rate nearly as copious and swift as Melons and was equally as scrupulous about standing her corner. And she smoked and swore even more than his sergeant.

Aside from these good points, he was impressed by what he had to keep remembering was a senior officer. Actually, when he thought about it, he was more than impressed. Jane Stanton was not only one of the lads, she was clearly clever and more than capable than most of the lads he knew. She also laughed at most of his jokes, which he found most appealing. Another bonus was that, unlike a lot of police officers, she did not appear to want to keep what she knew and what she was up to close to her impressive chest. It was only their second proper meeting and yet, if she was being straight with him, he had learned why the Special Project Unit was showing interest in his patch.

As he may have noticed, she had said with no trace of sarcasm that he could detect, there had been an increasing degree of illicit activity involving Eastern Europeans in recent years. This was true nationally, and specifically in and around the continental ferry ports. Of course, criminal gangs from behind what used to be called the Iron Curtain had been operating in the EEC for a long time, and particularly since the break-up of the old Soviet Union.

"One thing you can say about Russia under communism is that they kept a firm hand on unofficial criminals. And they kept them to themselves. Then along came Mr Gorbachev with all that *perestroika* and *glasnost* and huggy-feely stuff and started taking down the curtain. All very nice, but along with us being able to nip over and see Red Square much more easily, we also started getting visits from lots of not very nice people."

Another complication would be the entry of Poland into the EEC in a few years time, and that would not be the end of it, with Bulgaria and Romania not likely to turn down the benefits of membership. Of course, guaranteed freedom of movement applies to gangsters as well as tourists. "As I see it," she had said, "we've got plenty of home grown villains; why the fuck should we want to import lots more?"

"So you're down here looking for anyone with a Slavic accent and snow on their boots, or have you got names and faces?"

"A bit of both. We know about a few serious players from Russia who are moving into drug and slave trafficking in a big way. There's always been plenty of that going on, but now the Ruskis - and other Eastern Europeans - are getting organised. In the process, they're lashing around them a bit, knocking off the small fry to send out a signal."

Mowgley raised his eyebrows and almost put down his beer glass. "Are we talking about the Russian mafia moving onto my little patch?"

She shrugged. "Depends what you mean by 'mafia'. Lots of Slavs from all over the place like to claim they are part of the *Bravta*, which means 'brotherhood', as it helps persuade possible competition not to get involved."

"So how serious is it?"

"Very serious if you're a fairly small trafficker in drugs or women or other stuff. The big boys are sending out warnings they don't intend to share the pot with anyone. That's why those arms turned up in the flash bag."

"So you know about the arms?"

"Of course. It's my job to know about these things, Inspector."

"And what about the dead guy in my local?"

"I don't think that's got much to do with anything; we should have some more news by end of trading today."

"And the body on the boat? Just another coincidence?"

She shook her head. "Ah, Mr Burgess. Now you're talking. That is of special interest, and the main reason I'm here."

"So Burgess is or was more than a small time trafficker?"

"Don't know yet. It could be he was bigger than he looked - the best way to not arouse suspicion is to look skint. The guys with the big house, Range Rovers with tinted windows and trophy ladies are easy to spot. Posing as a small-time and not very successful boat trader would be a good excuse for travelling back and forward across the Channel. Anyway..."

She drained her glass and stood up, "I need a gypsy's. And I could eat a scabby horse. Do you fancy a Ruby?"

"Does the Pope crap in woods?" Mowgley set his empty glass down on the table top. "And I know just the place."

* * *

"Blimey, you were not wrong." She patted her forehead with a serviette and took a gulp of Kingfisher beer. "I always thought the best Lamb Madras this side of Calcutta came from my local Paki place in Southall. But this is the biz."

Mowgley smiled proprietarily and signalled to Bombay Billy for more beer. As he did so he noticed his hands had stopped shaking. Considering how madly Jane Stanton had driven her sports car from the pub to the Midnight Tindaloo, this was a good sign, and he felt able to roll a cigarette. "They reckon there are more curry shops per head of population in Pompey than anywhere else in the UK," he said, "or perhaps in India for that matter. It's the skates, you know."

"Skates?"

"Matelots...er, sailors. Having a curry after a runashore and a few shants is compulsory."

His companion raised a well-defined eyebrow. "Do you mind speaking the Queen's English, cocker? I understand matelot and runashore, but why 'skates'?"

In spite of being on his seventh pint, Mowgley looked uncomfortable. "Long story. Skates have the same sort and size sex organs as female humans. With a long journey ahead, the deckhands would nail a skate to the mainmast..."

"Okay, I get the picture." She pushed her plate away, took another drink and lit a cigarette. "That was bloody good. The guv'nor's a mate of yours by the look of it?"

"Very much so. I...er, keep a room here for when I don't want to drive home."

She looked at him through a cloud of smoke and smiled as if she already knew the answer to her question: "And where's home?"

He looked at her and thought it would be best to be straight. "It's in France. It's a farmhouse with twiddly bits not too far from Cherbourg."

"Nice."

"Not really; it's about as ruined as ruined gets."

"So why did you buy it, and why would you have your only home on the other side of the Channel? I know property is cheap there, but..."

"I didn't buy it. My ex-wife did. She just took the loan out in my name, and lumbered me with it after she ran off with the original owner."

"Yuk. And she got the house over here?"

Mowgley nodded.

"And what about the kids?"

"None."

She blew out a cloud of smoke and looked somewhere in her mind. "Me neither. It's good and bad, isn't it?"

He nodded again.

"So, what's the place in France called? I bet it's got some arty-farty Frog name."

"Well, it is a Frog place to be fair, but it's got a very plain name. It's called La Cour."

"Ah." She stubbed her cigarette out and smiled delightedly. "So that makes you..."

"Yes Ma'am. That's me. Inspector Mowgley of the Yard. Cheers."

* * *

"Right, Inspector. It's your turn. But not before you pour me another glass of that really crappy red."

Mowgley obliged. They had moved on from beer to wine, simply because they both felt the need to cut down on quantity after the big meal. They had also reached the stage of early intimacy brought on by drink, and were playing Question Time. As she had said, they were going to be working together, so it would be nice for both of them to know who they would be working with. As they were both used to interviewing suspects, they should take the same approach with their after-dinner conversation. So far, Mowgley had learned that Jane Stanton was as close as she was going to tell him to forty, had been married briefly but ditched her husband when she realised she was going to go further in the Force than he ever would. More importantly she would be earning more than him and didn't like the idea of living with a junior officer. Also he had cramped her style, couldn't hold his drink and was fairly useless in bed.

"Alright. Next one. Why did you join the Force?"

She looked into her glass and frowned. "Do you know, I really never worked that out or thought about it much. I suppose I wanted to do something a bit different, and there weren't that many openings for TV presenters or footballer's wives then. To be honest, I was always a bit of a bossy cow, and I could see the way things were going with equality and all that old bollocks."

Mowgley looked at her owlishly across the top of his glass. "So you don't believe in feminism and all that stuff?"

"Only when I can use it to my advantage. How do you think I got to this level at my age? Not by getting my tits out for the boys, that's for sure. Now it's your turn."

"What, to get my tits out?"

"No thanks, Inspector. What I want to know is why you joined up?"

"You won't believe it, but I did it as a bet."

"You're right, I don't believe it."

"Well, to be fair, it wasn't just a bet. I left school with a pathetic handful of bad passes at 'O' Level and drifted around from job to job on the buildings. I got to know a few coppers after the pubs shut, but not as mates."

"I can see that," she said, nodding at the tattooed letters on the fingers of his left hand.

"Anyway, I got fed up knocking up muck on some muddy site in the depths of winter. Then I met an old mate who had made sergeant, and he bet me I wouldn't get in. I did, and here I am."

"Here you are," she agreed. "Right. Any further questions?"

"Only one. Which football team do you support?"

"I can't bloody stand football."

"Nor can I. I knew you were a girl after my own heart." Mowgley stuck out a hand with a flourish, knocking over his glass of wine. "Put it there."

She took his hand, then nodded to Bombay Billy for the bill. "Are you fit, then?"

"For what...Marm?" Mowgley grinned with schoolboy lewdness at his superior officer. "I would invite you up to my place, but it's a bit untidy."

"You should be so lucky." She smiled. "But play your cards

right and who can tell? I think we are going to work together very well, Inspector Mowgley..."

Twelve

The man tweaked his face mask for the fifth time, looked again at his watch then checked the gauge on his tank. Two hundred bars meant he would have an hour below if he kept his breathing under control.

Always a stickler for procedure, he pulled sharply on the painter to ensure that the ageing Zodiac was lashed securely to the rusty mooring ring. Having tested that all was as it should be with a couple of sharp puffs into the regulator mouthpiece, he sighed contentedly and slid below the gently swelling surface. He shouldn't alone, but he had no regular diving buddy, and anyway did not want to share what was to come with anyone else.

The moment the water closed over his head he felt the magical change, and exulted in it. By passing from one world to another, he had metamorphosed from a slow-moving crippled lump to someone totally at home in what to others would be an alien and dangerous environment.

He smiled behind the mask and thought how apt the comparison to a fish out of water would be. On land he was a gimp; under the sea he could make any able-bodied non-diver look disabled. Beneath the waves, the leg and arm shattered and put back together like a bad jigsaw when he came off his bike all those years ago were no longer a handicap. His bloated body - the inheritance of enforced inactivity and a liking for takeaways and beer - no longer felt uncomfortable. Quite literally, his physical problems no longer weighed him down. Here, he felt free. He did not know why other people liked to dive, but for him it was not only a release from pain, although that was enough of a reward in itself. There was also the feeling of peace and solitude, and even euphoria at being in control of himself and his surroundings. And this was a great place to be in control beneath the waves. There were some cracking dives in this part of the world, and the Far Mulberry was one of the best.

It was an ill-wind, he had read, that was responsible for the creation of this popular dive site a couple of miles off Selsey Bill, just along the coast from Bognor Regis. The Far Mulberry was one of thousands of giant reinforced blocks of hollow concrete which would form temporary ports, harbours and pontoons off the coast of Normandy for the D-Day Landings. Having been constructed out of sight of enemy eyes, the caissons were floated out to sea and sunk off Selsey or Dungeness to wait for the call of Operation Overlord. A handful did not make it any further, and the Far Mulberry was one of them. A change in the tide and wind had swung the unwieldy hollow block savagely round, its back had broken and it had been scuttled. The only action it would see was as a target for bombing practice in the last year of WWII.

As well as divers from all over Britain and beyond, the sixty foot long, six thousand ton artificial reef also attracted a huge diversity of fish. He was wearing a Drager rebreather so the lack of bubbles would not disturb the residents, and a huge cloud of pouting enveloped him as he lazily finned to where the Far Mulberry sat. Visibility was as crap as usual, but it was a bright day and a little light filtered through the surface above his head.

Although he could see the looming, brooding shape and his was a familiar journey, he followed the course of the mooring chain, avoiding causing any damage to the line of lobster pots dotting the shingle and mud bed. With luck, he thought, he might pick up a couple of mature specimens. Ironically he disliked eating any form of fish or seafood, but a brace of live lobsters made good trade for a few pints in any food pub along the coast.

He reached the bottom of the chain which stretched down

from the buoy and took hold of one of the two ropes leading off to other sunken treasures. One was the remains of a landing craft which also had not made it across the Channel to the D-Day beaches. The other was what had been known in the trade as a cuckoo. This was an air-sea rescue float, designed to help airmen forced to ditch in the sea. Now, like the Far Mulberry and the landing craft, it was home to an aquarium's worth of sea creatures. The wrecks also gave an ideal toehold to all manner of marine growth, from hornwrack weed to sponges, anemones and the very suitably named dead men's fingers. As he thought about the options of visiting the craft or venturing into the encrusted and sharply-edged compartments in the heart of the Mulberry, he noticed something poking out beyond one corner. With visibility down to a few feet, he could not make out what it was, but it had certainly not been there when he had dived on the site just a week ago.

Rounding the edge of the caisson and avoiding a length of harpoon-like reinforcing wire, he reached for and switched on his Sola 800 torch. The powerful beam showed the mystery object was a small boat. Even with the duff visibility, he could see it was a cabin cruiser which would have been more suited to a canal or inland waterway than open waters. Perhaps, he thought, that was why it was keeping the Far Mulberry company. There was no obvious sign of damage and the boat was sitting upright on its flattish bottom, an oddly normal position which made it look even more out of place. Reaching the bows, he took hold of his torch in his right hand, and used his good arm to pull himself along the side towards the stern. Perhaps, he thought, it had been put there by the authorities who managed the site to add another interesting place to explore. That, though, was unlikely as he reckoned he would have heard about it on the Far Mulberry Fan Forum, and he had seen no new buoy marking its presence.

He continued hauling himself along the side of the boat, then paused as he thought he saw something moving in the cabin. Although he could not see what it was, it looked somehow familiar. Narrowing his eyes, he pulled himself closer to the plastic window which ran most of the length of the cabin and pointed the torch at the inside. When he saw what the object was, he dropped the torch, recoiled in shock and a burst of bubbles escaped from his suddenly slackened mouth.

What he had seen in the beam of light was a pallid human hand, and it had seemed to have been waving at him.

* * *

"So what's your excuse this time?"

"For what? The War of Jenkins' Ear? The sinking of the French Fleet at Toulon? The exploitation of the riches of India? Not guilty, squire. You must remember I'm Irish and Scots from a couple of generations ago. All we did was colonise the world with workers and great inventors and poets, not occupying forces."

Melons raised her eyes to the ceiling. "You know very well I mean what's your excuse for not having your phone with you yesterday? You can't say the battery's flat because I charged it yesterday morning, and you can't say you left it in your other jacket."

"Why can't I say I left it in my other jacket? In fact, I just did - say that I left it in my other jacket, that is."

"You can't say you left it in your other jacket because you haven't got another jacket."

"Oh." Mowgley frowned and looked out of the office window as he considered this inarguable statement of fact. He regarded a giant banana boat for a moment but found no inspiration there, so went from defensive to attack mode: "So why would you want to phone me? What occurred that you couldn't handle without me? Are you incapable of using your initiative? Did anything monumentous happen?"

"There's no such word as monumentous, but there was news of a couple of things I thought you might find of interest."

"Such as?"

"Such as my chum in the Path lab called with some unofficial advance information about the arms in the designer bag. *And* there's news about the body in the Gents at the Leopard. Which do you want to hear about first?"

"If it affects the re-opening of my local, I'd like to start with the body in the bog. But duty calls. Are the arms in the bag a match for the trunk in the cabin, if you see what I mean?"

"Erm, actually yes and no."

Mowgley gave her a full-strength Paddington Bear stare. "What do you mean, yes and no?"

"I mean yes I know what you mean and no, the arms don't match. As a matter of fact, there's not even a match for themselves."

Mowgley sat up. "Sorry pardon?"

"Well, for a start they're both right arms, so they couldn't match each other."

"Mmmm." Mowgley got his baccy tin out. "So there's either a couple of blokes walking around out there minus an arm, or..."

"Or there's another couple of bodies missing some parts out there."

"True. But there's something that's really puzzling me at this exact moment?"

"What?"

"Why have you abandoned the midget cigars and gone back to fags?"

Melons shrugged and inhaled deeply. "I thought about what you said and, for once, you were right. I was inhaling them and smoking as many of them as I usually do with cigarettes."

"I'm glad to hear you do listen to my advice sometimes Sergeant."

"So, then. What do you think about the arms and torso situation?"

"The trunk in the cabin seems pretty armless to me at the moment. Ha ha ha."

Mowgley made a failed attempt at a smoke ring while he waited for at least a grunt of appreciation of his pun. When it was not forthcoming, he told Melons that Jane Stanton had a couple of ideas about the torso.

"And what were they? I want to hear all about yesterday and how it ended up."

"Later. First I want to hear about the dead bloke in the cubicle."

"Only if you promise to tell me everything about you and DCI Stanton."

"'Me and DCI Stanton'? You make it sound like we're an item. We only had a drink and a Ruby."

"Okay. You can fill me in over a couple of pints at the Leopard."

"You mean it's open again, and Two-Shits is in the clear?"

"Yes and no again. That's another reason I tried to call you yesterday. The pub's open for business, but Two-Shits is not in the clear."

Mowgley began rolling another cigarette. "Elucidate, if you please, Sergeant."

"My contact at the Path lab says there is no suspicion of foul play. The guy simply killed himself by drinking too much of his own products."

"Go on."

"You remember he was the bloke with the tattoo on his arm we saw playing pool in the Leopard."

"His tattoo was playing pool? Now that is clever."

"You know what I mean. Anyway, he is or was a Polish lorry driver. He's been coming over regularly with foodstuffs we and his fellow countrymen enjoy. Jams and sausages and tins of delicacies and that sort of thing. Apparently, he was doing a bit of trade on the side with the local pubs, and thought he would expand into beverages."

"So far so good," said Mowgley, "but how comes you know all this?"

"Two-Shits told me. When I couldn't get you on the phone yesterday, I went round to the pub looking for you and your lady friend. I knew it was still shut, but reckoned you might have called in anyway."

"Good thinking, Batwoman. Continue, please."

"The place was still under the closure order, but Two-Shits was on his own in the bar, and very much in his cups."

"Do you mean skimmished?"

"I do, and well skimmished at that. Anyway I stayed for one and he wanted to talk and coughed the lot."

Mowgley sighed and shook his head. "Why is it that blokes will tell women stuff they would never tell another man? Never mind; pray continue."

"It's because they know they can tell a woman without losing face. Anyway, the driver appeared last week with a case of vodka and wanted to know if Two-Shits wanted to make an order. No duty to pay of course, and very, very cheap compared to what he called the British brands. He had a sample bottle and Two-Shits took a shot to check it was the real thing."

"And was it?"

"Yet again, yes and no. It had a recognised Polish brand

name, but my mate at the lab says it was forty percent methanol."

"Methawhat?"

"Drinking alcohol comes from ethanol. Methanol is the simplest chemical form of alcohol, and generally known as wood alcohol. As my contact explained, It's produced from carbon monoxide, carbon dioxide and hydrogen."

"Yum yum. And it's not the right sort of stuff for drinking?"

"Not really. They use it for antifreeze or for making diesel. It can be very toxic even taken in small amounts as it's poisonous to the central nervous system. Drinking too much can cause blindness leading to coma and death."

"I seem to remember a few sessions when I felt like that was happening. So our Polish friend was trying to set up a dealership in deadly spirits?"

"Quite. He even suggested that Two-Shits be the middle man and flog cases on to other landlords in the city. That could have been catastrophic."

"And what was the deal?"

"The guy would supply cases at £20 a pop, and part of the deal was that he could use the Leopard as a depot, and kip there for free. Luckily for a lot of future punters - if lucky's the right word in the circumstances - our Polish entrepreneur had a few pints and then took the sample bottle upstairs for a nightcap. Two-Shits assumed he'd made an early start until someone from the commercial park came in and said his lorry was still there. He had a look upstairs and found the poor man dead in bed with the empty bottle. He panicked and got WingCo to help him take the guy down the back stairs and into a cubicle in the Gents. Then he phoned 999 and said they had just found a body in the toilets."

"But why didn't he phone us first?"

"He said he tried your number, and when he couldn't get through he couldn't think of anything else to do. He figured that if they had found the guy upstairs and done a search they might have found the case and put two and two together. He hoped the CID would think the guy had wandered in off the street with his own bottle, then had a heart attack or whatever in the toilets."

"And did our colleagues buy it?"

"It seems so. They're a tad bemused that nobody found the

body at closing time or the next morning, but Two-Shits' lack of attention to detail in the health and hygiene department are well known. As it stands, the mystery is solved and the local paper's got a great story. Your local landlord is off the hook, unless you want to take it further."

Mowgley looked up at her with wide-eyed surprise, stubbed out his cigarette and got to his feet. "Take it further? Are you kidding? When he knows I know the real truth about the Body in the Bog, we should be good for free drinks and pastys until at least the next Millennium. C'mon, let's make our first collection." They had reached the outer office when Detective Constable Mundy caught up with them. "Excuse me Sir, have you got a moment?"

"For you, my dear, always," said Mowgley expansively. "How can I be of assistance, as long as it does not delay my arrival at the Leopard for more than a moment?"

"It's just that DI Donahay at Bognor called a few minutes ago."

"Ah, Buster. What did he want?"

"He said he had promised to keep you informed about any developments which might be relevant to our ongoing cases."

"I bet he didn't put it like that, but go on."

"He called to say a body has turned up off the coast at the Witterings. He can meet you there in half an hour if you want to have a look."

Mowgley looked at his watch. "At lunchtime? Did he say if the body had all its arms and legs and things?"

"No Sir, but he did say the body had been found on a sunken boat."

"And?"

"The boat has the same name as the one which our missing person was bringing over on the ferry from Caen."

Thirteen

"There you go; The Dun Cow. That's a boundary for me," said Melons triumphantly. And I still say the Fox and Hounds was worth at least eighty runs if you allow for ten horses in the hunt and the same again for the dogs. Then there's another four for the fox."

"Don't be ridiculous, Sergeant. The name of the pub was The Fox and Hounds, not The Fox, Full Pack of Hounds and Fully Subscribed Hunt."

They had been passing the time on the journey to Sussex by playing pub cricket. According to the Mowgley version, the basic rules were that the person who was batting scored a run for every leg which could be attributed to people or animals or even furniture connected to the names of the pubs passed during the innings. The Queen's Head was still in dispute, but the Jolly Drover on the A27 had scored Mowgley only two runs as there were no cows on the pictorial signboard. Melons had claimed six runs for The Milkmaid until her boss had pointed out that the traditional stool on which the lady was sitting should have had only three legs.

Melons shook her head and let out a cloud of exasperated smoke. "Even if it was a small pack of hounds, my claim is much more reasonable than you awarding yourself twenty thousand runs when we passed The Duke of York."

"As any schoolboy knows," said Mowgley as if talking to a

fractious child, "The Duke of York never went anywhere without marching his ten thousand men over the nearest bridge. Come to that, he would have been on horseback and had his officers with him, so I should have scored at least twenty thousand and twenty four runs. Whatever pubs we pass for the rest of the journey, that has to be game, set and match to me."

* * *

Inspector Mowgley got out of the car and smiled. He could smell good food.

This part of the English coastline seemed to specialise in small seaside towns which had seen better days, or perhaps never seen them. Although their former clientele now jetted off for holidays in the sun, there was still an echo of the past to be found in most of them. It was as if they were gamely hanging on, hoping the punters would one day return. A clue as to their mutual pasts was that seaside towns like these tended to have more cafes and takeaway shops than any similarly-sized inland community. As he stood in the car park next to the beach, it seemed to Mowgley that the signature smell of East Wittering was not the sea air, but fried food.

"I like it," said Mowgley, nodding admiringly at an elderly man sporting a Breton fisherman's cap and reefer, and a huge strawberry shaped and coloured nose which would have equalled the combined weight and size of those belonging to WC Fields and Leo McKern. "I wouldn't mind ending up like that."

"The way you drink, it's quite likely," said Melons. "I swear your nose has got bigger since we met. But perhaps that's all the lies you've told since then."

"Ha ha. No, I mean living somewhere quiet and shambling down to the shops each morning and going to the pub afterwards."

"But you go to the pub every day anyway, and you get me or Mundy to do your shopping. Aren't you living the good life already?"

"Hmmm. I suppose you're right, really."

* * *

A gaggle of dog walkers, a lone surfer, a trio of youngsters sitting on mountain bikes and members of what looked like a local television crew led them to where the police tape cordoned off a small area of the beach. Overhead a number of gulls were wheeling around as if as interested in proceedings as the spectators on the ground.

Drawn up in a circle within the tape were a dark blue Land Rover, a marked patrol car, an unmarked Volvo saloon and a trailer bearing a large inflatable boat with a very big outboard motor. Alongside the trailer was a dark blue van with its back doors open, and two officers in white coveralls were moving equipment from the inside. Beyond the gathering and at the water margin, a smaller inflatable boat was sitting on the concrete slipway. At the back of the heavily chequered Land Rover, a trio of fit-looking men were in various stages of undress as they peeled off wet suits and stowed flippers, face masks and air tanks into the back of the vehicle.

From previous acquaintance Mowgley knew the divers would be part of the regional Specialist Search and Recovery Team. They would all be serving police officers, but also expert divers trained in recovering anything from submerged vehicles, vessels and firearms to drug packages, hazardous chemicals and, of course, bodies.

After cocking a leg over the tape. Mowgley saw a body bag alongside and half underneath the Land Rover, and realised that the SSRT had already brought up the occupant of the sunken boat.

As they reached the group of vehicles, the back door of the patrol car opened and a man got out. He was about Mowgley's size and age, but much better dressed. Whether his hair was also better dressed could not be seen, as he was wearing what Mowgley believed to be one of the last remaining pork pie hats to be regularly worn by a serving police officer.

"Alright John Boy?" The man offered a hand the size of a small ham, and looked over Mowgley's shoulder to where Melons was talking to one of the divers.

"How do, Buster. Good to see you again."

"Nice to see you, but nicer to see your bag carrier. Is this the famous Melons?"

"It is, but if you don't want to join the bloke in the body bag, I wouldn't call her that."

"I get the plot. Do you want to speak to the finder?"

"That would be good," said Mowgley, "Is that him in the back of your motor?"

"Yep," said Donahay. "He seems a genuine sort of weirdo, if you know what I mean. Bit of a lad in his youth and then fell off his motor bike while out with his chapter or whatever you call them. He's not worked since then and took up diving 'cos he said it was almost like being back to normal when he was in the water. Nothing known except for a bit of youthful messing around when he was what the meeja used to call a Greaser. I expect you'll also want a word with the leader of the dive team."

"As long as there's time for lunch afterwards."

"You're not wrong, and I know the very place. A real pub just along the prom with sticky carpets, no juke box or piped bloody music, a surly landlord, satisfyingly dirty toilets and a barmaid with massive tits."

"But are they real?"

"The tits? I've not found out yet, but am told on good authority they swing quite naturally if one orders a bottle from the bottom shelf of the back bar."

"So far so good. What about the catering facilities?"

"Brilliant; the whole range. Pork pies, scotch eggs, pickled eggs, crisps and pork scratching."

"But no pastys?"

"Not the last time I was in."

Mowgley sighed. "Well, I suppose a man can't have everything." He looked across at the bag. "I take it that's our man in there."

"Correct. Do you want a look before the wagon gets here?"

"Now we're here, I suppose we might as well. Any ID?"

"Apart from the cabin ticket, strangely not. No money, no keys, no nothing."

"Mmmm" Mowgley scratched his chin. I don't suppose he had a tattoo of a tiger on his arm?"

"Don't think so, why?"

"No matter."

The two men crunched across the shingle to where Melons was standing looking down at the body bag. Alongside her was one of the dive team, bare-chested and still wearing the bottom half of his wet suit. Introductions were made, and after receiving a nod from one of the figures in white overalls, the dive team leader knelt and fiddled with the tag on the zip which ran in a 'D' shape along three sides of the bag.

He unzipped it a little, then looked up at Melons and then at Mowgley as if he were concerned about revealing what was inside. Mowgley made a don't-upset-her-whatever-you-do face, and the man saw Melons' darkening features and continued unzipping the bag before pulling back the top.

The face revealed was surprisingly reposed, and it seemed the man were asleep and not dead. Mowgley put his age at middle to late thirties. The face was unremarkable, with high cheek bones, full lips and a small nose with a slightly flattened bridge. There was no facial hair but a heavy shadow of stubble on face and head, which the man had obviously kept shaven. Although the skin was puffy and discoloured, there was no evidence of injury or suggestion of any length of time in the water. Mowgley knelt, pulled the zip down further and looked inside the bag to check both arms were where they should be. As he looked again at the face of the dead man, he noticed there seemed to be a slight upturn at the corners of his mouth, as if something had amused its owner before his violent death.

"Well, I suppose you could say he didn't know what hit him," observed Mowgley.

"All the damage is to the back of his head," said the dive leader. He nodded towards where the couple in overalls were watching. "Do you want me to ask if I can show you?"

Mowgley shook his head."No thanks, we're just off to lunch. Just tell us off the record what you found and what you think happened and I won't hold you to it."

The man nodded his appreciation. He knew that Mowgley was asking for his thoughts and theories as well as the facts and there would be no come-back if he volunteered something which turned out to be wrong.

"The boat was sitting by the north-west corner of the Mulberry," he said. "It was laying on an even keel. We didn't have much of a look because of what we were after, but didn't see any obvious signs of damage. It'll probably come up tomorrow when the lifting gear arrives."

He went on to explain that they had had to force the cabin doors, and had found the body laying on its back on the deck.

No attempt had been made to restrain it with ropes or

weights, but one foot had been caught under some shelving.

"He was half floating with his arms and hands moving a bit, which was what the guy who found him saw. The back of his head was well smashed in; some brain matter had exited the wound. we had a quick look around without touching anything but couldn't see what could have done the damage. That's not our job, of course," he added as one of the white-overalled figures approached with an officious stride.

"No, of course," said Mowgley thoughtfully. He thanked the man and looked at Donahay quizzically. "What do you think, Buster?"

Donahay took off his hat and scratched his balding pate. He looked down at the dead face, then at the approaching SOCO officer, then spoke: "Pub?"

"Good call," said Inspector Mowgley. "Good call."

* * *

"Are you thinking what I'm thinking?"

"Don't know," said Mowgley. "I was thinking that the barmaid's knockers were even bigger than our Twiggy at the Leopard. What are you thinking?"

They were on their way back to the Fun Factory, caught in the traffic build-up outside Chichester.

"I'm thinking that the body had to be our prime suspect for killing and dismembering David Burgess."

"Who, Igor, you mean?"

Melons nodded as she wagged a reproving finger at the driver of a BMW who was trying to bully his way into the gap between their front bumper and the back of a battered white pick-up van. "Well, he's of the right age and size and general description that the woman on the ferry gave of the bloke who booked the cabin in which Burgess, or what was left of him, was found. And the body in the bag also matches the description by the loader who waved what we think is the same man off the ferry, driving Burgess's van and the trailer with the boat on it which is now sitting on the sea bed off Selsey Bill. It would be a bit of a coincidence if it isn't the same man."

"True..." Mowgley paused as Melons held up a finger, reached inside her jacket and took out her phone. She answered it, listened and nodded twice before returning it to her pocket.

"Sorry about that," she said. "It was Stephen."

"Doesn't he know it's distracting to call someone when they're driving? What did he want?"

"He took a couple of calls from France on your mobile, which is, surprise surprise, in the drawer of your desk."

"Not a couple of offers for La Cour, by any chance?"

"Sorry, 'fraid not. One was from Yann Cornec, your private dick friend."

"Aha," said Mowgley brightly, that sounds promising. And the other?"

"It was from Guy, though I don't know why he phoned you and not me."

"Now now. I promise you there's nothing going on between us. What did he have to say?"

"He thinks we should nip over and see him as soon as possible."

"I bet he does, and so do you. What's the official reason or excuse?"

"The results are in from the French SOCO work on the boat in the marina at Carentan."

"And did they manage to identify the identity of the original owner of the pork chops?"

Melons shook her head: "Don't know, but they did find some human blood."

"Aha again. Do they know whose?"

"Not for sure until proper DNA testing. But it looks like it could belong to or have belonged to the body in the ferry cabin."

Fourteen

Melons frowned. "How rude. You'd think it would have apologised."

"Apologise? Don't be silly; it's a French seagull."

"You don't know that for sure. Seagulls are not visibly ethnic. It could be just visiting, like us."

"No chance. Its accent is completely different and it hasn't stopped squawking for the last ten minutes. And look at the way it's shrugging its wings. It has to be a Frog seagull."

Melons thought about his proposition, then shook her head in bemusement. "Have you ever thought what people would think if they could hear our conversations? They'd think we were mad, wouldn't they?"

"I think that's a rhetorical question, is it not, Sergeant? Besides, think about the crap that everyone else talks about."

"True."

Inspector Mowgley and Sergeant McCarthy were taking their ease outside a bar on the quay of the small Breton port of Le Légué. The bar was named for the seabirds which lived off the port, and a dense flock were wheeling and screeching overhead as a fishing boat made its slow way back from the bay of St Brieuc. Perhaps due to the excitement of the moment, a very large herring-gull had just made its mark on the table at which the couple were sitting.

Melons reached out just in time to stop Mowgley using his

sleeve on the white dollop, then wiped it up with a newspaper someone had left on an adjacent table.

"I was going to read that," he said in unconvinced protest.

"What?" Melons scoffed. "You can't speak French, let alone read it."

"I know, but I reckon if I looked at it enough I might somehow absorb the lingo."

"By osmosis, you mean?"

"If that's what absorbing stuff through exposure is called, yes."

"That's the same sort of logic as all those fat ladies who buy a Jane Fonda work-out video in the hope that watching it will make them lose weight."

"And what's wrong with that? Better than doing nothing, isn't it?"

Melons gave up and looked across to where a very large man in yellow oilskins was having a voluble discussion with the owner of an expensive-looking yacht moored alongside the quay. The reason for their discussion was obviously because the yacht was preventing the big man's dilapidated fishing smack from docking. The passengers of the sleek schooner were taking their ease in various poses around a nearby table, and were obviously too sophisticated to show any interest in the altercation. Other customers were moving their chairs to a better vantage point and ordering drinks so they could settle down and enjoy the *cinema*.

The decibel level of the exchange rivalled the shrieks of the birds, with the low rumble of the giant fisherman playing counterpoint to the high-pitched reedy and nasal delivery of the amateur sailor. After an extended bout of arm-waving and shrugging, the fisherman made a final well-I-warned-you lift of his massive shoulders, then signalled to the man at the wheel of the fishing boat. With obvious relish, the helmsman brought the spectacularly battered craft alongside the quay, with the sound of the labouring engine augmented by a painful rasping sound as its bows scraped along the gleaming hull of the yacht.

As the yacht owner's arm-flailing went into hyper-drive, Mowgley sat back, sighed contentedly and said: "I do like the way they do things here. If we were in England, the fisherman would have laid one on the yachtie by now, or vice-versa.

Here, they'll just enjoy a good shouting match. Apart from that and lots of other things and if it weren't for the weather, language and all these French people, we could almost be at home."

"I know what you mean," said Melons, looking at a dog which had cocked its leg at the base of a huge heap of cement bags next to a mountain of shingle being unloaded from a dredger which appeared to be held together by rust. "Some of the characters in the bar could make the punters at the Ship Leopard look respectable." She sat back in her chair, tilting her face to the weak winter sun. "However much you moan about France and the French, you like being on this side of the Channel, don't you?"

Mowgley gave the question due consideration, then said: "I like being here when I know I'm going back. I don't think I'd be so keen if I couldn't go home. I suppose I like being a temporary foreigner. Being somewhere where you can be yourself and get away with it."

"But you do that at home anyway."

The development of the debate was curtailed by the arrival of Capitaine Guy Varennes. He was a regional officer in the SDPJ, which was the French equivalent of the CID. This made him a rather influential contact as well as a good friend. At the moment, the Captain was bearing a tray of drinks and sidestepping and gliding between tables in the manner of a particularly flamboyant matador.

"I suppose that's why they make such good waiters." Mowgley observed.

"Who?"

"Your average Frog. They love showing off."

Melons bridled. "I think you'll find it's more likely that their good at it because the average Frenchmen don't have any Brit- type macho hang-ups about serving other people."

"Right," said Mowgley dryly. "French men not having any macho hang-ups? Watch out for that pig flying up there, Sergeant. You'll need more than a page or two of the local paper if it shits on us."

The drinks arrived with their bearer. "A flying pig?" asked Guy, "Have I missed something?"

The trio had convened on the north coast of Brittany so that the *Gendarmerie* officer could take them through the results of the forensic examination of David Burgess's boat at Carentan marina. As Mowgley observed when Melons booked their flights, it could all have been done by a telephone conference call or even an exchange of e-mails, but it gave them an excuse for a jolly. He added that it also gave Melons and Guy another chance to be at it like knives. As Melons reminded her superior, it also gave Mowgley the chance to talk business and money with Yann Cornec.

They clinked glasses, then Guy opened his briefcase, took out an official-looking envelope and handed it to Mowgley. "In case you are interested in the details, this is the report on what the team found in the boat at Carentan. A copy has been sent to your superior officer."

Mowgley looked puzzled at the term 'superior officer', then remembered he had one, took the envelope, then asked: "I hope it's not in French?"

Guy smiled to show he was not offended and realised Mowgley was making what he would call a joke: "Yes, I am afraid French governmental agencies do make a habit of writing their reports in French. But I am sure Catherine would have no problems translating it for you."

Mowgley nodded and handed the envelope to Melons. "The amount of time you spend billing and cooing in French, she must be totally fluent by now. At least in words and expressions related to shagging."

Guy frowned. "Billing and cooing? Shagging?"

"Never mind," said Melons. "Just his little joke. Can you run us through the main findings of the report anyway, Guy? You said on the phone that there had been a match?"

"Yes. As you can see from the letters on the envelope, I have been communicating with the big cheeses at the institute."

Mowgley looked again at the envelope: "So who or what is the IRCGN?"

"The *Institut de Recherche Criminelle de la Gendarmerie Nationale* has more than 150 specialist forensic experts, and it is to them we go for scientific investigations and analysis."

"And are they any good?"

Guy smiled. "You could say that we invented the idea of forensic science. I can tell you that it started four hundred years ago when an army surgeon studied the effect of violent death on the body's organs. We even have celebrity forensic scientists. Doctor Phillipe Charlier is known as the Indiana Jones of the graveyards, and has worked on dust and bones from your Richard the Lionheart and our Joan of Arc."

Mowgley made a sour face. "Something else you claim to have got to before us, then. Next you'll be claiming to have invented cricket."

"Actually," said Melons, "there's good evidence that they did."

"Yes, thank you Sergeant," interjected Mowgley. "Now can we get on? If you cut to the chase, Guy, what did your blokes find out?"

"As you know, a small amount of blood was found in the kitchen area and some hairs on a cushion in the sleeping area. We could not confirm that the blood or hairs were those of Mr Burgess, as you do not have any blood or DNA records. In fact, you do not have any sort of official records for him." Guy's tone was almost reproachful, and Mowgley raised both hands in ironic surrender.

"Not our fault, mate. It happens when someone is off the radar by choice or circumstance-"

"He means when there are no records of any sort about someone," explained Melons. "It is rare, but happens sometimes."

Guy looked unconvinced. "Or it could be that Mr Burgess is not actually Mr Burgess?"

"Believe it or not, we had thought of that," said Mowgley heavily. "It's not hard to get a Mickey Mouse passport."

Before Guy could ask, Melons explained the expression, then turned to Mowgley. "But why would a man in his line of business want to keep his head down? I can't think the profit margin on buying and selling small boats would make him want to go to that sort of trouble."

"You'd be surprised at how many people don't exist officially And we don't know if knocking out second-hand boats is all Mr B does or did."

"What do you mean?"

"Never mind for the moment, Sergeant. Okay, Guy, pray continue."

"Well, for whatever reason, we were not able to confirm that the blood or the hairs in the cabin of the *Belle Amie* was that of Mr Burgess. But there is some more positive news."

Mowgley made as if to speak, but Guy held a hand up and continued: "The DNA from the boat is an exact match for the DNA of the torso found in the cabin of the ferry boat."

Mowgley sat up sharply. "So why didn't you tell us when you were on the phone?"

Guy smiled. "I did not know officially until late yesterday. And of course, I was happy to take any opportunity of seeing you."

"Is there anything else your enquiries turned up, Guy?" asked Melons quickly.

"There is. My people talked to everyone who uses or works at the marina, and found that Mr Burgess was last seen two weeks or more ago."

"On his boat?" asked Mowgley.

"No. He was seen in a car, driving quickly away from the marina." Guy paused as if he had something of import to deliver.

"So was he alone?" asked Mowgley.

"No."

"Oh for God's sake, man, get on with it. Did you get a description of what the passenger looked like?"

Guy smiled. "Yes. He was said to be a man in his middle years, with a shaved head and a dark complexion. From the description, it is likely it could be the man you are also looking for."

There was a moment's silence, then Melons said, "So, that means the body in the ferry cabin was Burgess. And he was killed by Igor, who he knew."

"Not so fast, Sergeant." Mowgley stroked his imaginary beard. "All we actually can be sure of now is that the blood in the *Belle Amie* matches the blood from the body in the ferry boat cabin. As the great Sherlock said, you must eliminate the impossible before you can move on to the probables."

Melons sniffed. "I don't recall him saying that. Are you sure you don't just want to downgrade the level of Guy's discoveries? What other possibilities *could* there be?"

If he had one, Mowgley's response was forestalled by a tinny rendition of *I Walk the Line* coming from his jacket. As he began random patting, Melons raised an eyebrow.

"Blimey, wonders will never cease. You've actually got your

phone with you – and it's charged."

Looking unusually discomfited, Mowgley located the mobile and stood up. "Er... yes. I expect it's Yann. If you'll excuse me, I'll find a better signal..."

* * *

Mowgley feared flying even more than travelling by car. He knew the odds and statistics, but that just made things more complicated. From his perspective, there were lots more cars on the road than planes in the sky, and most were piloted by highly trained, skilled, and competent people. That was why air accidents were very, very rare. But it was hard to be logical when you knew that sitting in an aeroplane about to crash into land or sea was much more likely to be fatal than being involved in the average road traffic accident.

Although he hated flying, Mowgley quite liked some airports. He was particularly fond of elderly small, provincial airports, and Brest was a classic of its sort. A new terminal of acres of glass and steel was under way, but he knew it would not be a patch on the old one. Its low-level buildings sprawled casually away from the runways, and there was never a parking problem. Passengers were allowed to leave their cars more or less where they liked as long as they at least kept clear of the runways.

Smoking was almost compulsory in all areas, and it was often hard to tell if the uniformed customers at the bar were pilots returning from or preparing for a flight.

"Hello Big Boy. Is that a truncheon in your pocket or are you just pleased to see me?"

Mowgley turned sharply and realised he had been looking in the wrong direction. He flushed slightly, then said: "Erm, it's a collapsible umbrella, to tell you the truth."

"Really? I would never have thought of you as a collapsible umbrella sort of guy."

"It's not mine," he said defensively. "My sergeant gave it to me when she heard I was going off on my own."

"And is that your overnight bag? A Tesco carrier? At least you could have used one from Waitrose."

Mowgley shifted his grip on the bag uncomfortably. "I like to travel light, and the rest of my stuff is at the hotel in Morlaix where my sergeant and her boyfriend are staying."

"Ah." She nodded to the bar in the corner of the departure lounge. "Fancy a quick one before we get down to business?" Without waiting for a response, she set off, leaving Mowgley to follow with her wheeled suitcase.

She looked back and smiled as if at the contrast between the expensive suitcase and the shambolic man pulling it. "So what was your excuse for leaving them to it after my call?"

"I said you were a Frog private detective who wants me to do a favour for him. My sergeant knew I was meeting him."

They reached the bar and she slid on to a stool, raised a finger and got the instant attention of one of the barmen, something Mowgley had never come close to achieving. After ordering two bottles of beer and two glasses of Calvados in what he recognised as excellent French, she turned on the stool and said: "I do hope you are getting something more than a thank-you for doing this guy a favour, Inspector? As my dear old dad used to say, there's no taste in nothing."

Their drinks arrived. They raised their glasses, then Mowgley felt the fiery liquid hit the back of his throat and began to feel much more relaxed.

It had been a surprise when Jane Stanton called and asked where he was and what he was up to. When he had told her and made a clumsy attempt at a joke about wishing she were there, she had said she could be if he fancied a foreign pub crawl. She would get someone to book her on the next flight to Brest and let him know when it was arriving. All he had to do was lose his sergeant, who could have him back the next day. His mission after she arrived, she said, would be to show her the hotspots of Brest and find a good hotel with views over the bay. And it would be her treat – or rather it would all be courtesy of one of her imaginary street-level contacts. Anyway, it would give them a chance to catch up on developments with the body in the cabin and other matters appertaining.

Fifteen

At the height of World War II, the Luftwaffe caused considerable collateral damage on their frequent visits to the naval dockyard at Portsmouth. The Mowgley family had lived near the port, and his mother had never forgiven Goering for taking out the family greenhouse.

At around the same time in the Brittany port of Brest, the Allies had been even more heavy-handed. The near-total destruction of the town by bomb and bombardment while flushing the occupiers out had literally left only a handful of buildings standing.

In the post-war years, Brest had acquired a completely new centre of modernist glass and concrete buildings. In contrast, much of the port area had been left to its own devices. That made it much more to Mowgley's taste. Universal trendification had not yet come to pass, and seedy and ramshackle tattoo parlours, kebab shops and tough-looking dockside pubs sat at ease alongside the swish café bars where the *beau monde* came to eat and drink and see and be seen.

It was to the quayside that the taxi delivered Mowgley and his companion, at the entrance to one of the very few Irish bars in France owned and run by an Irish person.

McGuigan's bar was close to the water and full of character and characters. A major contributor to the bar's appeal was the way the customers, like the furniture, were appealingly mismatched. After a shift, burly dockers and deckhands rubbed shoulders with pretty young girls who were making a start to their evening on the town. McGuigan's had many of the ingredients of The Ship Leopard. This, from Mowgley's perspective, made it a pretty perfect pub.

At a bar offering Breton, French and European draught ales they settled on pints of creamy stout and took them to a cubicle beyond the eating area.

"Well," said DI Stanton, "I suppose this is what they call French Leave. Have you missed me? Was your journey worthwhile? What did the Frogs find in Burgess's boat? What have you got to tell me?"

Taking the top off his Guinness, Mowgley told her of his meeting with Guy and his passing-on of the news of the DNA report from the French forensic lab. But he omitted to mention the sighting of Burgess and his car passenger.

"So," she said, "the body in the cabin was our Mr Burgess after all."

"Mmmmm," responded Mowgley non-committedly.

"So now we need to know who done him, and why...and I reckon I've sorted the 'who' side of it."

Mowgley looked impressed: "Do tell."

"For starters, we've found Igor, the guy who went down with Burgess's boat. He was as we say in the trade, very well documented, though finding out about him took a bit of nagging of Interpol - or Europol as they now insist on being called - and what's left of the Russian National *Militsia* and associated bodies."

"So he's a Ruski?"

"Yes and no. He is or was a particularly unpleasant little chap, originally from a mid-sized town called Shali in the Chechen Republic. He disappeared from the local scene fifteen years ago after killing a dealer in a territorial dispute, then showed up on the records in Moscow five years later. From what we have it looks as if he dabbled a bit as a freelance, then decided it was a good idea to join in with an organised team."

"You mean he was in the Moscow Mafia?"

Jane Stanton took a considered draw on her cigarette.

"Sort of. People think that 'organised crime' is, well, organised, with affiliated gangs operating in agreed areas like some sort of hamburger chain franchise. But it ain't like that in real life.

There are around five thousand identifiable and organised criminal gangs operating in Russia, and the bigger ones like to do their stuff in the wider world."

"And Igor was a made man?"

"Arkady Doku Ayubkhan Arzu Basayav, actually. Or Arkasha to his close mates, if he had any. Anyway, Igor seems to have progressed by making himself useful to a team based in outer Moscow, generally enforcing and sorting out admin and competition problems by cutting off the odd hand or head while gradually moving up the ranks. Things were going along nicely for the commissars and the crooks, and then along came Gorbachev with all sorts of ideas which were going to rock the boat."

Mowgley raised his eyebrows. "You sound really clued up on all this. Do you speak Russian?"

She shrugged. "A bit. You could say that Eastern Europe is my speciality area. Anyway, Gorby started on with his programme for restructuring and openness - which is what *perestroika* and *glasnost* mean, in case you didn't know - and that changed everything. Same as all the others, the Moscow Militia always had bent coppers working with the crooks but when Gorby tried to clean things up they ended up more or less joining forces. As they got bigger and more influential, some of the branches of the brotherhood liked the idea of going international."

Mowgley fiddled with a beer mat. "So they started moving into the drug business in a big way in the rest of Europe?"

"Yes, but not just drugs. You'd be surprised what other lines they like to get involved in, and not just people trafficking and gun-running. But Igor's lot moved into drugs import and export in a big way, with the route going from Afghanistan to anywhere and everywhere in the EU. Igor was one of their action men. The thing about the drugs business is that it's highly competitive, and the best way to get a bigger slice of the action is to knock off the competition."

"Whoah." Mowgley emptied his glass. "Take me through this slowly, Ma'am. Are you telling me that Igor killed and cut up Dave Burgess because he was a piddling little competitor in the drugs business?"

Stanton shook her head and raised her shoulders in a not-sure-yet way as she reached out for his glass. "Watch this space."

"And are you sure Igor's our man?"

"Yep." Standing, she fiddled in her handbag then took out an unmarked brown envelope. "That's a copy of a sheet from his file, translated from the Russian. No DNA information, but the prints match up and the body hadn't been long enough in the water off Selsey to spoil his good looks. The woman on the ferry boat desk was sure he was the one who booked the cabin in which Burgess was found, and the deckhand was pretty sure Igor was the guy who drove Burgess's van and trailer off the boat. Same again?"

Mowgley nodded, handed her his glass and watched as she moved easily through the crowd to the bar.

After rolling another cigarette, he opened the envelope and pulled out and unfolded the single A4 sheet of paper. In the top right hand corner was printed a head-and-shoulders photograph. Another had been clipped to the sheet. The original shot was of a young man with thinning hair and a heavily-stubbled chin. He had a long upper lip and a small but firm jaw. His arched eyebrows gave him a quizzical look and he was looking quite neutrally at the camera, with no assumed show of bravado or menace. It was as if he had no interest in the proceedings. The photograph clipped to the sheet showed the same face, only older and deader and how it had looked when staring sightlessly out of the body bag on the shore at Selsey Bill.

Mowgley folded and slipped the piece of paper back into the envelope and put it in the inside pocket of his overcoat. Jane Stanton was still waiting at the bar, so he decided to visit the toilet.

Returning a few minutes later, he saw that she was still waiting to be served. At their table, their ashtray had been emptied and wiped clean, and the beer mat he had shredded had been replaced. A further addition was a plain white envelope, lying alongside the ashtray. He picked it up and turned it over and saw that it was sealed.

Looking across the room and seeing Jane Stanton in negotiation with the barman, he sat down, reached for his reading glasses and opened the envelope.

Inside was a single photograph. It had been roughly cropped, either to make it fit the envelope, or to edit out something or someone alongside the three central figures. Two were attractive young women, both wearing white overalls which had been left unzipped at the top to show a generous expanse of cleavage. They were sitting either side of a man at the wheel of what looked like a very expensive power boat. He was bare- headed and wearing the same sort of overalls as his companions, though the zip was drawn up to the throat. The girls each had an arm along the top of his shoulders, while he was smiling at the camera at the same time as pouring Champagne into three glasses he was holding. From what Mowgley could see of the surroundings, it looked as if they were at some sort of nautical festival.

Mowgley looked at the bar again and saw that Jane Stanton was waiting for their drinks to be poured. As he watched, she felt his eyes and half - turned and smiled over her shoulder. Then a man arrived at her side and put what seemed to be a familiar hand on her other shoulder. The man was short and slight, and wearing a woollen hat pulled down over his ears. Overall, his restricted height and the patchy, white-flecked beard and wire-rimmed glasses and drinker's nose gave him the appearance of a bibulous gnome. DCI Stanton glanced again in Mowgley's direction, and he could see she looked angry. She bobbed down to bring herself to eye level with the man, at the same time firmly taking his arm from her shoulder. As she did so, the man leaned forward and spoke quickly and obviously urgently, to which she made a brief response. The man turned his face away as if he had been struck, then disappeared into the crowd as Jane Stanton ferried the drinks back to the table.

"So what did he want?" Mowgley asked, nodding towards the bar.

Her eyes followed the direction of his nod, then shrugged. "What do they always want?"

"Whatever it was, it looked as if you weren't obliging."

"He was a bit old and short-arsed for my taste. Anyway, I didn't have any change." She lifted her glass and Mowgley followed suit, then asked: "Have you been here before, then?"

"What? No. You mean because the old guy spoke to me? I'd have a bet he taps up every one who arrives at the bar who looks a soft touch."

"Blimey, if he thinks you look a soft touch he must have been well-oiled."

Sixteen

Mowgley looked at the Heath-Robinson combination of propeller and jet engine as the D8 400 turboprop lifted off the runway. Not for the first time wondered how something so big and lumbering and clearly heavy could not only get into the air but stay there.

He shuddered slightly as he thought he would soon be sitting on board a similar machine. He did not know if Jane Stanton had a window seat and doubted she would be watching, but waved anyway.

"I wonder why we do that?"

Mowgley turned away from the expanse of glass overlooking the runways: "What? Fly? I often ask myself the same question."

Yann Cornec shook his bullet-like head. "No, wave at people in planes and trains and on boats. And it is even stranger that they wave back. We don't do it to each other when we meet strangers in the street or pass them on the auto route, do we?"

Mowgley gave the observation fleeting thought. "Perhaps they wave because they're going on a relatively long journey. Or we think we're wishing them luck in case the boat sinks or the plane crashes. Or it could be just a tradition." He took Yann Cornec's hand. "You found me, then?"

He shrugged. "I'm a detective. Once a public one, now a

private, dick, is it?"

"Only if you've been watching old movies. Fancy a beer?"

"*Pourquoi pas?*"

"Is that Breton?"

"No, it's French. It means 'why not?' but it usually means yes."

"Ah," said Mowgley, leading the way to the bar. "It's the same in English, especially if someone offers you a beer."

* * *

"Are you saying that, in England, men go to airports just to take the numbers of aeroplanes?"

Mowgley nodded solemnly. "Yep. And they do it with trains as well. I even know some blokes who spend their spare time in garden sheds, making model things out of matchsticks. Sometimes it's the Eiffel Tower."

Yann Cornec gave him the French equivalent of an 'are-you-taking-the-piss?' look. "But why?"

Mowgley shrugged. "It's what they do."

Cornec digested the thought and shook his head. "So how did your evening in Brest go?"

"I want to talk to you about that in a minute. But first, here's the stuff you wanted." He took a crumpled envelope from his overnight carrier bag and passed it across the table.

Cornec opened the envelope and looked at the single sheet of paper inside, then frowned. "So who is Arkady Doku Ayubkhan Arzu Basayav?"

"Ah, sorry, wrong envelope. That's a Russian mafia gangster. Ugly looking customer, isn't he?"

Cornec handed the envelope back. "I was thinking he looked a little like me. When he was alive, that is. So he is a customer of yours?"

Mowgley rummaged in his carrier bag and took out another rumpled envelope. "In a sort of way; he would have been a customer if he had stayed alive, I reckon. But this is the bloke you wanted to know about."

"Ah, very good." Cornec removed the sheet of paper from the envelope and looked at the photograph and nodded. "That is my man. So tell me about him."

"It's all on the sheet-"

"Please, save me the trouble of reading it now."

"Okay. It turns out Mr Humphries was, until a year ago, a uniformed officer in the Liverpool police force. He took early retirement, but it was a case of jumping before he was pushed." Mowgley noted Cornec's bemused expression but continued without explanation: "It seems your Mr Humphries made a speciality of turning a blind eye to - I mean overlooking - crimes on his patch, providing he got a backhander - a bribe. He got too greedy and was shopped - informed on - by one of his customers. He denied the allegations but he was bang to rights and was given the option of leaving the force or staying on and assisting his superiors in an enquiry into the allegations. Does that help?"

Cornec nodded and smiled: "If you are saying what I think you are saying, it is most helpful, and explains a lot. If we are to work together in the future, I think I must learn your sort of English, or you will have to restrict yourself to the sort of English I learned at school."

Mowgley held his hands up in acceptance. "Can I ask why your client was interested in a bent former Scouse copper?"

Cornec smiled again. "*En fait* - in fact - I am the client. This one is for me. Mr Humphries arrived in Brittany last year. He set up as a private detective a month later after buying a piece of paper and a territory from a franchise company."

"So he's competition for you?"

"Not really. He operates at the other end of the region, and his customers are all English. And they would rather not be his customers."

"You'll have to explain that."

"What he does is use his contacts in the British police to find out about any problems with English people who have come to live in Brittany."

"A bit like you, then?"

Cornec looked as if he was thinking about taking offence, then gave a very low-level shrug: "Not really. I need the information to pass on to credit agencies and other official bodies. Your Mr Humphries befriends English people and then blackmails them if they have done some bad things in the past or have-"

"Skeletons in their cupboards?"

"What?"

Mowgley held a hand up. "Never mind. So what will you do about this bloke?"

Cornec pushed out his lower lip as if considering his options. "Now I know about his past, I will go and see him and let him know I know. I don't care what he does as long as it does not harm my business, and he could be useful to me in the future."

"I see," said Mowgley, while thinking that he would not like to be in Yann Cornec's bad books.

The private detective tapped the table briskly as if to signify the conclusion of their business, then reached into the inside pocket of his expensive-looking leather bomber jacket. It was the third envelope Mowgley had handled in a bar in Brest. This one contained something which felt pleasingly pliable.

"Just to cover your expenses and to show my good intent for the future," said Cornec.

Mowgley weighed the envelope in his hand for a moment, then put it on the table. "Very kind, but let's call this one a free sample. Perhaps I can now retain you to do a little job for me?"

Cornec gave another low-level shrug and said: "Of course. The fee will be the same. What is it you want?"

"A bit of detecting work, starting with a lift to the quayside. But only after we've sealed our deal with another drink. It's a tradition where I come from."

Cornec smiled and raised his empty glass. "It is just the same where I come from, my friend. Just the same..."

* * *

Mowgley opened his eyes when the fire-engine red 1963 French Alpine soft-top screeched to a halt outside the Irish bar. He did not know about classic cars, and had hoped that such an obviously old model would not be capable of such speed and agility.

Inside, he headed for the bar and a swift apple brandy to calm his nerves.

"So what are we looking for?" Cornec asked.

"This bloke." Mowgley took out the photograph and pointed at the central figure. "It looks to me as if it was taken at some sort of knees-up, possibly on the quay here. It would be good if you could ask around the waterfront if anyone knows him."

Cornec looked at the photograph and then at Mowgley. "Why don't you just ask her?"

Mowgley followed his eyes to where the young woman who had just served their drinks was scratching her cheek as she stared at the ceiling and thought of all the better places she could be at and better things she could be doing.

"You think she might know him?"

Cornec nodded towards the bar and smiled indulgently: "I think it likely. She has her hair a different colour and length, but that is the woman who was sitting next to the man in the photograph."

Seventeen

"What do you think about doppelgangers, Sergeant?"

"I prefer Kraftwerk in their early days."

Mowgley held the phone away from his ear and gave it a Paddington Bear stare: "What are you talking about?"

"I thought you were talking about the East German electronic band which nearly made it big in the early 70s."

"No you didn't; you're just being arsey because I haven't called you for a couple of days and my mobile's been off. You should be pleased that I left you alone with your favourite Frog."

"Okay. I forgive you. I suppose you're talking about doubles. It is said that everyone in the world has a doppelganger - someone who looks exactly like him or her. Going by the average celebrity lookalike, I reckon it's a load of hooey. After nearly a quarter of a century they haven't found anyone looking remotely like Elvis, and if there was I'm sure they would have done. Why, have you found one - someone's double, I mean, not an Elvis lookalike?"

"Don't know yet. But either David Burgess has a double, or he's got or had a double life."

"Go on, then. I'm all ears."

Although she could not see him, Mowgley nodded in agreement. "They are a bit on the big side, which I suppose is why you wear your hair over them, and are so good at bogging other people's conversations."

"Guilty on both counts. That's what makes me so good at my job. But what about the Burgess lookalike?"

"All will be explained when we meet at Perros-Guirec."

"Perros who?"

"Guirec. It's a yachtie heaven and haven about an hour north of where you're snuggling up to Guy. According to the barmaid in this place, it's where Mr Burgess's doppelganger hangs out. Or where our man lives his other life..."

* * *

As the barmaid had said, Perros-Guirec was indeed a haven for those wealthy enough to own and keep a boat in the town's marina. Some also owned apartments in a block directly overlooking the water, where prices per square metre equalled or even excelled those in coastal southern England.

Mowgley and Melons were sitting outside a bar on the quay, waiting for the waiter. He was looking through the plate glass window at them as if debating whether they were worth the effort of serving.

"Whatever you do," said Melons, "don't wave and snap your fingers or we'll never get a drink."

"How did you know I was going to do that?"

"Call it feminine intuition or just a guess based on what you always do when anyone with a tray looks even slightly down their nose at you." She smiled sunnily at the window, then said: "So start again and take me through exactly what we're doing here."

"Well, as you know, while you've been at it with Guy, I had a meeting with Yann in Brest."

Melons ignored the dig. "But why Brest? His office is in Morlaix. Could it be that you had other business there?"

Mowgley did his best not to look evasive. "Tell you about it later when we're alone."

"But we are alone."

"You know what I mean. Anyway, we went to a bar on the quay, and someone left a photo of Burgess on our table while I was in the khazi and J-Yann was getting the drinks."

"J-Yann?"

"Just a slip of the tongue, Sergeant. Anyway. The bloke in

the photo had a couple of dolly birds on his arm and was sitting in a very expensive-looking power boat. According to the barmaid - who was also one of the birds in the photo - the shot was taken at a yearly summer beano in Brest called the Festival of the Sea. The girl said he was a really rich playboy type who dropped in now and then and knew how to give a girl a good time. Flash boat, flash car and flash clothes, and always happy to flash a wad of mazumah. She hasn't seen him for a month or so, but thought he had a boat and a flat here."

"Is that why Yann and Guy have gone to see the harbour-master or whatever they call it here?"

Mowgley nodded. "Yep. According to Belinda the barmaid, the Burgess lookalike's name was Harry."

"Harry what?"

"She didn't know and I reckon it was the sort of relationship that she felt she didn't need to ask. That's why Yann's taken the photo with him."

"Here they come now." Melons waved to her lover and his friend. "So you're telling me that of all the bars in Brest, you went in one where someone had a photo of our man and then left it on the table for you to find? Bit of a coincidence, what?"

"Not if whoever left it followed us there and left the snap when the coast was clear."

"But who would want to let you know that Burgess had another identity, and why didn't he or she just tell you?"

"Perhaps they didn't want me to know who they were."

"What do you mean? And don't say 'tell you later'; that always means you won't tell me later."

Mowgley held his hands up, palms out in a placatory gesture. "No, this time 'tell you later' really means 'tell you later'. In the meantime, what do you want to drink? Don't look now, but Guy just snapped his fingers at the waiter and it worked a treat..."

* * *

"So the marina boss knew the bloke in the photo?"

"Bloke? Ah, yes." Guy nodded. "He said his name is Ripley."

Mowgley looked up sharply: "Not Tom Ripley, perchance?"

"Yes, it is Thomas. Do you know him?"

"Not in person. But carry on, please."

"The man in charge of the marina says Mr Ripley has a big and very expensive boat. It is kept here but does not go out to sea often. He also has an apartment at the top floor here -" Guy pointed upwards with his glass "- but he has not been seen on the boat or in the apartment complex for perhaps two weeks."

Mowgley looked impressed. "I don't suppose you got the name of the boat or the number of the flat?"

"The flat what?"

"Sorry, the *apartement*." Guy and Yann and even Melons winced as Mowgley pronounced the word in his idea of French.

Guy exchanged glances with Cornec, then shook his head indulgently and said: "Yes, we have the number, but there is no pass key."

"That shouldn't be a problem." Mowgley patted the pockets of his jacket. "Do either of you guys have a credit card?"

Guy and Yann exchanged looks again, then the Breton said: "Surely you don't believe what you see on television about using a credit card to open a door?"

"No," said Mowgley quickly before Melons could spoil the gag. "It's just that I've run out of cash and wanted to settle the drinks bill. Boom-Boom."

Eighteen

Mowgley had been here before.

Not in this particular apartment block, but one very much like it in a trendily vulgar marina complex near Portsmouth. He supposed there were many more just like them all around Europe and probably the world.

They would have the same sort of location and the same sort of owners and even the same sort of smell, or lack of smell. The carpets were thick and luxuriant, and the lighting subdued. As an indicator of how important their owners of these waterside dwellings were (or thought they were), each of the identical doors lining the corridor bore a spy hole at eye level but no number on the door. This was probably because there were no letter boxes.

This block was so up-the-market that it could afford fresh flowers in the vestibule. It could also afford a concierge with nothing to do but take delivery of mail and messages. He also had to try and look as if he were happy minding rarely-visited holiday homes for people who earned more in a day than he did in a month.

The almost eerie thing about these places, Mowgley reflected, was that you never saw any sign of human habitation. No empty or full milk bottles by the thresholds, no prams or push-bikes at stair heads or wells, and no catalogues, phone books or junk mail on the mats. Most of all, no smells or noises of any kind. Everything was clean to the point of sterility, and he supposed that was how the sort of people who could afford to live here - or actually not live here - liked it. Like rich people always left more food on the plate than they ate, perhaps it was a status symbol to own a flat here and rarely visit it. Conspicuous lack of consumption, as it were.

The loudspeaker in the lift pinged, the door slid open with a haughty hiss, and the passengers stepped out to find themselves in a large area which would probably take offence at being called a landing. It had a particularly fulsome vase of flowers in one corner, and one wall was occupied almost entirely by an extravagant window which looked out across the marina. Apart from a set of gleaming chrome spotlights, the expanse of whiteness on walls and ceiling was broken by only a single door.

"Blimey," said Melons, "it looks like he's got the whole floor to himself. The landing's bigger than my flat."

Mowgley nodded. "It's certainly not bad for a bloke who lives in a caravan in England, and an old tub in Normandy." He looked to where the large picture-window framed the marina and its collection of toy boats. "I could put up with living here."

Melons brought him back to reality: "So you're sure Ripley is Burgess, then?"

Mowgley pulled at his lower lip: "Long as the odds are, we might just have stumbled across a true doppelganger. Or it could be that the photograph is of Burgess, posing as Ripley, but not really being him."

"So you're saying there could be, however loony the theory, a real Tom Ripley who owns this flat and is the image of Burgess. Or it could simply be that Ripley is Burgess's alter-ego?"

"That sort of thing. Anyway, whether or not Ripley is Burgess, we still don't have any firm evidence he's no longer with us."

"But what about the DNA from the body being the same as the blood on the boat at Carentan?"

"Ah," said Mowgley portentously before reaching out for the bell-push, "there's the rub."

Guy and Yann, who had been watching the exchange like spectators at a tennis match, looked at each other and made near-identical shrugs before the *Gendarmerie* officer asked:

"Why are you doing that? There was no answer when we used the entry phone in the foyer."

"I just wanted to see if it had musical chimes," replied Mowgley, looking disappointed at the discreet buzz coming from within. "The last time we were doing this, the doorbell played *A Life on the Ocean Waves*. I was hoping for *La Mer* or somesuch."

"I see," said Guy, who obviously didn't. "But you would like to see inside?"

"If you reckon you can get that door down without causing too much damage or upsetting the neighbours or fetching the police."

"As you have perhaps not seen, there are no neighbours," observed Yann, reaching into his bomber jacket, then nodding towards Guy, "...and the police are already here." Pulling out and unzipping a small black case, he took out a metal ring on which were strung a number of variously shaped and sized metal rods.

"I'm disappointed," said the Inspector as Yann Cornec approached the door.

"Why, did you want to kick it down in the traditional way?" asked Melons.

"No, it's just that none of those keys looks anything like a skeleton."

* * *

Generally speaking, Mowgley had observed that most single men fell into one of two categories when it came to housekeeping. They were, like him, unconcerned slobs, or tidy on a scale ranging from organised neatness to Obsessive Compulsive Disorder. Often and unlike most women, they lived at the extreme ends of the range.

If his apartment was as it was when he had last occupied it, Mr Ripley/Burgess was clearly a person who disliked clutter. He also clearly disliked soft furnishings and furniture and curves, and preferred straight edges and corners where possible. He also disliked keeping and displaying any items which would give clues to other aspects of his character.

Apart from the bedrooms, where some softness was inevitable, there was little concession to cosy comfort in the penthouse apartment. There were no curtains, and the Venetian-style blinds were all partially opened to the same precise angle. The floors were of highly polished parquet with not a rug to break the geometric lines. In front of the window overlooking the marina and taking up most of one wall sat a smoked-glass table. Though he had no tape measure to hand to prove it, Mowgley would have placed a significant bet on the six dining chairs being the same exact distance from each other and the table.

As severe in design as the other pieces, a low sideboard ran along one wall, and against another stood its twin. Like the rest of the furniture, they were supported by chromed metal legs, and also like the other furniture, the main components were matt black in colour. In contrast, the walls of the sitting room and four bedrooms were a pure white, broken only by the narrow-framed picture each bore. Again, Mowgley would have had more than a modest wager that the frame on each wall occupied its precise epicentre. Unsurprisingly, the drawings were in black and white.

Earlier exploration of the three bathrooms and kitchen had confirmed the same constancy of style and material and colour, or lack of it.

"Well now," said Mowgley, embracing the main room with a sweep of his arm, "nothing like a nice, cosy, lived-in home, is there? And this is nothing like a nice, cosy etcetera. Unless there's evidence to the contrary, I'd say this place has never been lived in."

"Either that or it's been cleaned up really professionally," observed Melons.

They had spent an hour going over the apartment, and the search had revealed not much more about its owner than the fixtures and fittings. The designer clothes in the wardrobe and drawers in the master bedroom appeared not to have been worn. There were no electronic gadgets or photographs, and not even a book by the bedside. There was a pristine towelling dressing gown hanging on the back of the bathroom door, and the glass shelves were neatly lined with expensive male toiletries and unguents. In the cabinet above the hand basin was a set of hairbrushes and a comb and a tube of toothpaste, neatly squeezed from the bottom. Alongside was a small box of proprietary painkillers, a bottle of English mouthwash and a reel of dental floss. Next to the cabinet and on a small shelf by a power point was a top-of-the-range shaver and an electric toothbrush.

In the kitchen, the fridge was empty except for a large bottle of unopened mineral water and a cardboard container of tomato juice. The eight-ring cooker, chopping board, chef's knives and other preparation equipment looked as unused as the clothing in the bedroom. Clearly, the owner preferred to eat out.

They had agreed to leave the clothing for the forensic team when the apartment received an official visit from the *Gendarmerie*, but Guy had taken the shaver, hair and tooth brushes and other small items in case Mr Burgess/Ripley returned in the time between their departure and the arrival of a police guard.

"That's us done, then, unless anyone has any ideas?" Mowgley looked at where his watch would have been had he owned one. "I see it's coming up for lunchtime, my friends. Reckon there will be anywhere I can get a pasty round here?"

As he stood up, he saw Melons looking thoughtfully at the sleek cordless telephone in its docking bay on the glass topped table. "What are you thinking?" he asked. "We already checked the answer phone thingy and it's been wiped. And Guy is going to get us a list of all calls made to and from this number."

"Yes, but there is something else we can check."

"Okay, I give in. What?"

"Three police officers and a former police officer, and none of us thought about checking the last caller." She looked at Guy. "Don't tell me you don't have that service."

He smiled and held up his hands in an apologetic gesture. "Yes, of course. But it only works if the call was not answered and the answering machine did not start." He pointed at a green light on the front of the sleek device. "As the machine is active and had been wiped-"

"But if someone called and hung up before the answer phone kicked in, the number would still be there, yes?"

"Yes. You have just to dial 3131."

Melons did, listened for a moment, then wrote in her notebook and put the phone back in its docking station.

"Stop looking so smug," said Mowgley. "It was probably

someone selling double glazing."

"If it was, they must have a wide sales area."

"What do you mean?"

She handed her notebook to Mowgley. "It's a mobile number, and British."

"Oh." He looked at the number, then closed the notebook and handed it back to his sergeant. "Well done, Mel-Catherine. We'll look into it when we get back to HQ."

She looked disappointed. "I could call young Stephen now and get him to start working on it?"

"No, really," he said, "it'll wait." What he did not add was that the number Melons had written down was familiar to him, and one that he had called many times in recent days.

Nineteen

Detective Inspector Mowgley stared gloomily at the windscreen and tried to stop his eyes following the metronomic motion of the wipers. "On days like these," he sighed, "I can see the attractions of living in France."

Melons thought of her lover across the Channel: "So can I, but not because of the weather. Anyway, it's bound to be raining just as hard on your house in Normandy. And the roof leaks."

"I know, but the rain seems less...wet in France."

"True. But think of what you'd miss, apart from me. You won't find many boozers like the Ship Leopard in France."

Mowgley refused to be comforted and lapsed into sulky silence as he thought about the pros and cons of a voluntary or enforced exile. Perhaps it would not be too bad, as with all the frequent crossings he was beginning to feel almost at home on the other side of the Channel. But it was true what Melons said about the lack of Ship Leopards in France.

Apart from the Daily Telegraph crossword, caff fry-ups, Indian curry shops, white sliced bread and hard cheese, what Mowgley missed most when in France was a proper English pub. Not the poncy sort of place which was really a restaurant, but a proper bang-on boozer with sticky carpets and no need of a sign to tell you where the toilets were located.

As he reached out to increase the volume of the Johnny

Cash classic already thundering from the audio system loudspeakers, the car in front braked sharply and swerved towards the kerb. It was a big, black 4x4 with tinted windows and huge chromed bull bars.

Melons winced as a sheet of dirty water erupted from beneath the nearside wheels of the top-of-the-range Nissan. Most of the members of the small queue waiting at the bus stop saw what was coming and jumped back to avoid a drenching. But an elderly lady was less agile.

"Bastard!" Melons was reaching for the blue light button on the dashboard of their unmarked car when Mowgley put a restraining hand over hers. She looked across at her senior officer as the vehicle accelerated away. "Surely we're going to do him? It was no bloody accident. He did that just for fun."

"Don't be so sexist, Sergeant. The driver could be a female. And what could you charge him or her with? Driving without due care, or being in possession of an offensive vehicle?"

"I'm sure we could think of something. There's the way he's doctored the licence plates for a start. 'GBH' my arse. Surely you're not going to let him get away with soaking that old lady?"

"Certainly not, Sergeant. I just wanted the chance to say: 'follow that car.'"

* * *

"How did you know?"

"What?" asked Mowgley as they followed the 4X4 into the car park of the Ship Leopard. "That he was coming here."

"As a trained and naturally gifted observer, I had noted that the same vehicle was here yesterday and the day before at around this time. I have also observed the driver, who by his lavish spending and pathetic chat-up lines, is either having it off with Twiggy or would like to so do. And from the company he's been keeping together with the resale value of the car and his bodily ornaments and several other more subtle indicators, I suspect he's doing a bit of Class 'A' dealing. There's also the fact that I had young Mundy look his index number up and check him out."

"And what did Stephen turn up?"

"It transpires that our man has a number of known and

dodgy associates. Mundy has been keeping an eye on his movements elsewhere, and I have been noting his movements in here."

"Are you telling me that for the last three days when I thought we were having our usual lunch at the Leo, we've actually been on obbo?"

"Correct, Sergeant."

"And naturally, you'll claim the bar bills - which I've been mostly settling - as exes?"

"No good getting older if you don't get smarter, Sergeant. The thing is, we don't want to spook our man. That's why I told you not to pull him over."

"So he gets away with drenching the old lady?"

"Far from it. As I often say, watch and learn. Now please get the beer in and bring me a menu so I can decide what I will order for my luncheon."

"Why do you want a menu? You know you'll have pasty and chips like every other single day we come here at dinner time."

"Yes, but I would hate to be thought a creature of habit."

Melons made for the bar and gave their order. Waiting for her change, she watched as Mowgley walked across the bar to where a group of men were sitting around a table. To a palaeontologist from a distant star, they might be seen as members of some sort of sect which required them to daub their clothing with paint, plaster and other substances. In fact, they were merely wearing badges of their trades. As tradition also demanded in the building profession, there was also a competition for who could display the most outrageously distressed tops, trousers and footwear. Being proper tradesmen, they were of course forbidden by custom from wearing overalls.

After a general acknowledgement, Mowgley spoke to the biggest and easily most colourfully daubed man in the group. His mother and wife knew him as Trevor, but to the other regulars in the Ship Leopard it was inevitable that he was known as Bob The Builder.

After greetings and words had been exchanged, Bob left the pub and Mowgley joined Melons at the bar.

"So what's occurring?" she asked. "Are you arranging to have Bob and his boys give your room above the Midnight

Tindaloo a makeover?"

Mowgley made no reply, lunch was served and they made their way to their permanently reserved table. Silence ensued for several minutes, then Melons pointed her knife at the man who had splashed the old lady and said, "I wonder if more men are going balder earlier."

Mowgley paused with a forkful of pasty, chips, mustard and brown sauce en route to his mouth. "Eh?"

"I was reading that you lot are less hairy than in prehistoric times. And all the science fiction films show men and women with bald heads. It's something to do with central heating, apparently."

"What, in caves?"

"Don't be silly. Because we live in a much warmer environment nowadays, we don't need so much hair."

Leaving some of the forkful on his shirt front, Mowgley filled and then emptied his mouth, then said: "Your logic is a bit wonky, Sergeant. For a start, nobody can really know what things were like in prehistoric times, as they were, well, prehistoric. And you only have to watch the adverts on telly to see women have got more hair than they know what to do with. That's why they keep swinging it about in slow motion. I think you'll find it's just the fashion that blokes who are losing their hair at an early age shave their heads rather than go for a Neil Kinnock comb-over."

"But shaving their heads just draws attention to the fact that they're balding."

"I know that and you know that, but they hope you might think that they have shaved their heads for reasons of fashion."

"But that's a daft fashion."

"Do you as a woman want to start a debate about silly hair fashions?"

"No comment."

They continued with their meals as they - or rather Melons - discreetly watched the subject of their conversation. Thinking of a possible confrontation, she noted that the shaven-headed man was not as tall or broad as Mowgley, but at least a decade younger and clearly in better shape in spite of a sizeable beer- belly. Despite the weather and probably to show off his brawny, tattoo-embellished forearms, the man was wearing what looked like an expensive short-sleeved silk shirt. On his right wrist he wore what was probably a genuine Rolex watch. On his left was a chunky gold bracelet which, if real, would have cost as much as the watch. His hands were so big that he wore his bulky sovereign ring on a little finger. His beige slacks were immaculately creased, and his black loafers looked as if they had been put on the first time that morning. With his tiny ears, lack of neck, wide, long upper-lipped mouth, flat nose and fleshy face badly pitted with past acne scars, he looked to Melons like a modern-day Mr Toad. The impression was reinforced by his arrogant demeanour.

"It somehow makes what he did worse."

Mowgley looked up and across the bar. "What, you want to nick him for bad taste?"

"The fact that he is so fussy about his own clothes but didn't care what happened to the people in the queue. Why would he want to ruin their day?"

"That's exactly the point. It's a cruel world and the *hoi polloi* have always taken joy in seeing other people in trouble. Some people delight in inflicting pain and sorrow, as you should know. Why else do yobs shoot swans and throw kittens off the top of high-rise blocks? I reckon it's because they can't think what it would be like to be in someone else's shoes, or how they would feel if someone inflicted misery and pain on them. That's why they need reminding sometimes. Ah, here comes my man."

Bob the builder arrived at their table, carrying a bundled-up plasterer's apron which he put on their table before returning to his colleagues. Making a show of it, Mowgley undid the bundle to reveal a hammer and four six inch nails.

"What's this," asked Melons. "Are you joining the Masons? You always said you wouldn't join any club which would have you as a member."

"Actually, that was the great Groucho Marx, but I concur." He looked across the bar to where the shaven-headed man was watching. "I just wanted matey to see what I was doing."

"Why?"

"It will make it sweeter, somehow."

"What will?"

"Granny's revenge." Mowgley stood, picked up the bundle and before leaving, pointed at a table near a window overlooking the car park. "In a minute, shift to that table and I'll see you back there."

"What's wrong with this one?"

"Humour me. The view's better from that one."

* * *

"That was good going."

"What was?"

"Building an ark so quickly. I assume that's what you were doing with the hammer and nails after all this rain we've had. Or do you plan to do some DIY on your place in France next time over?"

"Not really. It's falling to pieces without my help."

Deciding not to spoil his good mood with thoughts of the downside of owning an uninhabitable home more than a hundred miles from where he worked, Melons lit up a cigarette, then asked: "Are you ready to talk business?"

"If you must. What bit of business do you think we should talk about?"

"All those things you keep telling me you'll tell me about later, for a start. And I have a couple of pertinent questions."

"As long as they are not also impertinent, Sergeant." Mowgley rolled his eyes and sighed theatrically. "Oh, alright then; go on."

"What I want to know is what you really reckon to the Burgess forward slash Ripley scenario. And I mean what you *really* think is going on. And what you know that I don't about the case. You clearly believe that Mr Burgess is still with us in whatever incarnation. That means you know something I don't, or you've been cosying up with someone in the know. You may think so, but I am not unobservant or stupid. I can tell when you've been having secret assignations and also when you are smitten. The two may of course be connected."

Inspector Mowgley took a long pull on his lager, looked deliberately evasive, then asked: "On what do you base your assumptions?"

"For a start, you were lying when you said all the calls you were taking in Brittany and since were from Yann Cornec. And I think you were seeing someone else apart from him in Brest."

"How do you know?"

"Unless you've changed your sexual orientation, you don't go all dopey and moonstruck when you've been speaking to a bloke on the phone. And you looked really smug when you arrived at Perros Guirec. And I know when you know something I don't. You should never play poker."

"I don't. Anyway, what you've got is hardly proof of anything."

"There's more. I have positive proof you've got a new contact."

"In what form?"

"You remember when you gave me your phone to recharge yesterday?"

"Yes?"

"Normally I have to bully you into keeping it topped-up. You must have wanted to be sure not to miss any special calls."

"So? That's just me being conscientious."

"Hah!" Melons looked at him for a moment, then took her notebook out and laid it on the table as if introducing a new piece of evidence." I have to admit that I took a look at your call history before I charged your phone."

"My *what* history?"

"Quite. I knew you wouldn't even know how to find your past calls, let alone delete them."

Mowgley looked genuinely evasive. "So...?"

"So the same number came up a dozen times."

"It's probably Yann's number..."

"Don't be silly. His is a French number. You've been taking calls and making them to this number every day since we were in Brittany last week. And there's something which is really strange."

"Which is?"

"It's the number of the person who was the last caller to Mr Ripley's fancy flat in Perros Guirec."

* * *

"And that's absolutely everything?"

Mowgley nodded. "Absolutely. You now really do know everything I do."

She pursed her lips: "Except what's going on with you and bloody Wonder Woman."

"I've already explained all that; as you already knew, she's down from the Met's Special Projects Unit to check out some Russians who are planning to bring stuff in big time. She's not trying to get anything on us or drop us in the shite. All the evidence says that something big is going on and our little patch is going to be a fairly important part of it. She could have done things by the book and buried everyone in paperwork and had Cressida Doodad breathing down our necks. Working together this way it keeps things simple, and it limits those in the know. You can't argue with the logic of that."

Melons looked as if she easily could, and said: "Since when did I get lumped in with all those people who don't need to know about a job you're on?"

Mowgley sighed. "That's not even worth answering. For a start, I've been as banjaxed by this one as you. Passing on every little detail of my meetings with the DCI wouldn't have helped you. And anyway, she gave me a direct order not to reveal the details of our meetings."

Melons made an explosive sound of mock amusement. "Yeah, right, I know how attentive you are to orders. And anyway, I only wanted to know what you know, and now I do." She looked hard at him and then continued, "...I hope. I'm certainly not interested in what goes on between you and her behind closed doors, or wherever else you do it. You're old enough and certainly ugly enough to look after yourself in that respect. But just how serious are you about her? I hope you're not getting in too deep."

Mowgley bridled. "Less of the old enough and ugly enough, if you don't mind. And what do you mean by getting in too deep?"

"I mean all this health and hygiene stuff and playing your favourite Country and Western records at full volume. And how you look like a lovesick horse when even her bloody name is mentioned."

"For a start I don't know what a lovesick horse looks like. And as you of all people should know, sometimes when men and women work together, they find a mutual attraction -"

"I can see you being attracted to her, but what do you think she sees in you?"

"Bloody cheek. Just because you go for some smoothie who's obsessed with his appearance and can't pass a shop window without looking in it, it doesn't mean all women have your taste."

"No, but I just can't see Madame Stanton being attracted by your particular sort of rugged, homespun charm. Look at her clothes and her car, even the bloody fags she smokes. She goes for top-of-the-range in everything."

"So?"

"So I'm just saying. There might be more to it than her wanting your body. I don't want to see you getting hurt."

"Thank you for your concern, Sergeant. Now what was that other question you wanted to ask me?"

"What did you do with that hammer and nails?"

"As I said, all will be revealed."

Melons shook her head in despair. "You've been doing your Judge Dredd bit again, haven't you?"

"If you mean administering a bit of instant justice, I must hold my hands up."

"But why not just let Mundy get him on the dealing thing? And what if he has an accident because you spiked his tyres?"

"Do you think I'm an amateur? I let one of his tyres down as well. He ain't going anywhere soon. Mundy will see we get him for the peddling, anyway. This was just a little extra."

"So what do you think you've achieved?"

"For a start it'll cost him a few bob and at least a smidgeon of aggro to get his car sorted - and it should get his blood pressure up. With luck he might have a heart attack. And natural justice will have been dispensed."

Melons sighed: "But the old lady will never know."

"No, but I will."

"But this only works if Mr Toad knows who did it and why, doesn't it?"

Mowgley stood up and drained his glass while holding out a hand for hers. "That's where I'm going now."

"You're going to tell him you've done his tyres? He won't be best pleased."

"I shall be more subtle than that, but he's seen the hammer and nails and I'll make sure he gets the plot."

"He's not going to be a happy bunny when he sees what you've done to his shiny motor, is he?"

"Quite. Especially the new paint job."

His sergeant looked up sharply. "The paint job? You just

don't know when to stop, do you? What if he gets nasty? He's a big bloke."

"It's okay, lovey. I've got a police officer with me, haven't I?"

Twenty

"Well, you certainly know how to give a girl a good time."

"You said you liked a punt," said Mowgley defensively, "*and* this is the members' stand."

Jane Stanton looked at the rain-soaked sky through a hole in the corrugated-tin roof and smiled ruefully: "When I said I liked a day at the races, I meant I like going to Ladies Day at Ascot. This is the first time I've togged up to go to a dog track." She turned on one high heel as she surveyed her surroundings. "Mind you, considering the state of the rest of the city, I suppose you could say it's quite upmarket. Funny enough, in a way it reminds me of you."

"What, you mean entertaining, friendly and guaranteed to give you a good time?"

"Not really. More like shabby and run-down and well past its prime. But balanced by being endearing and not at all pretentious, and with bags of character."

"Thanks," said Mowgley, "I think."

They were taking shelter at Portsmouth's premier and only racing venue. Close by the waterside scrap yard where Mowgley had until recently lived on board a defunct lightship, the official name for the dog track was The Portsmouth Greyhound Racing Course. The stadium had been built in 1931, making it one of the oldest greyhound tracks in the country. As even its most ardent supporters would admit, it looked it.

The facilities were basic by the standards and expectations of modern times, and some wags claimed the toilets pre-dated the stadium by at least a century. The imaginative publicity material risked falling foul of the Trades Descriptions Act by claiming that the Course 'attracted a huge following, with the young and trendy set rubbing shoulders with traditional greyhound purists'. This, concluded the blurb, imbued the stadium with what it called a 'distinct feel'.

Although, like most of the dogs that appeared there, the stadium was on its last legs, it had attracted big crowds in the years before television. This was also a time when conditions in many people's homes were so unappealing that they were pleased to escape them.

Another incentive for attending in the heydays was that there were no betting shops or any other licit way of placing a wager off-course. Visiting the local barber shop or building a relationship with a bookie's undercover runner was always an option, but by going to the dogs, the punters could see the racing, rub shoulders with local celebrities and legally place a bet.

As they do, times had changed. Like many of the house dogs and some punters, the stadium was in terminal decline, but Mowgley liked the collection of tin-roofed, ramshackle block and concrete buildings set around a poorly-maintained cinder track. He liked the place's take-it-or-leave-it attitude, and most of all he liked the sort of people who turned out in all sorts of weathers to watch a handful of dogs in pursuit of a bundle of rags that looked nothing at all like a rabbit.

There was even a quite complex caste system, with the bookies and dog owners at the top. Mowgley's father had been an owner, and the detective could still see him at the finishing post, posing for a photograph and standing proud and tall with the plastic winner's trophy held aloft.

Following this family tradition, Mowgley had once owned the back nearside leg of a greyhound. It had been called *Surprise Surprise*, and as its disenchanted syndicate of owners had concluded, it was a genuine surprise when it finished a race.

"So have you made your selection, Marm?"

"I think so. I just picked the names I liked and made a lot of marks on the card. Is that right?"

"You'd probably have done better with your eyes shut and a pin. But you'll certainly have more chance than the form-studiers and tipsters. Dog racing, like my life, seems to follow a curiously unpredictable pattern."

He took her card and walked across the stained concrete decking to where a handful of bookmakers were trying to look as if they would not much rather be at home in front of the telly. He stopped where a very elderly man was standing on a low pair of steps, resting his hand on the shoulder of his assistant. Henry Cutts had been making a book in the city since before the War, and had, it was generally agreed, seen it all. His endless tales of turf wars, stings and outrageous good and bad fortune for punters and those who took their bets had kept Mowgley entertained when he was a schoolboy glass-collector at the track.

As well as telling tales, Henry had many told about him. One night after official closing time in the Member's bar, Mowgley had asked him if it were true that after the War he had conducted his business from a brand-new Bentley with £20,000 in very used notes locked in a metal trunk which was welded to the floor of the boot. This was said to be because he disliked and mistrusted the banks and the taxman equally and did not like to leave his money alone in the house. He was also said to protect his stash with a German Luger pistol he liberated from an SS officer before shooting him with it just after hostilities had officially ceased.

After looking affectionately back into the long-gone past, Henry had shaken his head and said "Course it weren't true: It was a Rover not a Bentley. Only a mug would want to be noticed by the taxman."

Back with Jane Stanton and having moved to slightly less damp conditions in the bar, Mowgley ordered drinks and took them to a table in a quiet corner.

"You really love it here, don't you?" She leaned forward to allow him to light her cigarette.

Mowgley snapped the Zippo shut and looked around the bar fondly. "Guilty, Marm. For me, it's got everything. A comfy bar, interesting people and even more interesting toilets. You get a bit of entertainment watching the dogs stumble round the track in return for doing your money, and there's an endless supply of pastys."

"Another part of traditional British life you'll miss if you go to France, then?"

Mowgley's face clouded over. "Bugger. I didn't have the dog track on my list. I don't think they do this sort of thing over there."

"There's lots of horse and buggy racing in Normandy, I hear." Mowgley made a face. "Not the same as a night at the dogs.

I find all that prancing around in camp and colourful outfits a bit dubious. And that's just the jockeys."

She smiled, drew on her cigarette, looked at him thoughtfully, then said: "If you don't want to go into exile, I might be able to help you out."

"Like shooting Madame Cressida Double-Barrelled?"

"It doesn't have to be that drastic. I know some people who could help."

"What, the Old Boy routine? Can you really see me in the Smoke, dashing around in cars with squealy tyres and all tooled up? I'd probably shoot myself in the foot. And I'd have to learn a whole new vocabulary with all that 'it's gone pear-shaped, guv' stuff."

"At your age I didn't mean changing location or jobs. You've got to remember there's all sorts of options for people like you and me."

"What do you mean, options?"

Jane Stanton looked at him thoughtfully, then tipped her head back blew a long stream of blue smoke at the polystyrene-tiled ceiling. "Tell you later, perhaps."

"That's my line."

"I know."

Mowgley reached for his baccy tin. "You seem to know a lot about me and where I am and what I'm up to and all sorts of other stuff."

"It's called being a detective. Part of my job is doing my homework and finding out who's who and what they're up to anywhere I'm going to do a bit of work."

"Quite. But you don't seem to like to share stuff that I might have an interest in."

"Like what?"

"Like our putative trunk murder victim having a nice little

pad in Perros-Guirec."

Except for a look of mild bemusement, she did not react. Then she asked: "Perros what?"

"As I reckon you know full well, Mr Burgess has got a penthouse gaff or had a penthouse gaff in a flash marina on the north coast of Brittany."

"Really?"

"Uh-huh." Mowgley took the photograph of Burgess as Ripley from an inside pocket and laid it on the table. "And he's got another name. But you'd know all that, anyway."

Again she did not react, and he continued. "I went there after someone left this for me in the Irish pub in Brest. You know, the one you'd never been to before."

Her expression did not change. "Did you find him?"

"No. It was empty and the place had been cleaned up professionally."

"You mean he'd had a cleaning company in?"

"Please don't take the piss, Ma'am. Someone had stripped it but left obvious things like hairbrush and razor. Almost like they wanted us to lift prints or DNA."

"Ah." Again she aimed a stream of smoke at the ceiling. "So what are you saying?"

"Someone seems to be trying to give me a leg-up. It's getting like a game of Cluedo. Except I'm stumbling around mostly in the dark, and you're keeping me there by choice. Oh, and we checked the phone line at the flat. The last caller was you."

As she opened her mouth to speak, the loudspeaker above their heads crackled and a frustrated radio DJ announced the next race with a pun that even Mowgley thought unfunny. The wind blew open the door leading to the stand and a flurry of rain rattled on the windows overlooking the cinder track. Jane Stanton looked across the table steadily for a moment, then stubbed out her cigarette and took a sip of her drink before responding. "Okay, it's a fair cop. I suppose now it's all gone pear-shaped I'd better put my hands up to it."

Mowgley gave her a Paddington Bear stare to show he was not amused. "I reckon so, Ma'am."

She reached for her cigarette packet. "As I probably should have told you, Burgess or Ripley is or was one of my contacts. It was because of him I came down here.

"For a small-time boat trader? That's all he was?"

She continued to look at him for a moment, then leaned forward and took a cigarette from the packet. "Alright. Active listening mode, please."

Mowgley gave a neutral nod. She waited for him to light her cigarette, then picked up her lighter. "Burgess was regularly importing class 'A', using the boats he brought over. It was a pretty good cover, actually. Customs and Coastguards are always on the lookout for regular travellers, but he had a good excuse. And he always looked and acted as if he was just about scraping a living."

"But with the penthouse and his lifestyle in Brittany, he must have been doing pretty well?"

"Very well. Unlike most people who use boats to bring stuff in, he went to a lot of trouble. His speciality was making up lead ballast ingots with up to a kilo of cocaine inside."

"That sounds a bit tricky."

"Not if you put the gear in heatproof metal boxes and then sink them in the molten lead."

"So what put you on to him?"

"At the back end of last year, he did a smallish deal for some heroin with one of our undercover people. That's where I came in. When they pulled him in and put the frighteners on, I turned up and gave him the chance of staying out of nick if he gave me all his contacts. We had heard he was working with some pretty dodgy people, but we didn't have a clue as to how deep he was in."

"And how deep was that?"

"He was working for the Russians I told you about. They were using him as their local man in this area, and to help them make the right contacts and set up the system for getting stuff into the country in a big way. He was delivering the boats and gear to marinas along the south coast, and in the process helping set up a processing and distribution network for them."

"So you made him an offer he couldn't refuse?"

She nodded and toyed with her glass. "I said I would let him keep going if he kept me in the know."

"That was a bit dodgy, wasn't it?"

She shrugged. "Better to wait for the big fish than take a small one, I reckoned."

"Not so small if he could afford his lifestyle in Brittany."

"That was because he was being a silly boy and ripping off the Russians."

"So you didn't know about the Ripley incarnation?"

"I honestly didn't to start with. He called me in a panic just before Christmas and said he thought the Russians were on to him. Then came the body on the ferry. I thought it was him until I got a call from Brittany. We met over there and he came clean. Or said he was coming clean."

"Do tell."

"He said that the Russians had tumbled what he was up to and sent Igor to deal with him. That's where the plan for him to disappear came from."

Mowgley frowned. "Killing people and cutting up bodies sounds a bit advanced for a simple drug smuggler."

"According to Burgess, it was all Igor's idea. Burgess told him he had a pot of cash and a big stash, and Igor saw it as a good opportunity to go into business on his own."

"So where did the torso in the cabin come from?"

"According to Burgess, Igor found a would-be illegal immigrant who was of the same age and size and body-type as Burgess. The poor sod was supposed to be smuggled over in Burgess's boat. Instead, Igor got him drunk on the crossing, killed and cut him up and threw the spare parts in the Channel. Then he took the boat off the ferry with Burgess hidden inside."

"So how did Igor end up in the boat beneath the Mulberry?"

"Burgess said he had to make up a story about the money and stuff he had set aside to keep Igor sweet, and anyway, he was sure Igor intended doing for him when he got his hands on the stash. Anyway, according to him, he told Igor the goods were hidden in one of the air pockets on the Mulberry. He planned to strand him out there and push off with the boat and disappear. But when they arrived, Igor tried to kill him and Burgess acted in self-defence."

"Hitting a bloke from behind with a blunt object don't sound much like self-defence to me."

"Me neither, but that was not my worry. Igor was not a very nice person and I wanted Burgess to get me to the big boys."

"So what happened?"

"He was going to give me the heads-up when the first big shipment was coming in and how and where. Then he stopped answering my calls. I went to his flat at Perros-Guirec and found it clean, and that's where we are now."

"So your idea of coming over to Brittany wasn't just because you were missing me?"

"No. Believe it or not I was going to bring you into the loop, but when we spoke on the phone I thought it would be a good idea to come over and find out what you were up to. I also thought it would be a bit of fun, which I hope you agree it was."

Mowgley looked at her but made no comment, then said: "So what do you think has happened to him?"

"I honestly don't know. Either he's done a runner and set up another new identity, or the Russians have got him. Either way I'm buggered. If we can find him, we've got a chance of getting to the big boys."

"We? So I'm included now?"

A look of irritation passed across her face. "Be fair. I couldn't tell you any of this until I was sure you weren't involved somehow."

"Ah. So you thought I might be at it and making an even better job of appearing skint than Burgess. Are you going to tell me who gave you that idea?"

"I asked around before I came down, and believe it or not, some people think you couldn't lie straight in bed."

"And what do you think now?"

"I know how you lie in bed, and I think you're a very unusual bloke and not at all the sort of man I am used to dealing with." She picked up her glass and looked reflectively at him over the rim "You just might be the straightest copper I've met in a long while."

* * *

The loudspeaker crackled and whined again before the wannabe DJ announcer reeled off the evening's results in a contrived mid- Atlantic accent. Mowgley was on his way to the bookies' enclosure, and had left Jane Stanton in the bar while he walked around the cinder track and thought about what she had told him.

"Who picked all the winners, son?" asked Henry Cutts as he ruefully handed over a thick wodge of banknotes, "I bet it was that bramah party you were with in the bar?"

Mowgley nodded and explained that the lady was not only

a bramah party, but also a police officer of senior rank to him.

"Well now," observed the old man, winking one rheumy eye, "better at playing the game than you. And tasty, and lucky. You want to watch her son."

"You're not wrong there, Henry," observed Mowgley thoughtfully as he looked through the bar window and watched Jane Stanton making a call on her mobile, "You are certainly not wrong."

Twenty-one

Caught in the headlights, the big dog-fox paused, tail nonchalantly aloft and one paw raised in a somehow fastidious manner. Rather than being transfixed with fear, it seemed unconcerned. After a moment it tilted its head to one side and seemed to look at them as if querying or challenging their intrusion into its world. Then it lost interest and slipped away into the darkness shrouding the wasteland behind the stadium.

"Cheeky sod." Jane Stanton took her foot off the brake and pulled away. "It wasn't worried by us at all."

"Living in this town, it was probably thinking about mugging us."

Mowgley liked foxes and their cleverness and apartness. He thought it would be too much to say he identified with them, but he admired the way they lived on the edge of society while making a living from the opportunities cropping up in a big and wasteful habitation. Like some of the human denizens, he thought as they drove on into the dark heart of the city.

Like the fox, Mowgley felt at home abroad at this time, and the later the better. When he was not trying to sleep, the small hours were his favourite time to be out and about. And it would not be long before night became day. As was customary after the last race, the bookies and privileged punters had arrived in the bar to celebrate or drink away their disappointment. That had been followed by the inevitable lock-in, and suddenly dawn was waiting in the wings.

He looked out of the window and, considering how much he had drunk, was surprised at how clear-headed he felt. Hardened drinkers sometimes said they had drunk themselves sober after a long, spread-out session. This claim did not stand the test of logic, but he did find he sometimes entered a state of clarity and even acuity after a drawn-out and carefully managed drinking marathon.

Not many people had been out on any sort of marathon on the previous evening, he reflected. They had so far not encountered a single car since leaving the dog track. People were spent out after Christmas and the extra-special New Year celebrations, and Portsmouth was almost eerily quiet. With a few exceptions, the late-night pubs and clubs and eating places were shut and revellers long gone home. An unusual and almost uncomfortable blanket of stillness lay across the sleeping city.

It was as bright as day on the dual carriageway, but the light washing the road and buildings was a jaundiced yellow. One of the sodium-vapour street lamps lining the road was flickering intermittently, constantly changing the texture and appearance of its immediate surroundings. As the bulb re-ignited, Mowgley saw a hooded figure slumped with its back against the steel upright of the post. The next burst lit up a young and untroubled male face. Their eyes met as the car passed him and Mowgley nodded and half-smiled as if to reassure him he was no threat. There was no response. The youth's expression was as incurious as that of the fox before the hood masked his face as he leaned forward and vomited into his lap.

Mowgley raised a hand in a pointless gesture of sympathy and farewell. "Have you ever noticed why all spew looked the same, regardless of what the up-chucker had been eating?"

"Can't say I've thought about it much," she said. "It's not the sort of thing that keeps me awake at night."

They drove on in comfortable silence, past the new and elaborate sign welcoming visitors to the city by the sea. It had been designed and built by a woman who liked to be known as a creative blacksmith. According to the local newspaper, the work had cost the city taxpayers more than ten thousand pounds. Mowgley suspected it would soon find its way to an unfussy scrap yard where it would be valued at a fraction of its cost. Perhaps it would be best to pay potential thieves *not* to nick it, he thought.

They drove on past a row of darkened shop fronts and reached some more flickering lights. They were flashing to announce the presence of the city's leading lap-dancing club. By the steps leading up to the entrance of the former theatre was a fleshy figure, its top half barely contained in a jacket at least one size too small. The man was standing in the traditional doorman's stance, head retracted into straining collar and meaty hands crossed at crotch level as if protecting his most sensitive parts. He was watching dispassionately as a tall thin young man tried to open the back door of a black taxi. After several fruitless attempts, the driver got out, opened the door, pushed his fare inside and drove away.

They reached a junction where five roads met, and Jane Stanton brought the car to a stop as the lights changed to red. A police car pulled up alongside, and the driver gave Mowgley a hard look. He responded with an inane tongue-lolling grin. The officer shook his head in resignation, then, as if to demonstrate his privileged position, drove away before the lights turned green.

"I bet if I'd been driving he would have given us a pull," said Mowgley.

"Why? Because you look like a drinker?"

"No, because, even nowadays, when a woman is driving a man after the pubs shut, your average plod assumes she's only being allowed to do so because the old man has had a few and she's had to stay on orange juice."

She lifted her hands from the wheel in a don't-know gesture, then drew away from the lights. As he reached for his baccy pouch, Mowgley noticed a Range Rover sitting at one of the junctions. It was a new model, and the overhead lighting made the black finish and smoked windows gleam. The way was clear but its driver seemed in no hurry to pull away after they passed it. Mowgley also noted the car had its lights off.

Having navigated the city centre, they took the seafront road alongside the ancient common where Richard the Lionheart's army had camped and on occasion rioted before setting off on yet another Crusade. Pompey, he thought, must have been nearly as rough then as it was now.

A few minutes later and Jane Stanton had pulled to a stop opposite the Midnight Tindaloo. It was the first time Mowgley had arrived to find the restaurant in darkness.

He reached for the seatbelt, then remembered he had not bothered to secure it. Twirling an imaginary Sir Jasper moustache, he said: "I could ask you up for a nightcap and to see my etchings, but I don't have any booze on the premises and the only etchings are on the wall of the communal toilet. There are some interesting bite marks on the khazi door, though."

She shuddered theatrically. "Thanks but no thanks. I'm knackered and it's an early start tomorrow, or should I say today. I'll give you a bell this afternoon to see if you want to come out to play. We could go back to my hotel after. There ain't no bite marks on the toilet door, but the bed head has a few notches on it. Not put there by me, of course. Yet."

"Sounds good to me, Ma'am."

Mowgley got out of the car, waved and turned away, patting his overcoat pocket to check for his keys.

He was a few paces down the alleyway when a bulky figure stepped out from behind the overflowing dump bin. The man was wearing a ski-mask, but in spite of the bad light, Mowgley recognised the brawny tattooed arms, expensive watch and sovereign ring. He also noted the baseball bat the man was casually dangling from his left hand.

"Ah," said Mowgley in a light-hearted tone which did not match his mood, "Mr Toad. Does Ratty know you're out at this hour? And how's your motor?" By taking this tone, Mowgley knew he ran the risk of increasing the level of possible injury coming his way. But he also knew it would let the man know that Mowgley knew who he was.

The figure made no response beyond stepping further away from the dump bin to allow another figure to join him. His face was also hidden by a ski-mask, and he was taller than Mr Toad but less broad. He was wearing a set of dark-coloured overalls and heavy boots, and was also carrying a baseball bat. This was not good news, as the odds against Mowgley finishing the encounter upright had now lengthened considerably. Instinctively, he put his shoulders back and rocked forward on his toes. This would help to be ready for what was coming. It would also make him look bigger. While he did so, he considered his options.

As he considered how limited they were, the silence was broken by the toot of a car horn. As if it were a signal, the men started to move towards him. They walked slowly, shoulder-to-shoulder and almost taking up the full width of the narrow alleyway.

At the approach of danger, an unbidden process began inside Mowgley's body. He did not know it, but his adrenal gland immediately released a surge of epinefrene, a hormonal transmitter. At the same time, his respiratory rate increased quite dramatically and blood was shunted away from his digestive tract and directed to his muscles and limbs. Nature had now seen to it that he was better prepared to fight or run.

Another of his body's instinctive reactions was to make him fear that he might shit himself.

Mowgley had read somewhere that whenever the Admiral Lord Nelson was in a gathering of senior naval officers, the talk would inevitably turn to the best manoeuvres when confronted by an enemy. There would be much discussion about taking the weather gauge and the pros and cons of being broadside or bows-on to the foe. At some stage the nation's greatest seafaring hero would be asked for his views on the way to deal with the enemy. It was said that he would reply: "Gentlemen, I have always found it best to go straight at 'em."

Generally speaking, Mowgley was in agreement with Nelson. This inclination was not because of courage or foolhardiness, but based on experience. In any unequal confrontation, the side with the advantage of numbers would expect their opponent to at least hesitate, try to negotiate, or turn tail and run. From the playground onwards, Mowgley had found that running encourages pursuit, and, for some perverse reason, the punishment was invariably greater when the runner is caught.

Also, an unexpected reaction is generally agreed by experts to give an edge in battle. Mowgley had found this to hold true in a hundred scuffles, arrests and out-and-out brawls.

Accordingly, he waited until the two men came within a few paces, then put his right hand in the inside breast pocket of his overcoat, held his left arm out straight with palm out and shouted very loudly: "Stop! Armed police officers!"

His claim was technically true as he was fully limbed, and it gave the masked figures a momentary pause. As they stopped, Mowgley breathed deeply, lowered his head and went straight at them.

He chose the lighter of the two men, and felt teeth go as the top of his head smashed into the ski-mask. The wearer gave a muffled shriek and fell backwards under the force of the charge.

In films, fights are invariably depicted in a way which does not happen in real life. Crisply delivered kicks and punches rarely miss their target, and those struck obligingly fall down or even fly through the air. In reality, Mowgley had always found fighting a much messier and unballetic affair. People swing and miss, or punch and kick to no real effect. Confined space makes things more difficult, and this fight was taking place in a narrow alleyway containing a number of obstacles. They included the dump bin and at least a dozen black sacks stuffed to bursting point with two week's worth of leftovers from a busy Indian restaurant.

With Mowgley on top of him and already scrabbling for possession of the baseball bat, the man landed heavily on a pile of bin-liners. The top bag split under the impact, spewing out what, in happier times, would have been for Mowgley the evocative aroma of Jalfrezi Chicken. But his mind was elsewhere. Having got a grip on the wrong end of the baseball bat with his left hand, he used his right to swing a punch at the ski-mask. As he did so, the bags shifted and the man rolled to one side, causing Mowgley to miss and his fist to hit the alley wall. The pain in his hand was as nothing as the bat wielded by Mr Toad smashed into the back of his head.

As the flow of oxygen to his brain was interrupted, Mowgley did not see stars, but there was a flash of light before he entered that semi-conscious state of fear, bewilderment and confusion when boxers hang on to their opponents as if they were lovers.

A fortunate result for Mowgley was that the blow drove his head down and forward, bringing it smashing again into the face of Ski Mask 2. The prone figure screamed through broken teeth and bucked violently. This caused more bags to break and move, and as Mowgley slid to one side the next blow from above missed his head, found a bin liner and created a fountain of curry sauce.

Heading into unconsciousness, the detective lay on his back, watching almost dispassionately as Mr Toad raised the baseball bat above his head.

Then there came the dull crump of an explosion and a light brighter than the brightest day filled the alleyway. When Mowgley re-opened his eyes, he saw that Mr Toad was standing, arms raised in a frozen tableau in the centre of a ring of fire. In spite of his condition and situation, Mowgley was reminded of the painting of an Old Testament prophet on the wall of the Bethesda chapel he used to attend on Sundays for the free cup of tea and sticky bun. Then, all was dark again, and the detective drifted away as Mr Toad began to scream.

* * *

"Why the fuck do people always ask that?"

"What?"

"'Are you alright?' They only say that when it's pretty fucking obvious the person they're asking is nowhere near alright."

Jane Stanton helped Mowgley up to a sitting position and to rest his back against the alley wall, then began gently wiping his face with a wet-wipe. "Well, excuse me for saving you from a very nasty beating and possible death, Inspector."

Mowgley did not respond, but moved his head gingerly and regretted it as the wound came into contact with the rough surface of the alley wall. Stanton continued dabbing at his face: "What I meant was how bad do you feel? Where did he get you? Is anything broken, do you reckon?"

"No, but I got a good one on the back of my head."

"Oh that was lucky, then."

"Lucky?"

"Hitting your head instead of anywhere a bit more fragile."

"Har har." Mowgley risked another fingertip exploration, then asked: "So what happened to Mr Toad? I didn't imagine that he was on fire, did I?"

"He was more sort of...scorched. He legged it with his mate, so he can't be that bad. And why Mr Toad?"

"It's a long story, and don't change the subject." Mowgley winced as he nodded towards where a pump-action shotgun lay on the floor. He was not a firearms specialist, but it appeared to be no different from a standard shotgun except its stock had been sawn off to leave only a pistol-style grip. "That doesn't look much like a flame-thrower to me."

"Ah, you mean the dragon's breath thingy."

"The what?"

"The cartridges are loaded with magnesium pellets. They can be used as an emergency flare at sea, but they're becoming popular with dealers who want to scare the shit out of the opposition. Or us. This one was taken off a bloke who was going to use it on a mate of mine. I forgot to hand it in and it's been in the boot ever since."

"Did you know what was going to happen when you fired it?"

"Not really. I changed my mind about those etchings you offered to show me, then when I was getting out of the car I heard you shout. I guessed you were in trouble so got the gun out. I saw you on the floor and your Mr Toad with the baseball bat, so shot over his head to unnerve him."

"You did that, alright."

"Anyway, we can talk about all that later. I think we'd better get you to A&E. That's a lot of blood on your face."

"Erm, not really." Mowgley ran a finger down his cheek, then licked the tip. "I can't be certain, but I reckon that is a prime example of Bombay Billy's secret recipe for North Indian red curry sauce."

Part Three

Twenty-two

"So what happened to you agreeing to keep me in the loop?"

"What loop? Can't you see I'm busy?" Mowgley was trying to see the back of his head by using a combination of the new mirror on his office wall and a make-up compact he had found in his sergeant's handbag.

"The loop you promised to keep me in when we last had this conversation." Melons reached out impatiently, took hold of the compact and held it at the correct angle. "Going by your smug look of late, I suspect you've made a breakthrough in the Trunk Murder. So I think I could be forgiven for feeling left out in the cold."

Mowgley made as if to speak, but Melons wagged a finger in his face: "And don't you dare tell me you'll tell me later. Or say 'to tell you the truth', which always means you're about to lie. And when you say 'to tell you the *honest* truth', it means you're going to tell a really big lie."

As he had no defence against the charge, Mowgley continued to explore the bald spot on the back of his head where the wound had been stitched. Then he adopted a hurt expression, touched the bald spot and gave a groan. "To tell you the honest truth, Sergeant, If I'm looking smug it's because I'm just feeling happy to be alive."

Melons paused in mid-wag, looked at him keenly, then said

grudgingly, "I suppose I can see why, though it could be argued that you brought it on yourself."

"That's debatable. And if the person you disrespectfully refer to as Action Woman had not been on hand to frighten Mr Toad off, you could now be prostate with grief and making plans for what outfit to wear to my funeral." He closed the compact and handed it to her. "And you'd be wondering if you had any chance of getting my job, or if not, if your new boss would be as easy to manipulate as your old one."

"Agreed, although I think you mean 'prostrate'. But I still don't understand exactly how she scared them off. It's true she's quite a scary-looking woman, but even so..."

"I would tell you how she did it, but I of course was out of it when she arrived in the very nick of time. Anyway, here comes Young Mundy. Perhaps he can shed some light on it all.

After a polite knock on the door frame of the glass and hardboard partition cube which counted as his superior's office, the son of the former head of the city CID entered, notebook at the ready.

"Is this a good time, Sir?"

"Depends on what you want to tell me about, son. If it's that I'm behind with my subs for the office lottery syndicate, no, it's not a good time. If it's to tell me Madame Hartley-Whatsit has run off with the bird with the cropped hair and tattoos and big knockers who works on the desk at HQ, very much is it a good time."

"It's actually an update on Mr David Brimmigan and his...colleague, Sir."

"Ah." Mowgley leaned forward and put his elbows on his desk and steepled his fingers: "I'm all ears, Constable. Should I know this Mr Brimmigan?"

Mundy adjusted his tie and looked at his notebook. "I think you know him as Mr Toad, Sir."

"Or perhaps it should be Turd of Turd Hall. Anyway, pray continue."

"As I reported earlier Sir, Mr Toad and his colleague-"

"When you say 'colleague', I'm assuming you mean his slimy oppo, Ratty?"

"Er, yes Sir. As I told Sergeant McCarthy earlier, Mr Toad and...Mr Ratty arrived at the A&E department at the Queen Alexandra hospital at around 3.37a.m. on Tuesday. They were seen almost immediately and given treatment. Mr Toad had suffered second degree burns with blistering on the top of his head and right side of his face and upper right arm, and superficial first degree burns to his left hand and forearm."

Mowgley tried not to look pleased: "Sounds painful. And what about Ratty?"

"He had a broken nose, fractured left cheekbone and severe damage to his mouth, involving the loss of two front teeth and the breakage of others. They both had initial treatment but refused to be admitted."

Melons leaned forward and prompted him: "Did they say how they got their injuries?"

Mundy consulted his notebook again, turning over a page before answering. "Yes, Sergeant. They said they had been involved in an accident with an outboard motor."

"Ah." Mowgley unsteepled his fingers to roll a cigarette. "So how did you track 'em down?"

"After you told me the likely nature of their injuries and a general description and possible time of arrival at the hospital, I was able to speak to the nurses and doctors who treated them. There were photographs of the injuries, and I was able to identify and confirm that the man with burns was the man I have been tracking under your direction with regard to his involvement in drug importation."

Mowgley whistled appreciatively. "Good Boy. That's the way to make a report. I hope you're paying attention, Sergeant. So what news is there on what they've been up to on the drug front, Munders?"

DC Mundy closed his notebook and looked fleetingly at a pile of paperwork on his superior's desk. "As you know from my reports Sir, I have been working with the relevant agencies, and following up your request for more information on Mr Toad."

"And has your research proved fruitful? Is he well-breeched?"

"Well Sir, he has a large house on a private estate in East Wittering, and a top-quality R.I.B."

"A whatter?"

"A Rigid Inflatable Boat." Melons volunteered. "They're like a large dinghy with, as the name suggests, rigid bits."

"That doesn't sound very flash for your average filthy-rich

dope dealer."

"On the contrary," she said. "Nowadays a RIB goes with the top-of-the-range Range Rover with smoked-out windows as standard accessories for your image-conscious Class 'A' peddler. They're also just the job in southern coastal waters for nipping across to France or Holland and back under cover of darkness - or rendezvousing with a yacht in mid-Channel. The ones with really big and powerful outboards can set you back a hundred grand and reach speeds of up to 50 miles an hour."

Mowgley made a mock-pained face: "Surely you mean knots, Sergeant?" He turned back to Mundy and smiled encouragingly. "Anyway, let the lad continue. Where did you say Toadie keeps this posh dinghy?"

"It's moored at a marina in East Hayling, Sir-"

"- just round the corner from where your metal-detectorist found the Hermes bag," interjected Melons. "And the marina manager says Mr Toad usually takes it out once a week and brings it back the next day before having a slap-up meal with bottles of shampoo all round."

"Ah." Mowgley said. "The plot thickens. So what's his excuse, Stephen?"

"Excuse, Sir?"

"For having a big house and tasty boat and car and throwing lots of money around. What does he claim to do for such a good living?"

"He's a director of a property development company, Sir."

"Another surprise. And you've had the money boys on to him and you've run him past your mate at the Inland Revenue?"

"Yes Sir. According to the company's books, they are making a lot of money from not much activity."

"And you're keeping HM Revenue and Customs and our friendly local Coastguard informed?"

"They've put together a joint observation and possible arrest proposal, but Mr Brimmigan has not appeared at the marina for a week, probably because of his injuries."

Melons held up a hand as if to plead for permission to speak: "And have your enquiries revealed exactly how Messrs Toad and Ratty really came about their injuries?"

Mundy looked at Mowgley, who nodded, then back at her: "Er, no Sergeant. They've not lodged any complaint, and the

Inspector told me not to bother to go down that line of enquiry."

Melons sniffed and reached for her cigarettes as she looked accusingly at Mowgley. "Humph. I bet he did."

Mowgley gave her his village idiot look then smiled again at Stephen Mundy. "So, to summate Constable, the relevant agencies are keeping an eye on Mr Toad and itching to do a bit of watery stop and search the next time his rib thingy makes a quick trip across the Channel and back?"

"That's right, Sir."

Mowgley stood up, stretched and moved towards where his overcoat was draped over the filing cabinet. "Well done indeed, Stephen. I hope the sergeant has learned from your example of attention to detail and thoughtful investigation. Actually, I reckon she should be happy to buy you a beer or two at the Leopard this very lunchtime in appreciation of the lesson. Thank you for your time, and see you there."

Mundy closed his notebook, looked uncertainly from Mowgley to Melons, then began to back out of the office.

"Just a moment, Constable." Melons eased herself off the corner of Mowgley's desk.

Mundy hovered at the doorway. "Yes, Sergeant?"

"For a start, you don't have to back away from the Inspector as if you were leaving a royal presence. But what I would like to know is, as she is specifically here to investigate illegal drug movements in the area, I hope you've been keeping DCI Stanton in the picture about Mr Brimmigan?"

Again, Mundy looked at Mowgley, who again nodded assent. "No Sergeant, I haven't spoken to her. Inspector Mowgley said not to bother her as she's not worried about small time independent operators."

Melons shook her head. "I see. Thanks Stephen."

Mundy was almost out of the office when he turned back: "One other thing Sir, if I may."

Mowgley paused with one arm down the wrong sleeve of his overcoat: "If you must, Constable."

"It's just that we've had several calls asking for you. The last one was just before you arrived. Jo and I tried to get hold of you on your mobile each time, but only got the messaging service."

"What did he or she want?"

"He wouldn't say, Sir. Just said he needed to talk to you

and you would know why."

"Did he leave a number?"

"No Sir. I checked and he called from a phone box in the square at Petersfield."

Melons frowned: "So why did you go to that trouble of finding out where he called from?"

Mundy gave her a self-effacing look: "It wasn't a lot of trouble, Sergeant. I just phoned the number and waited until someone picked it up and then asked the lady where she was."

"Oh."

Mundy continued: "He seemed very nervous, and it was strange that he was so keen to speak to the Inspector but wouldn't leave any contact details."

"How was it left?"

"He said he would call back later today."

Mowgley looked at his virtual watch and frowned. "So why didn't you give him my mobile number?"

Mundy looked at where Mowgley's phone was lying on the desktop, then said: "I knew you didn't have it with you, Sir."

"Fair enough." Mowgley began to put his arm in the correct sleeve. "Fair do's. So did the mystery caller at least leave his name?"

"Yes Sir. He said to tell you it was Tom Ripley."

Twenty-three

Mowgley stood at the window overlooking the port, his shoulders hunched and lips moving slightly as he counted the last of the cars moving slowly over the linkspan and into the belly of the giant boat.

In a similar moment of office ennui, he had marvelled at and tried to calculate how many vehicles could be swallowed up by the new breed of super-ferries. After working out the approximate floor area of the three car decks and trying to divide that figure by the average vehicle wheelbase, he had given up and gone down the pub.

As he sighed theatrically and began forecasting the nationality of the next lorry to arrive on the quay and how many wheels it would boast, Melons arrived to suggest she could pick up a couple of pastys from Greggs. "And," she said brightly, "there's a tray of lager filed under 'S' for Stella in your filing cabinet."

"It's not the same as being in the pub," said Mowgley, doing a fair imitation of a sulky child. "Anyway, the pastys from Greggs would be fresh."

* * *

The call came at just after two o'clock.

Mowgley did not know what he expected Burgess's voice to sound like, but it was not at all as he had imagined. For whatever reason, that was invariably so when he met someone for the first time after speaking to them on the phone. Burgess/Ripley had a light voice with a flat delivery and a Portsmouth accent. He spoke with a sort of hurried persuasiveness, and sounded to Mowgley more like a salesman making a cold call than a Class 'A' drug-dealing killer.

"How do I know you're Mowgley?"

"How do I know you're Tom Ripley - or Dave Burgess or whatever other names are in your portfolio?"

A brief silence, then: "Did you find the leg of pork at Carentan?"

The detective wrinkled his nose at the memory. "Hard to miss it."

Another silence, then Mowgley said "Anyway, nice to hear from you, but I thought it was me who was looking for you. Why are you changing the rules?"

"I need to talk to you."

"You have my full attention."

"Not like this."

"Ah. Then why not come into the office? And why are you phoning me and not your usual contact?"

"You must be fucking joking."

"Just a thought. What do you want to talk about?"

"I want to do a deal. I can tell you the truth about what's been going on, and you won't believe some of it."

"I'm sure I won't..."

* * *

"It's very nice."

Mowgley put his glass on the marble table-top and looked around the waterfront bar. "Do you think so? It's a bit over-the-top for my liking." He nodded at his drink. "That looks more like a specimen tube than a sensible beer glass."

Jane Stanton smiled wearily. "As you well know, matey, I meant the bag."

"Oh, that," said Mowgley casually.

"Yes, that. It's supposed to be the same make as the one

on the beach with the dope and arms in it, isn't it?"

"Don't worry, I didn't nick it from the evidence room. And what do you mean it's *supposed* to be the same make?"

She paused, fingered the handle of the large bag sitting on the table. "Well, you know it's not real, don't you?"

"I think it is, Ma'am. It demonstrably has shape and form. Though some people say we live in a hologram of our own making and I could be imagining all this."

"Don't take the piss, Inspector. How much did you pay for it?"

"What a question to ask. Are you telling me it's a knock-off?"

"I'm afraid so."

"How do you know?"

"Believe me, any girl would know. It's lots of little things, and some not-so-little things. For a start, it's made of plastic, not crocodile skin."

"Oh."

"And, without wishing to hurt your feelings, if it was real you wouldn't be able to afford it."

"You mean the real thing costs more than fifty quid?"

"A bit more, yes."

"I'll kill that Dinger Bell."

"Who he?"

"He's taken over from Terry the Trader as head purveyor of hooky gear on my patch. But he swore it was real and had come from a container load arriving from Bangladesh."

"I don't think they make Hermes bags in Bangladesh, or ship them by the container load's worth."

"So how much does the real thing cost?"

"You wouldn't believe it, and it would only upset you if you knew. But never mind, it's the thought that counts." She picked the bag up and put it down by her side. Mowgley noticed that she used just two fingers, as if handling something distasteful or soiled.

Mowgley looked puzzled. "But does it matter if it's real or not if most people wouldn't be able to tell a fake from a real one?"

She looked down at the bag and gave a slight grimace. "The sort of people who would have a real one would know. And it would matter to them."

"And you're one of those people?"

"I guess so."

He shook his head in mock sorrow. "It's always about money, isn't it?"

"It usually is. What's new?"

"Seriously. I mean everything's about money. That poor sod on the ferry boat would still have his bits joined together if it weren't for money. All this drug smuggling and killing is just about money."

"Just like dealing in shares, you mean, or being a banker? I'm afraid that's how it is with most things, Inspector, and especially so with drug trafficking."

Mowgley emptied his glass. "I suppose it is. So what would you do about drugs if you were in charge? Would you go for legalisation?"

"It would bring the price down, that's for sure. And it don't work this way. Look what happened with Prohibition. It was just the same, with all the killing for control of the market. Personally, I don't think they should legalise."

"Why not?"

She smiled and reached for his glass. "I'd be out of a job, wouldn't I?"

* * *

They had moved on to another pub overlooking the harbour. When Britain ran the biggest and most powerful navy the world had seen, there had been seventeen ale houses and knocking shops laying in wait at the main dockyard gate. Nowadays there were just three public houses, and their drink selection, food offerings and interior decor would have been unrecognisable to the ghost of a sailor from just a couple of generations before.

Jane Stanton had managed to leave the fake Hermes bag under the table at the previous pub, and Mowgley had allowed her to think he had not noticed. She smiled as he returned from the bar with a tray bearing two glasses, two bags of crisps and a packet of pork scratchings.

"So this is our working lunch. As I've said before, you certainly know how to give a girl a good time, don't you?"

Mowgley tore one of the bags of crisps asunder.

"You also said that was part of my charm."

"Did I? Blimey. I thought it was your suave manners and boyish good looks that I fell for."

"I thought it was that bottle's worth of Jim Beam you knocked back on our first date that had made your knees go weak."

"Date? Have we ever had a date? How quaint."

"Quaint is sometimes good, I reckon." They clinked glasses and drank, and Mowgley looked across the bar to where an enormously fat woman was organising her session at a fruit machine. She had moved two bar stools in front of it, and at first he thought she was going sit on both. Then he saw she was using one on which to rest her glass, cigarette packet, an ashtray and a bag of coins. Having gone through what was obviously a very regular ritual, the woman lit a cigarette and leaned her head sideways to avoid the smoke, then reached for the bag of coins.

"I wonder why they do that?" Mowgley said.

"What, eat so much they can hardly walk? Because they can, I suppose."

"I meant keep trying to win when they know the odds are so stacked against them."

Jane Stanton took a cigarette from her bag. "Don't most losers do that?"

"I suppose so. Perhaps she'll be lucky this time."

"What, you mean she'll be lucky if that bar stool doesn't disappear up her arse? I wouldn't bet on it."

"I suppose not." He looked at her thoughtfully, then said: "Anyway, have you thought any more about tomorrow evening? Do you want to come?"

"Did you tell him I might?"

"To be honest, your name didn't come up. But he did say I had to be on my own. I got my sergeant to drive me over to the meet yesterday. It's a good place for him to watch all approaching roads and who turns up, and beat it if he doesn't like what he sees."

She toyed with her cigarette, then swirled her drink around the bottom of her glass. "Well, we don't want to spook him now he's got back in touch. Perhaps it's best I'm not around. Did you ask him why he'd gone shtum, by the way?"

"As I said, your name didn't come up."

"Okay. So how are you going to get there? Is your bag lady taking you?"

"I can drive, you know. I just prefer not to."

She tapped her cigarette on the side of the ashtray. "So, what's the plan?"

"I haven't got one, really. He says he's got a lot to tell me."

"And you reckon what he gave you over the phone about a shipment coming in next week could be puckah?"

"Don't know. He could have just been trying to keep me happy."

She nodded, then said: "It is a bit of a schtoomer. Did he say anything specific about what it is he wants to tell you - or what he wants in return?"

"No. Just that I wouldn't believe some of it."

DCI Stanton looked at her glass thoughtfully for a moment, then sat up straight and said: "Okay. If you're up to going on your own, best to hear what he has to say and make another meet. Just be very careful."

Mowgley frowned "Are you saying you don't want me to bring him in? If anyone found out, I'd be dead in the water."

She tapped her cigarette on the ashtray again. "True. But what options do we have? If you nab him or I bring a team along, what have we got?"

"A serious drugs dealer and maybe a multiple murderer as well? Ain't that a bit of a catch?"

She nodded. "Okay. But the problem is that he's our only lead to the Russians. If we can cop the big guys and break up their whole network, that would be a real result. If we stick him in a cell and be nice to him, he'll be in charge and just give us enough to get what he wants. Don't forget I've been this way before."

"Yeah, but it's all very much what Bramshill calls risk-intensive, isn't it? If it all goes wrong, Burgess stroke Ripley literally gets away with murder."

"True, but if it works and he stays loose and gives you everything he knows over time, we pull a whole troupe of big-time Russian gangsters who intend flooding this end of the country with tons of gear. This way, if he does disappear again, the shit won't come your way - or mine. I reckon it's got to be worth the risk. Anyway, if you take over as his contact and let him stay out there, who's going to know? I'm certainly not going to tell anyone. Are you?"

He looked at her silently for a moment, then shook his head. She finished her drink and put the empty glass on the table.

"Okay then. Another one before we go back to the hotel?"

He looked at his wrist and the watch which wasn't there: "Bit early isn't it?"

She shook her head. "Don't worry, we can get a curry on the way if you're having withdrawal symptoms. Besides, we need to talk some more about tomorrow; you need an early night. And the bed head needs some more notches."

Twenty-four

The sails of the old mill reflected the thin light of a watery moon. It was a clear and cold evening, and the mackerel sky was shot through with feathery bands of red.

The expensively restored building stood beside a coach and cart route to London which was already ancient when the mill was built. Nowadays the highway sat at the bottom of the hill on which the mill stood, and ten thousand cars a day roared angrily by. The juxtaposition of old and new was a reminder of how times and things had changed, and of times past.

When Mowgley was a child and the mill in ruin, he had believed that the single sail pointing up at the sky from the domed roof was the barrel of a giant gun, ready to shoot down German bombers before they reached the city dockyard.

He would see the mill on the last Sunday of every month when the family car would chug past on its way to the county town of Petersfield and a picnic by the lake. The journey was less in distance than most people travelled to work now, but it had seemed a great adventure.

On arrival and as respectability required, his mother would lay a crisply clean and ironed white tablecloth on the grass. Then she would lay out plates, and carefully arrange on them the corned beef sandwiches, sausage rolls, hard-boiled eggs and pickled onions. There would also be a couple of light ales cooling in the shallows of the lake, and a bottle of pop for Mowgley.

After they had eaten, he would be allowed to wander off and fish for sharks, or take on a horde of Japanese jungle fighters who were hiding in the bushes at the water's edge. His mother would clear away the remains of the picnic and go for a walk around the lake, while his dad would take a snooze. On the way home, they would stop at a pub for a watery beer for his father, a port and lemon for mum, and a dumpy bottle of lemonade and packet of not very crispy crisps for him.

Sometimes it rained on the day of the picnic, but they went anyway, sitting defiantly on the wet grass in plastic mackintoshes. Mowgley realised in later years that his dad had insisted they made the trip whatever the weather just because they could. Theirs had been one of only two private cars in the street. It was an elderly Vauxhall, hand painted by a previous owner in maroon. The chrome flutes along each side of the bonnet became ever more rusted, and his father had let Mowgley paint them. He had used a gloopy grey his dad had got from a mate who worked in the dockyard, and his dad so liked the effect they had painted the whole car. As Mowgley heard his father say to his mother, if it was good enough to keep battleships from rusting, it would be just the job for Tin Lizzie. He smiled as he recalled how cars were like members of the family and had names in those distant days.

A savage blast jerked him back to his present situation. He looked into the rear-view mirror, and saw it was filled by the radiator of a huge lorry. The driver obviously thought he was travelling too slowly, and was trying to bully him into increasing his speed or moving to another lane. As usual, Mowgley's reaction was to hunch over the wheel like an old man and slow down to about half the speed limit. After sitting on the back bumper of the unmarked police car for a few minutes, the 16-wheeled Euro-truck shrank in the mirror, then pulled out and roared by with another prolonged blast. Immediately, it pulled sharply in front of the car and slowed to even less of Mowgley's pace. But the driver soon tired of the game and pulled away, sticking his arm out of the window and giving Mowgley a one-fingered salute.

The detective thought briefly about switching the flashing blue lights on and pulling the lorry over to have some fun, but accepted he had more important business to hand. In truth, he also did not fancy the idea of overtaking the juggernaut, then manoeuvering the relatively flimsy car into its path. He contented himself with taking one hand off the wheel, making the shape of a pistol, then aiming a volley of shots at the lorry's wheels and imagining the catastrophic outcome.

* * *

The Iron Age farm was the idea of an entrepreneurial academic who could see there could be a profitable future in the past.

The slogan on the sign by the entrance said *As Old as the Hills*. It was a clever line though not strictly true, as the site of the farm had been moved three times in thirty years. But in whatever incarnation and location, the collection of huts, ancient cereal fields and animals set in the swelling Hampshire Downs had proved a popular attraction.

At this time of night, the site was shrouded in darkness, with only a faint drone and loom of light coming from the distant motorway. Mowgley had known the farm was unattended at night, and the nearest dwelling place was a hamlet more than a mile away.

At the end of a bumpy track off a minor road, the large car park was lit by a single sodium lamp on a tall post by the open gateway. The car park was empty except for a van which had once been white. It sat alongside a post and rail fence at the furthest point from the entrance, and as he drove in, Mowgley reflected that Burgess had made a good choice of venues.

With the site sitting in a literally commanding position at the top of a hill and with little distracting light pollution or noise, he would be able to see and hear vehicles approaching from a distance. With the help of the single light, he would also be able to watch the car park from the safety of the darkness beyond the fence and take action if he did not like what he saw. Also, Mowgley considered, the van might not be his, or even a decoy. His getaway car might be hidden elsewhere and easily accessible from where he watched.

Mowgley got out of the car and walked across to the van. As he had guessed, it was unoccupied. Looking around as he considered his next move, he heard a noise. It had been a shuffling and scraping sound, as if something heavy was being dragged across the grass beyond the fence.

He fleetingly reflected how it was true about hairs standing up on the back of the neck at times like these, then took a couple of deep breaths as he patted the bulge in the top inside pocket of his overcoat.

Apart from training sessions and the odd assignment in the early years of his attachment to Special Branch, he had never carried a gun. The comforting bulge was made by a torch, and it was not the standard police issue model. The casing of the heavy-duty Maglite was made of anodised aluminium, held six chunky batteries and was over a foot long. It had a satisfyingly weighty feel, and was favoured by some US police officers over official equipment for subduing troublesome customers. Mowgley had confiscated it from one of the rowdier members of a stag party which had invaded the Ship Leopard some years previously. It was usually to be found in his filing cabinet next to an ornate brass knuckleduster (also confiscated) and a full-scale replica Bowie knife. He eased the Maglite from his pocket, pushed his shoulders back and walked towards the fence.

* * *

Standing on the lower rail and holding the top one with his right hand, he used the other to point the torch in the general direction of the noise.

The beam travelled across a muddy patch, then picked out a rusty water barrel and a battered feeding trough. At the trough stood what appeared to be a cross between a sheep and a goat. Obviously used to inquisitive visitors, it looked towards the source of the light, then returned its attention to the contents of the trough.

Letting out a long sigh, Mowgley was about to step back down to the car park side of the fence when another sound broke the stillness. This time it was instantly recognisable as a prolonged and piercing scream.

* * *

Over the fence and beyond the paddock, he found and followed a rough path of compacted lumps of chalk, its borders lined with large and irregularly shaped pieces of flint.

The screaming had stopped, and now he could hear a continuous snuffling, grunting and squelching. At the end of the path, something large loomed out against the night sky, and he saw it was the first of a huddle of huts. In the light of the Maglite, he could see the walls were of mud, topped off with neatly conical straw roofs.

Beyond the huts, his torch picked out a small, fenced-in patch of ground, where it looked as if someone had been successfully cultivating weeds. Beside the crops patch was an unsuitably modern shed, probably holding tools and equipment, and then a chest-high enclosure, made from interwoven lengths of split wood. It was from here that the grunting and squealing was coming.

The noise grew louder as he reached the enclosure, stood on tiptoe and leaned over to point his Maglite at what was within.

Up to their pendulous bellies in mud were four enormous pigs. Beneath a coating of more mud, they appeared to be pig-coloured, except for large and ragged patches of black along their prominent spines. The excited animals were formed roughly into a circle, tails to the walls of the sty and snouts colliding as they fought over something long and dark.

Leaning further over, Mowgley saw that it was a bag, tied roughly at the top with a length of blue polypropylene rope. Squealing and buffeting and barging with mounting frenzy, the pigs were engaged in an increasingly furious attack on the bag, which was torn in several places. Something red and pink and white glistened in the beam of light, and Mowgley used both hands to steady the torch.

When he made out what the pigs were eating, he dropped the Maglite into the mud, fell on his knees and vomited violently on the grass.

Above him, the moon broke free of the feathery clouds and bathed the scene in a gentle, silvery glow as the pigs continued their feasting.

Twenty-five

Chin in hands and elbows propped awkwardly on knees, Mowgley waited for the inquisition to begin.

The poster on the wall behind the Chief Superintendent's desk showed a beaming black policeman standing alongside an equally ecstatic Asian woman constable. In front of them and slightly to one side was a diminutive and equally enraptured WPC of Far Eastern ethnic origin. The group was completed by a beaming male officer, mouth open to show off his perfect teeth. He was white, and had a square jaw and the sort of bushy moustache sported by the butchest member of The Village People.

The wording assured the reader that the modern police force was dedicated to diversity. The poster was obviously well intentioned, but Mowgley knew of no Asian or black officers in the city. Nor any with that sort of moustache and teeth. There was, to be fair, an elderly Bangladesh man who worked as a glass collector in the police club, and a large and jolly West Indian woman who served up meals in the canteen.

Hearing a non-committal grunt, Mowgley turned his attention to the top of the head of the woman who was probably responsible for the poster being displayed on the wall.

Chief Superintendent Hartley-Whitley was pretending to be reading his report for the first time. As he had noted during his first encounter with her, the standard managerial ploy gave her the excuse to keep him waiting and in suspense, and also time for her to make little grunts or shakes of her head especially designed to unnerve him.

He looked across to where Jane Stanton was sitting on a chair placed against the wall alongside the giant desk. Like the mock reading of his report, he knew the positioning of the chairs was part of the routine. Their location meant he would be facing both senior officers, like an accused man in court. Their relative positions also indicated which way the shit was going to fly. Instead of being cast as a co-conspirator, Jane Stanton was literally lined up with the Prosecution.

The air of a courtroom scenario was heightened by the middle-aged woman sitting alongside the desk. She had a large pad resting on one, crossed knee, and she was obviously there to take notes which would if possible be used in further evidence against him. He had already noticed that, like a prejudiced jury member, she had been looking disapprovingly at him as if her mind was already made up as to his guilt. Or perhaps she was giving the sour looks just because he was the only man in the room. To test his theory, he gave her his idiot smile, which made her look even sourer. Perhaps, at the end of the inquisition, she would take delight in handing her boss the black cap. He gave her an even more cretinous leer, and sought pleasanter sights.

Jane Stanton sensed he was watching her and looked up from doing something with her mobile phone. She smiled encouragingly and closed one eye conspiratorially. He returned the smile and the wink, heartened by the way she refused to be part of the game.

He sat up straight, then pulled at the knot of the tie that Melons had selected and insisted on putting round his neck. It felt very uncomfortable and he wondered if it were true that colour could affect mood. Perhaps it was Melons' little joke that the tie was black, and the last time he had worn it was at the funeral of a colleague.

The situation took him back to another time when he sat in a silent office, fiddling with a tie and waiting for judgement and punishment to be delivered. At Mowgley's secondary school, it had been a rule that caps were to be worn on the journey to and from it. At a time when pompadour haircuts were paramount, it was a rule that was inevitably broken. Outside the gates, ties would be removed and caps stuffed in blazer pockets and rolling swaggers and face-contorting sneers would take over as pimply boys paid homage to the Kings of Rock and Roll. It was generally agreed that Mowgley had one of the best - which meant lairy - combinations of swagger and sneer. But his ego had taken a knock when an elderly lady had stopped him in the street and asked if he was feeling unwell. When assured he was not, she had sympathised with his disability of a club foot.

Being discovered breaking the dress code was punishable by three strokes of the cane, delivered by the assistant head master. A wiry little man, Gus Grainger was a keen golfer, and renowned for the club head speed he could achieve at point of impact with the ball. At the school he was renowned for the pain he could inflict on the fingers of any pupil caught in a misdemeanour. At a reunion many years later, Grainger had recalled Mowgley's frequent visits to his office, and observed that the beatings had obviously done him no harm, and probably a bit of good.

Mowgley had taken pity on the decrepit old man and agreed, but wondered sometimes if those painful encounters were actually part of the reason he quite enjoyed beating people up when they deserved it.

Back in the present, Mowgley resumed his study of the top of Chief Superintendent Hartley-Whitley's head. In spite of himself, he felt his chest tighten as she came to the end of his - or rather Melons' - report.

It irritated him that, after all these years and having seen their shortcomings, weaknesses and constant cock-ups, he still felt nervous and intimidated in the presence of authority figures. Looking at the cause of his unease, he remembered the advice given by an old trouper to a new singing star who was in an agony of nerves at the prospect of meeting the Queen at the end of a Royal Variety Performance. "Just think of her sitting on the toilet with her knickers round her ankles, lad," had been the advice, "then you'll realise she's no different from thee and me. But remember not to laugh when you meet her."

Mowgley tried but quickly abandoned the ruse it as it made him feel queasy. Perhaps, he thought, it would work if he imagined having sex with her over the desk...

"Are you feeling ill, Inspector?"

Mowgley jerked upright and felt a further lurch of his bowels as he wondered if he had groaned aloud or just in his head. She might even have read his mind. Then he realised she had been watching him as he imagined rolling up her regulation uniform skirt and finding a hairy penis beneath her regulation blue knickers. The worse thing had been that it was much larger than his.

"Er no, Ma'am. Just that my tie's a bit tight."

She made no reply, looked down at the sheet of paper, then dropped it into a filing tray. Mowgley noted that she handled the paper in much the same way Jane Stanton had picked up the knock-off Hermes bag.

More silence, then CS Hartley-Whitley leaned forward, interlocked her fingers in the approved manner and regarded him steadily with what he knew would be a carefully contrived neutral expression. Having readied herself, she nodded to the secretary to indicate that the inquisition was about to begin.

"I have to say, Inspector-"

No you fucking haven't, but you will, you sadistic cow...

Mowgley's bowels churned and his facial muscles twitched and he broke into another sweat before he realised that he had thought the words and not spoken them aloud.

"-that your report raises more questions than it answers."

Full marks for originality, bollockface. Mowgley realised he was on safe ground with the insubordinate thoughts, and the technique was definitely helping settle his stomach.

"My first is quite obvious..."

Then why ask it, droopy tits?

"Why did you not report your proposed meeting with Mr Burgess so that an action plan could have been put in place?"

Because, you silly mare, you would have totally fucked it up and a shedload of woodentops would have turned up at the wrong place, or by mistake turn up at the right place with flashing lights and sirens and warn him off from miles away.

He cleared his throat. "I did not have time to report it, Ma'am. I only got the call a half hour before Burgess insisted we meet. Had I not gone straight to the site, he might have taken fright and left."

The CS gave him a look which suggested that Burgess's

death was his fault. "It would have been better for him if he had left, of course. But the urgency of the situation would not have stopped you from calling in on your way to the meeting place. You do know how to send as well as take calls on your mobile phone, I assume?"

Ah, got me there, fuckface. Time for the big porkie.

"Yes, Ma'am. As my sergeant confirmed, I did call in from my car to report my situation and destination. The signal was bad, and by the time we had re-established contact, I was at the site and I had to cease communications for obvious reasons."

"What 'obvious reasons'?"

Gotcha.

"I obviously couldn't use my mobile while approaching the meeting on foot in case it spooked - alarmed - Burgess."

"Mmmm." Hartley-Whitley grimaced her disapproval and perhaps disbelief. "Yes, we have spoken to your...team...at the ferry port. They have confirmed your calls and exchanges though there is no record of them. The term 'closing ranks' comes to mind. It sounds like you took some trouble to get your stories right. But why did you not contact DCI Stanton? Did you not have her number, perhaps?"

Har de har. What a card you are, you fat trout.

"Yes, Ma'am, I did. As I said, I had communication problems, and when I did get through I asked my sergeant to pass the message on to DCI Stanton. By that time it was too late for her to take any action, again of course."

Hartley-Whitley looked as if she was thinking about being offended by his dig, then looked across at Jane Stanton. She nodded, uncrossed her legs, adjusted the hem of her skirt and said: "That's true, Ma'am. I left the city as soon as I heard about the meeting, but got there too late. Burgess was dead, and Inspector Mowgley and a SOCO team were in attendance. For what it's worth, I would have done exactly the same as the Inspector. He was given no warning and had to make a decision and then act on it."

Both the Chief Superintendent and her secretary looked at Jane Stanton as if she was letting the side down.

"Even if it was the wrong one?"

Stanton looked levelly at the Chief Superintendent. "It only appeared to be the wrong decision because Burgess was dead when Inspector Mowgley found him. It's sometimes difficult to understand the full picture about an operation if you weren't there and only read about it after the event. When you are on the job, you have to think and act independently, and not always go by the book."

Hartley-Whitley's head snapped back as if she had been struck, and her secretary's eyebrows arched with shock that someone should speak to her boss in such a manner. To Mowgley, it seemed that Hartley-Whitley was clearly so upset not only because of what Jane Stanton had said, but that she had broken ranks. There was silence as Stanton held the senior officer's eyes, and Mowgley restrained himself from punching the air in delight.

Yes! That's my girl!

"I beg your pardon, Inspector?"

Hartley-Whitley's expression was thunderous. "What did you say?"

Oh Shit.

* * *

Mowgley raised his glass. "What a woman."

Melons frowned. "Who, me or Hartley-Thingummy?"

"Don't be silly. We are talkin' Chief Inspector Jane Stanton. You should have seen the way she faced the Devil's dyke down. She certainly saved my bacon."

"And I suppose my falsifying the telephone log and records, rehearsing the office staff and generally putting my job on the line was no help?"

"Of course, but that's what I expect from you."

Melons shook her head in pantomime despair. "Sometimes I just don't get you. You hardly turn a hair about being battered by a couple of gorillas in an alleyway, but you looked like you were going to pooh yourself when you set off for the interview with Madam H-W. Then some hard-nosed bint from London doesn't drop you in it, and you think she's *numero uno*. What a funny man you are."

"Not at all. Don't forget she also scared Mr Toad and his mate off and saved me from a real pasting."

"Scared him off? More like cooked him."

"She deliberately shot over his head - and she wasn't to

know what was going to come out of the end of the barrel. All I'm saying is that she bailed me out and put Cressida Thingie in her place."

Melons sniffed. "You know how it works. Shotgun Sally doesn't have to work for her. And from what you say, she doesn't have to answer to anyone, not even a Chief Super. Anyway, what's next?"

Mowgley looked at his empty glass. "Another pint, I reckon. And perhaps the Dish of the Day? I wonder if it's pasty 'n' chips?"

"Har de Har. As you well know, I meant where do we go with the case?"

"Well, to start with we wait and see what the Path boys have to say about Mr Burgess and how he died."

"I thought it was pretty obvious. Wasn't he in the process of being eaten by pigs when you arrived at the scene?"

"Yes, but I reckon he was well dead by then."

"I thought you heard him scream?"

"I heard *a* scream, Sergeant. That might have been his killer or killers."

"And why would they do that?"

Mowgley shrugged. "Dunno. Maybe to make sure I would come and have a look and find him while there was still enough of him left to identify."

"But why would they want you to know it was Burgess?"

"Pass."

"So what about the shipment?"

"What shipment?"

"The delivery of Class 'A' he told you about on the phone."

"Ah. Not our scene."

"What do you mean, 'not our scene'?"

"It's over to DCI Stanton now."

"What?" Melons banged her empty glass on the table top hard enough to draw looks from the bar, where Builder Bob and his colleagues were standing. "It's our case and it started on our patch, and the bloody boat is bringing the stuff into our ferry port. How comes that means it's not our scene?"

"Now, now, Sergeant," Mowgley chided her while smiling reassuringly at Builder Bob, "you must try not to be so possessive. The fact is that, according to the late Mr. Burgess, the lorry with the gear on will be loaded on board a French ferry at the French port of Caen next Thursday evening. That means its technically French business. Can you imagine what it would be like if we let our Frog counterparts in on it and then tried to keep them from nausing it up? What's going to happen is that Jane Stanton will have the heavy mob from the Met aboard on the way over, pretending to be Brits returning from a booze outing."

"A load of mouthy blokes with cropped hair, bomber jackets and big beer guts? Do you think they'll be able to disguise themselves as Brit booze cruisers?"

"Hopefully. Anyway, they'll be there to make sure nothing untoward happens on the crossing, like a transfer to another lorry or whatever. Jane reckons they might even get a look in the back. Plan 'A' is then to follow the load off the boat and to wherever the delivery is being made. They could stop it on the quayside, but then they'll never know where it was headed. The SPU will also have bodies in the port and every other concerned agency is in on it, so we don't have to do anything but provide a welcoming committee and introduce the boys and girls from the Special Projects Unit to the Leopard when the dust has settled. Does that meet with your approval?"

"I still think we should go over a day or two before the crossing and be on the boat to keep an eye on things."

"No you don't. You think you should go over a couple of days before it all happens so you can do all sorts of unmentionable things with your French bit of stuff."

"That's not the point-." Whatever the point was that Melons was going to make, it was lost as she reached into her jacket, took out her phone and held it to her ear.

Mowgley watched as she listened, nodded, shot a glance at him and replied: "Okay, thanks for that. I'll pass it on."

Closing the phone, Melons put it back in her jacket.

"Well, don't keep me in suspense. Who was it? Have we won the Lottery?"

"No. It was your drug squad mate. He wanted to know why you don't keep your bloody phone with you, and to say you might be interested in a shout they've just had."

"Try me."

"There's been a body found in Buckland, and it looks like an overdose."

"There must be more to it than that for Hoppy to think I'd

be interested."

"He said you knew the deceased. Someone called Cottage Grove Pete?"

Twenty-six

"So why is he called Cottage Grove Pete if he doesn't live in Cottage Grove?"

"Obviously, because he *used* to live in Cottage Grove."

"Oh."

There was a parking bay further along the road, but they left the car on yellow lines and walked across the cracked paving slabs to where a uniformed officer guarded the steps to the basement area of the old house.

It was one of the few remaining original dwellings on the outskirts of Portsmouth, and looked ill-at-ease amongst the forest of Council-owned maisonettes and high-rise blocks. Though he had not stayed long in the city, Charles Dickens had been born not far away. His birthplace was now a museum, but the installation of twee period lampposts and railings and other aspects of the general gentrification of the immediate area had not reached this grim quarter. Most cynical tenants would have forecast it never would.

The three-storey house must have been quite elegant in its youth, probably belonging to a naval officer or wealthy local merchant who liked to live a respectable distance from where he made his money. Now it belonged to an entrepreneurial kebab shop operator, and was home to a dozen benefit claimants with drugs and drink problems, or both.

Mowgley nodded amiably at the constable, who risked an

engaging smile at Melons before telling them that they had beaten SOCO to it. Reaching over, he opened the gate so they could descend to what would have been called the garden flat when the property had one.

Melons scowled at the PC, then looked down into the basement area. "Blimey, your mate drank a lot of milk, didn't he?"

Mowgley smiled as he looked at the dozens of empty bottles clustered beneath the sash window overlooking the small front yard. "Pete liked his milk when he couldn't face anything solid, but it's an old druggie den tradition. It was a sort of primitive alarm system in case the drug squad or any other uninvited guests tried to affect an entrance through the window."

"Did it work?"

"No, but like I said, it was a tradition." He touched one of the bottles with his toe. "I bet they were all around the doorstep as well when Hoppy arrived."

The much-battered front door was ajar, allowing a little light and air to venture within. In the hallway, a path had been cleared through an ankle-deep tide of what must have been several years' worth of circulars, voting reminders, official envelopes and flyers for local takeaways. A rusty bicycle with one wheel was propped against a wall beneath a monochrome poster bearing the symbol of the Campaign for Nuclear Disarmament. All three walls, the ceiling, the single door leading off the hallway and a considerable amount of the carpet had been painted a deep red. A frayed lead dangled from the ceiling, its socket holding a bulb which had been painted to match the general colour scheme.

Mowgley avoided the Tibetan prayer bells as he pushed the door open and entered the living room. It smelled of age, damp and decay, but above all a rank, musky odour.

Melons wrinkled her nose. "Crikey, what is that pong?"

"That's the smell of the Sixties, Melons. Patchouli oil, or hippy perfume. It was used by people like Pete to mask the smell of unwashed clothes and bodies, but mainly to cover up the reek of shit."

"You mean they didn't bother to wipe their bums?"

"Not that sort of shit. Cannabis resin, marijuana, pot, grass, weed or whatever you liked to call it. In those days, the term of choice was shit. We didn't have a bike shed, but Pete and I had our first toke behind the boiler house the term before we left school. It didn't do much for me, but it changed his life. The world moved on, but as you can see, Pete preferred to stay in 1966."

"So he was a close friend of yours?"

"Not really. Just someone who was a mate at school and then drifted away. Funny how much that happens."

Someone had pulled down the heavily embroidered shawl which served as a curtain for the front window, but the glass was so dirty it was difficult to make out details in the room. Mowgley found and tried the light switch, and both he and Melons started back as the room was filled with a hugely loud and distorted cacophony of sound. He flipped the switch and the ear-jangling combination of guitar and organ stopped.

"Jesus," said Melons. "What was that? Another early warning alarm?"

"No. That's The Nice, unless I am very much mistaken."

Looking up, Mowgley saw a bayonet plug in the overhead light socket. Its lead ran to an old-fashioned record player on a low coffee table in the middle of the room. The fabric-covered machine was a classic Dansette, and probably of about the same age as its owner. Alongside the Oriental brass-topped table on which it stood was an incongruously elegant chaise-longue, and Mowgley deliberately avoided looking at the huddled shape sprawled on it.

He turned instead to the posters lining the wall opposite the window. One had occupied a million bedsit walls in the Sixties, and showed the head and shoulders of a darkly handsome young man in a beret. He had long hair and a beard with a wispy moustache, and was looking with earnest solemnity towards a revolutionary future.

Next to Che Guevara was a full-length shot of Janis Joplin in action with the Full Tilt Boogie Band, and alongside that a poster advertising an appearance of The Nice. The cult 1960s rock band had taken its name for a slang term for being high on drugs, and it was their manic version of 'America' that had been sitting on the Dansette's turntable.

"All the usual suspects, eh, Jack? Just Ravi Shankar and the Indian-looking bird from the cover of the International Times needed for a full house."

Mowgley turned away from the posters. A short, stocky man was standing framed in the doorway leading off the living room. Even in the gloom, Mowgley could see that his small and neatly-featured face was shining from the recent attention of a razor, and that his close-cropped hair was parted unusually high above one ear. He was wearing a narrow, dark tie, with its small, exactly symmetrical knot just visible through the gap in his buttoned-down, pastel-shaded shirt. His navy blue Crombie overcoat looked immaculate, and the creases on his grey slacks appeared sharp enough to cut paper. The man's loafer shoes looked box-fresh, and his overall appearance was in sharp contrast to the tawdry room. Apart from having his trousers tucked into his navy blue socks he still looked, thought Mowgley, like the Mod he used to be.

Mowgley touched his forehead in recognition and salute. "Thanks for the call, Hoppy."

The man shrugged and walked over to shake Mowgley's hand. "Thought you'd like to know before they came and carted him away."

Mowgley looked at the shape on the day-bed and nodded. "I guess it was you who switched the music off?"

"Yep. It was still playing when I arrived. That model had an automatic record changer."

"Of course."

They stood side by side and looked down at the body. It lay on one side, knees tucked up in a foetal position. One arm was drawn up to the chest, and the other dangled over the edge of the chaise-longue. The thin grey hair was pulled back into a pony tail, emphasising the near-skeletal features. The eyes were shut and the face seemed in repose and surprisingly unlined.

The stocky man spoke first: "Not in a bad shape for someone who used to forget to eat for weeks at a time and ingested more stuff than in the stock room at a busy Boots."

Mowgley nodded. "He always was a survivor. I met him a few years ago and he said he put it down to eating a Weetabix each morning, and always cleaning his teeth, whatever state he was in."

Together with surviving the ravages of a dedication to the exploration of mind-expanding substances, Cottage Grove Pete had also survived any number of coups or take-over attacks by up-and-coming dealers over a long career. As well as an old school friend of Dave Hopkirk, he had been a useful contact for the drug squad and thus under their general protection.

He had retired as a full-time dealer a decade ago, and had become something of an icon for younger members of the drug- using community.

Pete had attained almost mystical status as someone who had been at the centre of the drug scene in the late Sixties, even if he could not remember most of them. His tales of unrestrained excess with green LSD-flavoured sugar cubes and Lebanese Gold cannabis resin were the stuff of legend and grew with the re-telling. It was often said by fans of the era and attitudes that he had allegedly not slept during the long and hazy summer of 1969. When Mowgley had asked if the tale were true, Pete had modestly denied it and said he had dozed off on several occasions at the Isle of Wight festival of that year. He had, he added, never seen what people saw in Dylan.

"Do you mind if I have a look around?"

DI Hopkirk looked over to where Melons was standing near the door to the kitchen, and nodded. "Of course not. Just watch out for the fleas. They must be on some of Pete's gear, 'cos their jumping really high."

"And there was me thinking you had come on your pushbike." Mowgley bent over and began tucking his trousers into his socks. "So who called it in?"

"Anonymous female," said Hopkirk. "About an hour ago. Sounded white and not that young. Might have been a mate coming round for a session, or a punter. Pete had obviously let her or them in." He nodded down at the body: "Could have been they jacked up together and then she panicked when Pete stopped breathing."

Mowgley knelt down and looked at the slim syringe dangling from his old friend's arm and saw that the barrel was half-filled with blood. It was common practice for serious users to flush blood back and forwards into a vein to ensure that all the heroin had made the journey. It was also a way to revisit and prolong the moment, a bit like a pubgoer taking his time over the first sip of ale, Mowgley reflected. He then saw that Pete had used a tie as a tourniquet around his upper arm, and grunted with sad amusement.

"What?" asked DI Hopkirk.

"It's our old school tie," said Mowgley. "He used to hate wearing it."

On the floor by the body was a silver foil container of the type used to hold pies. The bottom was a rusty brown colour, and beside it was a spoon and plastic lighter.

Mowgley briefly rested a hand on Cottage Grove Pete's shoulder. "Do you reckon it was a bad cut? Not like Pete to fall for that, I would have thought?"

"Dunno yet. I haven't had a good look around. There's been talk of some dodgy gear doing the rounds, but there's always street gossip. As you say, it wasn't Pete's style to go for really crap stuff."

Mowgley stood up and nodded. Heroin was always cut by the time it reached street level, and it depended on how many hands it went through as to how and by how much it was adulterated. In the old days, the preferred cutting substance was a simple sugar powder officially used as a baby laxative. Before that, quinine was popular. More unscrupulous or desperate dealers would use talcum powder to make a batch go further. Nowadays, competition meant that less adulterated heroin usually arrived at point-of-sale. But the quality still depended on who was doing the buying and the selling, and how desperate or greedy they were.

"Did your chum have a sweet tooth, I wonder?"

Both men turned to where Melons stood in the doorway leading to the kitchen. She was holding up a small yellow cylinder with a black tube sticking from the top.

"Find me a junkie who hasn't," said DI Hopkirk.

"What is it?" It's before my time I reckon, but it must be making a comeback. It's something called a Sherbert Fountain. There's a dozen of them in the kitchen cabinet."

"Anything else?" asked Mowgley.

"Only a few cockroaches which appear to have starved to death - or maybe overdosed. Oh, and did Pete like to do a bit of home baking?"

"Only stuff in teaspoons far as I know," said DI Hopkirk. "Why do you ask?"

"There's a couple of open flour bags in the bin. The labels are in Russian - or something seriously Eastern European."

Twenty-seven

"That's an 'L' and an 'I'. Ten bonus points to me."

"Rubbish. We said five for all Eastern European countries."

Mowgley wagged a finger: "Yes, but Lithuania is not technically Eastern Europe, and anyway it's a special case."

Melons scrutinised the list on her lap. "It doesn't say anything about Lithuania being special here."

"Ask any Lithuanian, Sergeant."

They were sitting in an unmarked car on the dock alongside one of the linkspans connecting ship to shore. The bellow of heavy engines issued from its bowels as the ferry disgorged its cargo of giant lorries. Once over the bridge, all vehicles were under the direction of a team of strategically-placed men in high-visibility jackets. Like cricket umpires, each had his own style and delivery of signalling. Some also enjoyed exerting and abusing their authority when tired, angry, bored or just because they could. Sometimes this would involve no more than delaying cars of a colour and make they did not like. If in a really bad mood they would send individual or whole lines of cars on a circuit of the docks which would eventually bring them back to where they had started.

Melons looked up from her list of country identification codes as approved by the International Organisation for Standardisation and shook her head resignedly: "Did you collect cigarette cards as a kid?"

"I'm not that bloody old. Why?"

"If you had, I bet you would have cheated."

"How can you cheat at collecting fag cards?"

"You would have lied about what you had, even to yourself."

"Rubbish."

They sat in silence, then Mowgley gave a gasp and thrust an arm in front of his sergeant's face: "I don't believe it - look at that!"

Melons automatically followed the direction of his pointing finger. "What? What is it?"

"It's a seagull. There - flying over that crane!"

"Big deal. So what...?"

"I claim a Norbert! That's fifty points and game set and match to me!"

Melons looked at Mowgley's triumphant expression, and then at the linkspan as a lorry bearing a distinctive logo and red livery colours of the Norbert Dentressangle freight forwarding company rolled on to the quay.

A sort of Gallic-style Eddie Stobart haulage company, Dentressangle had fans and followers on both sides of the Channel.

Before Melons could protest, her phone rang. She looked at the number display screen, frowned, then took the call.

After a brief exchange, her frown deepened and changed to a look of dislike, and she handed the phone without comment to Mowgley.

"Where are you?" asked the caller.

Mowgley nudged Melons and pointed at a Romanian-registered lorry trundling over the linkspan. "In my office. We're having a meeting. Where are you?"

"On the deck, just passing that Round Tower thing at Spithead," said Jane Stanton.

"Is it going okay?"

"Sort of. The paperwork and manifest says the lorry's full of French food products."

"What sort of products? Horsemeat and snails?"

"Funny enough, there's loads of snail shells in fancy packaging. It's all gourmet lines, like truffles, fine mustard, duck *confit* and -"

"Duck what?"

"Never mind. We had a look while one of our lads was having a drink and a chat in the bar with the driver, but there was nothing to see. According to the driver, he picked the load up from a depot outside Paris. He's taking it to a warehouse in South London for onward distribution. Quite clever really. All those cans and jars with really strong-smelling stuff in them would be just the job to put class 'A' in. And you can bet the Frogs would wave the rig through on the nod as it's stuffed full of their top gear."

"Quite. And what about the driver?"

"Hard to say at this stage. We didn't want to get too chummy. But he likes his drink and he's not that straight as he offered our bloke a deal on a case or two of bouillabaisse at a knock-down price or a swap."

"Boulawhat?"

"Posh fish stew."

"Oh, right. I don't think that's an indicator that he's a wrong 'un. More like par for the course for a lot of drivers, especially if they're carrying something tradeable. So what's next?"

"We've got a van and two cars on board, and a couple of cars at the gates. We won't lose him for sure, but we won't make a move until he's got to where he's going and finished unloading. Anyway, I'd better go; we've just passed that old ship, so we must be getting close to the docks."

"I think you mean Admiral Lord Nelson's historic and glorious flagship, HMS Victory."

"Whatever. I'll give you a call when something's occurred. As he's supposed to be heading for South London, you might want to come up and join us for a celebration drinkie at our local."

"Can't wait. Well, good luck."

"Thanks - and don't forget to keep your head down."

"That's a Roger, Ma'am."

* * *

An hour later. Mowgley, if not keeping his head down, was adopting a low profile.

Melons had moved the car into a line of vehicles waiting to board the overnight ferry from Caen for its return journey. She had also vetoed Mowgley's proposal that they should have a high-profile shouting match so that observers would think they were a typical holidaying couple.

The unloading of the *Falaise* had begun on time, and the suspect lorry was rolling off the linkspan and away from the quayside, an anonymous white van in its wake.

Mowgley watched the vehicles head towards passport control: "Are you sure that's the one?"

"Well, it's the right freight company, nationality and licence plates. Or so you said Burgess said. So what do we do now? Surely you're not going to follow it?"

"I think not, but we could just see it off the premises." As Melons started the engine, her phone rang.

"Aren't you going to answer that?" Mowgley asked, "It could be DCI Stanton to tell us they've left the boat. Don't forget she thinks I'm in the office."

"Okay, but why did you tell her that?"

"Just being prudent. Go on, then - answer it."

"I would if I could get my hand in your pocket. You didn't give my phone back after speaking to your lady friend."

He reached for the phone, flipped the cover and, after a fumble, pressed the right button. "Jack Mowgley?"

"Hello mate, Hoppy here. You alright to speak?"

"Yes mate. Just sitting on the dock of the bay, watchin' the ships roll in. Then I watch them roll away again. Yeah..."

"I hope you're not wastin' time just to make the dock your home, yeah..."

"Alright, smartarse. I know you know your Otis. So what's to do?"

"Got the result on Pete, and the flour bags your lady spotted. And the sherbert fountains."

"Good man. So was it some bad gear that did for Pete?"

"Sort of. The H itself was really good quality. It was almost pure, white diamorphine."

"So he overdosed?"

"Hang on and I'll tell you. People rarely overdose on heroin, no matter how neat it is. That's an urban druggie myth, or rather a non-druggie myth. What usually does for users is if the stuff's got something nasty in it."

"And did it?"

"Not half. It was cut with Fentanyl."

"Fentawhat?"

"Fentanyl. In simple terms for a layman like you, it's a pain reliever and then some. It's actually a hundred times stronger than morphine. It's pretty new, and can be deadly. It's caused a good few deaths already when loonies have got hold of it."

"So if it was good stuff otherwise, why would Pete put this Fentanyl gear in?"

"That, my friend, is the question."

"Ah." Mowgley nodded thoughtfully. "And was the stuff in the bag that my sergeant found cut with the Fentanyl?"

"No. It was flour, just like it said on the label."

"So why would Pete have a couple of bags of Polish flour in his kitchen?"

"Pass. Perhaps he was in a bit of a state and wandered into a Polish grocery shop and liked the look of the bags. More likely the H was in the flour."

"But you just said the flour was clean."

"It was. What I mean is that there could have been some plastic wraps of heroin in the bags. Buried in a kilo of white flour would be as good a place as any to hide white heroin, I reckon."

Mowgley nodded again. "Ah. Right. And what about the sherbert dabs or whatever they were?"

"Now you're talking. The sherbert showed a low level of contamination with the same stuff as in the syringe. You know Pete's off-the-wall sense of humour. He probably had a bit of fun passing the sherbert fountains round and inviting his mates to take a dip with the liquorice tube - or even snort through it. I reckon sherbert and H would give you a right buzz in the nasal cavities."

"Sounds about right for Pete. So tell me more about the flour bags."

"The labels said it was best *maka*. Apparently that's Polish for flour. There's an address and website number on the bags, so we're following it up."

"Maka? Is that M.A.K.A. with a funny little squiggle under the 'A'?"

"Yeah, that's it. How did you know?"

"I'm just reading it off the side of a bleeding great red truck. Can I call you back, Hoppy?"

Part Four

Twenty-eight

"And women complain about builder's bum."

Mowgley winced theatrically as the young woman bent forward and began to squeeze into the gap between the bench seat and table. They were screwed to the floor, and the struggle had caused the waistband of her jeans to move southwards. This had revealed a huge, pimply white cleft. It looked, he mused, like one end of a giant and very unripe peach.

The movement also revealed a straining scarlet thong, and a small tattoo of a gaudily coloured and badly-drawn butterfly.

Mowgley watched in fascination as the billowing motion of the flaccid flesh caused the butterfly to appear to flutter across the vast, swaying expanse of arse.

He shuddered and shook his head as if to clear away the image. "I wonder if she knows what she looks like from behind?"

Melons looked up from the *Daily Telegraph* crossword at him and then across at the tableau. "She probably doesn't care. Do you?"

"Do I what? Care about what she looks like from behind? You know, I think I do."

"You mean the sight of her size and what she's wearing offends your aesthetical sensitivities?"

"You'd have to tell me what aesthetical means before I

could give you an honest answer. You know I think people should eat and dress how they like."

"Well then, what's the problem? She's just dressing how she wants."

"No she's not. She's dressing how other people say she should dress. The desire to be fashionable has caused her to lose any sense of reason, judgement and understanding of what she looks like in that kit. Even her best mates will be having a good laugh - literally behind her back."

Melons looked at him with an expression which was a mixture of exasperation and bemusement: "For Christ's sake, when did *you* ever worry about what you looked like?"

"True. But then I'm not trying to look like this."

"You mean you're a genuine, committed slob."

"Um, yes. Suppose I do, really."

Defused by this concession, Melons returned to her crossword.

Across the aisle, the young woman was now seated, and apportioning her stomach above and below the edge of the table. As she let out a relieved sigh and picked up the plastic-coated menu, Mowgley wondered if she was aware there was no table service at Ginger's Caff. This would mean she would have to extract herself and then repeat the whole insertion routine at least twice. Then he saw she was waving to get the attention of a man standing by the counter.

He was around her age and as tiny as she was titanic. He was wearing what looked like a child-sized green t-shirt, very baggy jeans and terminally scuffed trainers. As well as being painfully thin he had badly hunched shoulders, and the resulting posture made it look as if he had been hung from an invisible hook with his feet just touching the floor. While the woman's waistband was under constant assault, the man's jeans hung perilously on his hips and looked ready to succumb to gravity at any moment.

Mowgley had observed in recent times that a higher-than-average number of very fat women seemed to favour the company of small, severely underweight men. He had seen many examples in the local supermarket, with vast, wobbly women towing diminutive partners in their wake like small pet dogs. It appeared that the man at the counter was there to order her breakfast. Or perhaps, he thought, she was sizing him up *as* her breakfast.

At the head of the queue, Detective Constable Mundy had been served and was closely inspecting and selecting cutlery and condiments from a table beneath a sign advertising the house specialties.

"I wonder why they always have pictures of the stuff on offer."

Melons looked up again and tapped her Biro against her teeth:

"*Rubbish in a Chinese Harbour.* What do you think that could be? It's four letters," she added helpfully.

"Bollocks."

"No, that doesn't fit."

Mowgley refused to continue the game, and said "Do you think anyone doesn't know what fried egg, chips, bacon, sausage and beans on a plate looks like?"

"Everyone who's not British might have a job visualising the presentation. Maybe, as the marketing boys would say, Ginger thinks a photo makes the proposition more enticing."

"Yes, but the photos don't show all the grease or the cracks on the plate or the thumbprints on the egg."

"Pictures of models are usually airbrushed; why not Ginger's Big Fry-Up, Mug of Tea Included?"

"It's just that the doctored photos don't look as nice as the real thing."

Their conversation was put on hold by the arrival of Stephen Mundy with a heavily laden tray. Putting it on an adjacent table, he laid Melons' bacon sandwich and mug of pallid tea in front of her, then gingerly handed over Mowgley's All-Day Jumbo Breakfast. He held the plate, Melons thought, as if handling a particularly gruesome item of evidence.

"Just think," she said, "If this was the Middle Ages you'd have to taste it all to see nobody was trying to poison your leader."

Mundy smiled nervously, then started to peel off the top of his blueberry-flavoured yoghurt.

"What's the game, Constable?"

"I just didn't see anything I fancied, Sir."

"I didn't mean that. I meant you've been short changed." Mowgley pointed an accusing fork at the poster on the opposite wall. "It clearly states that Ginger's Jumbo Breakfast consists of said jumbo sausage, two eggs, two slices of bacon, a fried slice, a piece of toast, black pudding, fried tomato, beans and chips. As you will agree, there is no toast on this plate."

"Actually, the menu says fried slice *or* toast, Sir. I chose fried bread because I thought you might prefer it to toast."

Mowgley re-examined the poster. "Ah. Good deductive work, Young Stephen. I rest content."

They attended to their food for a few moments, then Melons asked: "Did you have a nice holiday, Sir?"

Mowgley waited until his mouth was almost empty of a mixture of tomato, jumbo sausage and cremated bacon before replying. "I don't think a three-day leave of absence to attend a series of briefing sessions on a current case and modern policing procedures should be classified as a holiday, Sergeant."

"Oh, sorry. We-I-thought you were having a knees-up in London with DCI Stanton and her Special Projects buddies."

"I could hardly refuse any invitations to team-building after-work activities, and I had to show those London geezers that we carrot-crunchers can keep our ends up in the pub."

"And elsewhere, no doubt," said Melons into her mug of tea.

"Anyway," said Mowgley, choosing to ignore her aside, "going forward, have you been busy on our current caseload? I would have appreciated a daily briefing."

"Had you taken your phone with you, that would have happened. And when I called DCI Stanton to ask if you were still alive, she said she would get you to call back. That did not happen."

"It would have done had there been an emergency. Anyway, moving on if we may, I hope you have some positive reports to make?"

Melons nodded. "We certainly have, thanks to Stephen. But before we start, can I ask why we have come to Ginger's Caff for the briefing?"

"I thought a working breakfast was the way a progressive and forward-thinking team should move into the future, Sergeant. Now DC Mundy has done his homework on the flour lorry, I thought it would also be a team-building exercise to come somewhere different for the updating process. Besides, walls have ears and all that."

Melons looked around to see if that were the case, then said: "You don't mean you think someone in the office is listening in to what we say and passing it on? Or that the new Super has had the place bugged? Or that she's got Dickie Quayle snooping on us."

Mowgley waggled a forkful of chips at his sergeant. "Many a true word and so on. It's just that we need to exchange information, then make a plan of action. I wanted to be somewhere away from the Fun Factory, and even the Leopard is barely open at this time. And nobody does an all-day breakfast like Ginger."

"That's true." Melons looked at Mowgley's plate as she finished off her bacon sandwich, then wiped her face and hands on a paper napkin before taking a cigarette from a packet on the table. "Okay, I believe you. Not. But before Stephen gives us the SP, can you tell us some more about your chum's drugs-bust disaster?"

Mowgley looked at her as disapprovingly as possible for a man holding a fork which was dripping egg yolk on his shirt front. "You really should not be so disrespectful of a senior officer, Sergeant, or display such petty *schadenfreude*, especially at this time of the morning."

"Schaden-what?"

Mowgley regarded his shirt and frowned: "Dunno. Just sounded right. Young Mundy, can you shed some light on this?"

"It's a German expression for taking pleasure in other people's misfortunes, Sir."

"Thank you, but she already knew that." Mowgley absent-mindedly dipped his finger in the egg yolk on his shirt and licked it clean. "Anyway, in answer to your question about the covert ops mission, I have to report it was from any perspective a bit of a nause-up."

"In what way?"

"In the way that it all went pear-shaped when they had followed the alleged consignment of Class 'A' all the way to South London and swooped."

"Swooped?"

"You know these specialist teams, especially from the Met. They grew up thinking *The Sweeney* was real. I think some of them break the door in when they get home after work. Apparently, they watched the truck unload, then the off-site commander decided they should pull the driver and impound the stuff pronto. I'm told it was quite chaotic. Blokes in bomber jackets arresting passing schoolchildren, dogs biting their handlers, and French grub all over the place. Snail shells and trampled-on pâté everywhere."

"And what was the outcome?"

"Egg, or I suppose it should be *oeuf*, on face all round. They went through the whole lot and just about everything else in the factory, and nothing to show for it except for a couple of illegal immigrants."

"So the information from Burgess was duff? Doesn't that put you on the spot?"

Mowgley forced himself to stop watching the young woman at work on her All-Day Breakfast. Like many seriously obese people, she ate daintily and self-consciously. He wondered if this was restricted to her public eating, and when alone or with her consort, she shovelled her food in, or even got him to do it.

He wiped his hand thoughtfully across his mouth, then said:

"No, I don't think Burgess's information was necessarily duff; it could be that they switched trucks or called the trip off when they found out we'd been given the info. And I don't like to think how they could have found out he'd told me about it. Either way I'm in the clear thanks to you recording my chat with Burgess. We - that's the Special Projects people, DCI Stanton and me - still reckon there's a regular system being set up by the Ruskis for bringing in gear through our port. That's why I tasked you and Stephen to do the interesting research stuff about the flour shipments while I attended the boring seminars in London. Was your time well spent?"

Melons looked at Mundy and nodded and smiled in encouragement. "You could say that. Do you want to start, Stephen?"

DC Mundy nodded, wiped his plastic spoon with a paper serviette and put it and the empty yoghurt pot on to a nearby table before taking out his notebook. Then he cleared his throat, smoothed his already smooth hair, and began:

"I've been working with the ferry company, our *Gendarmerie* friends -" he glanced at Melons, who again smiled in encouragement, "- and Europol."

Mowgley looked impressed and also nodded his encouragement, and Mundy continued: "The lorry you saw is owned by a French-based specialist haulage company which seems to have only one significant customer and only a handful of vehicles. The company offices are registered in Paris, and there's a depot at Verviers, close to the borders of Belgium and Germany."

Mowgley shook his head as if to clear it. "So far, so confusing. I suppose there's no way we can cut to the chase?"

Mundy looked almost rebellious. "I'm afraid not, Sir." He looked at his notebook and continued: "The Polish company whose name was on the bags of flour Sergeant McCarthy found at your friend's flat is the same company whose logo and name you saw on the side of the lorry. Polskie Factos Maka is part of an association of Polish flour millers, and has its main plant in Poznan. They have a huge capacity and produce hundreds of thousands of tons of several varieties of flour for home consumption and export around the world."

Mowgley held his hand up. "So what makes Polish flour different from the local stuff? Why would people pay the price to have it delivered thousands of miles?"

"Polish regulations concerning the production of flour are very specific and different from other countries, Sir. There are five types of wheat flour produced for making anything from noodles to sponge cakes or pizza. Then there's their rye and potato flour..."

"But even so, what makes it worth shifting the stuff all that way from there to here? It must be thousands of miles?"

"It's a bit like British expats paying through the nose for a tin of corned beef in a French supermarket," said Melons. "It's a taste of home. Remember that Big Kevin at the Leo makes a nice living taking hundreds of day-old white sliced loaves across the Channel and selling them to Brits in Normandy and Brittany."

"True. So it's a legit business, then."

Melons nodded. "At last count, there were reckoned to be 700,000 ethnic Poles living permanently in the United Kingdom. If you allow for illegals and how things have moved on, it must be the best part of a million now. Or more. They like their bread and they like it made their way. That's why there are so many Polish bakeries and shops selling flour at twice the price of a bag of McDougal's."

Mowgley nodded. "And a good excuse for bringing loads of it over."

He held out an inviting hand to Mundy. "Pray continue, young Stephen."

Mundy cleared his throat, consulted his notebook, then said: "The lorry you saw was part of a weekly shipment bringing different types of flour from the mills at Poznan to a Polish - run company in London. The company is linked with the flour mills, and uses their name. From there it's bagged or sent in bulk to bakeries and shops or direct to customers around the country."

"And how does it arrive at this factory?"

"It comes in 100 kilogram compound tubs, and is bagged into various sizes at the factory."

"Okay, I'm getting it so far. And how long has this been going on?"

"According to the ferry records and the flour mills, just over a month."

"So what happened before?"

"Apparently, there were other arrangements. The contract was awarded to the new Paris-based haulage company last October, and the first run took place just before the end of the year."

"Do we know why they changed the routine? Did the mill get a really low quote or for some other reason an offer they could not refuse from the haulage company?"

"We don't know that yet, Sir. But what might be significant is that the flour mill changed hands at the end of last year."

"And who bought it?"

"That's not clear, yet, Sir. According to Guy and his Europol *feducier* specialists, the trail is long and tangled, but they're working on it."

"Mmmm again. Whoever owns the company, the delivery set-up doesn't really make sense, does it? Call me picky, but unless they've moved it, isn't Poland in Eastern Europe?"

"It is, Sir."

"So would it not be shorter and quicker and cheaper to take the flour from Pozwhatsitsname to Calais then across to Dover and onwards, rather than much further west to Caen and then through our port and then on to the place in London?"

"Exactly what *we* thought," said Melons. "It's close on a thousand kilometres from Poznan to the depot at Verviers, then it gets interesting. From Verviers to Calais is another 300k, while taking the Caen option is double that. The distance to the factory from this side of the Channel is about the same."

Mowgley frowned. "So what conclusions do you draw from that inconsistency? Is the new logistics company that crap at geography?"

Melons looked uncomfortable. "I doubt they're that crap. It could be that they chose to go to Caen and across to us for some other reason."

"Yeah, right. You mean the haulage company has a special deal for that route, or the drivers get better treatment on the Caen run?"

Melons raised her eyebrows and shrugged. "Don't think so. It could be..."

"Don't hold back, Sergeant. It could be what?"

"If they are bringing dodgy stuff with the flour, maybe they see our port as a soft touch in some sort of regard. Or they may even have some sort of special arrangements to make it worth coming the extra distance..."

Twenty-nine

It was raining as they left Ginger's caff. Melons suggested they take shelter while Mundy fetched the car, but Mowgley said he wanted to walk.

She looked at him with mock concern. "Are you feeling alright? The car's at least three hundred yards from here."

"Bloody cheek. Just wanted to walk my breakfast down and have a fag. It tastes better in the open air."

In truth, Mowgley was feeling nostalgic and wanted to revisit his past. The funfair lay on their route along the promenade, and once upon a time it had been, for him, a magical alternative to a grey post-war world. Forty years ago he would have been hanging around, breathing in the sights and sounds and testing the penny machines to see if anyone had left a copper in the works or the coin cup.

Even now he could recall the unique fragrance of simmering onions, hot dogs and hamburgers, the sickly-sweet tang of candy floss, the greasy smell of deep-fried doughnuts, and the over-arching odour of tobacco, beer, sweat, cheap perfume and the sea.

"Have you noticed how onions cooked in water smell like stale sweat?"

Melons sniffed and shook her head. "I think you'll find it's low tide and that's the sewage outfall."

"I don't mean I can smell it now, although I can. I was

remembering it from a long time ago. Do you think that's possible?"

"After years being cooped up with you in a car, is that a serious question?"

They walked past the shuttered arcades and stalls and below the rusting skeletal contours of the Wild Mouse ride. It was surprising how little things had changed in this part of the city, he thought, but perhaps that was because they couldn't build on the sea - yet. One day the fair would be replaced by blocks of flats with silly names, but now he could still walk where he had spent endless summer holidays all those years before. In a new millennium and a very different world, the link with the past felt somehow comforting. People said travel was good for you, but there was a lot to be said for staying in the same place, he reckoned.

"Are you sure you're okay?"

With an exaggerated start, he looked down to where Melons had laid a solicitous hand on his arm. "Absolutely. Why?"

"Didn't you know you were groaning? Perhaps the jumbo sausage was off."

"I was not groaning," said Mowgley in a deeply offended tone. "I was singing. That's my old school song."

* * *

Their arrival at the car park coincided with a French ferry easing its way past the Round Tower and through Spithead. This was the relatively narrow gateway to the harbour and port which gave the city its name.

When here, Mowgley was always struck by the incongruity of the gaudy colours and sleek lines of modern shipping against the backdrop of stone walls and natural defences which had protected the port for a thousand years. Today there was also the contrast between the monstrous ferry boat and the relatively tiny sailing boats and other small craft passing or clustering round it as if for protection from predators. With their size and shape, sheer sides and windows rather than portholes, modern ferry boats put him in mind of hotels which had been uprooted from the land and floated in the sea.

At this time of day and year, the car park was almost

barren. Ten yards from their vehicle, a curl of exhaust smoke showed that the black Range Rover with tinted windows sitting by the pay-point machine had its engine running.

As Mundy unlocked their car, Mowgley nodded at the windscreen "Pass me that ticket will you, son?"

Mundy paused with the door half open, and turned to look quizzically at his superior.

Mowgley held his hand out. "I said give me the ticket. It might be useful to the bloke at the machine."

"But it's almost expired, Sir. I only took an hour-"

"Never mind." Mowgley spoke testily "Just give me the bloody ticket, will you?"

Mundy did so, and he and Melons exchanged bemused looks as Mowgley began to walk towards the Range Rover, holding the ticket aloft.

As he got closer, the vehicle began to move. It backed away slowly, then at a faster pace and with a slight squeal of tyres. The reaction of the unseen driver was unusual enough for Melons and Mundy to exchange glances again, and then begin to walk quickly across the car park.

As the driver of the Range Rover put it in forward gear and began to head towards the only exit, Mowgley broke into a lumbering run. Incongruously, he was still waving the ticket.

He got close enough to lay a hand on the bonnet before the driver gunned the engine. As it shot past, the mirror caught his elbow and the force spun him round before he landed on the wet tarmac. He was laying there with his eyes closed against the rain when Mundy and Melons arrived.

"Whatever you do, for Christ's sake don't ask me if I'm alright."

"I wasn't going to." Melons nodded to Mundy to help Mowgley to his feet. "I was just going to ask what that was all about."

"Search me, Sergeant. Just trying to do a fellow human being a small favour, and that's the thanks I get. Perhaps he thought I was going to ask if he wanted his windscreen cleaned."

Thirty

Mowgley leaned forward to peer through the rain-riven windscreen at a roadside sign. "Blimey, this bloke really is crap at navigation, isn't he? How long has this been the way to London?"

After a short wait on the quayside, the target lorry had been cleared to leave the port and they had followed it out of the gates and on to the motorway. They had expected the Renault eighteen-tonner to follow the standard route to the M25, but the driver had chosen the coastal road eastwards.

"Are you sure this is a good idea?" asked Melons from her unaccustomed position in the back seat.

"Letting Young Mundy take the wheel? I reckon so. He doesn't drive anywhere near as madly as you, or go berserk and use profane language when another road user upsets him. I can safely leave the jack handle within his reach – and we might need to do a nifty bit of reverse parking at some stage."

"Ha Ha. As you know well, what I meant was this going-it-alone routine. Did you not learn from the aftermath of your rendezvous with Mr Burgess? I bet you haven't told anyone that we're trailing a truck possibly carrying a shipment of Class 'A' drugs on behalf of a splinter group of the Russian mafia."

"You win your bet, so pay yourself, Sergeant."

"Thanks. But you still haven't said what we're doing here."

"It's quite simple, Sergeant. If I had told DCI Stanton about our theory on the flour lorry shipments and she chose to undertake another official operation, how would she and we look if it turned out to be another dud? This way we can have a discreet decko at what occurs at the other end. If it's nothing, then no harm done. If it's something, we can give her the nod and she can have all the glory. And anyway, it's nice to get out of the office - even on a day like this."

"But if there is any dodgy stuff on board that lorry, we're not going to be able to do anything about it, are we?"

"Obviously not. But the whole point of all this is that the Ruskis are supposed to be setting up a regular delivery route. If this is the means of carriage, Jane and Co will get 'em next time. And, if you want to be anally official about it, they're going through my patch, so this all falls under our remit. Besides, I want my revenge if they're using my port because they reckon we're a soft touch. All clear now?"

Melons remained silent and contented herself with making a face at his back. Mowgley relaxed, then shrank back in his seat as DC Mundy made a swift manoeuvre to maintain the approved three-vehicle buffer between tail and tailed. After opening his eyes and unclenching his fists, he reached out and laid a hand on Mundy's arm. "Nicely done, Stephen, but can you give me a bit of warning when you're going to do something a bit sudden?"

* * *

"It's for you. Dougie." Melons passed her phone to Mowgley, who took it.

"Yes, Douglas?"

"Alright, Sir?"

Mowgley scowled at the phone. As usual, Detective Sergeant Quayle managed to make the use of the title sound derisory. In any service of a previous generation, they would have called it dumb insolence. Nowadays, there was nothing much Mowgley could do to avenge himself except give Quayle the dirty jobs and let him know he knew what the sergeant was up to. At some Christmas booze-up in the future, he might give in to sudden temptation and give Quayle a slap, but he had promised himself to defer the pleasure until he wanted to opt for an early if not honourable retirement. "Yes, thanks, we're having a lovely time, Sergeant. What about you?"

"Just calling in to confirm that the Range Rover you had a fight with in the car park was more than likely a clone."

"Don't take the piss, Sergeant."

Quayle's voice took on an overly officious tone and content, which was, in itself, Mowgley knew, a form of insolence: "Sorry Sir. The registered keeper of the vehicle is a Mr Nicholas Cronin. He lives in a nice barn conversion in a village outside Wokingham."

"Anything known?"

"Nothing much. Just a load of parking tickets and a couple of speeding fines. He's sixty-eight and a retired tax specialist for a big import company. Buys a new motor every eighteen months, and got this one at the end of last year."

"He don't sound like the sort of bloke who tears around in flash cars with smoked-out windows while collecting speeding and parking tickets."

"That's what I reckoned, Sir. I think it's a case of *cherchez la femme*. That means 'look for-'"

"As I said, don't take the piss, Sergeant. What woman?"

"Mr Cronin has a very young and very blonde wife, Sir. I think she's probably the one who picked up the tickets."

"Can't he afford her a motor of her own, then?"

"She's got a nearly box-fresh Porsche in the garage, but has blown her points and is off the road for three years, officially. From his and her manner, I reckon she got him to buy the Range Rover and the smoky windows and put it in his name. He's probably taken the hit for the speeding and parking fines she's clocked up."

"But you don't think it was her or him in the car park."

"Very unlikely, Sir. When I got her on her own and pressed her a bit, she coughed that she was with her boyfriend in London all that day, allegedly doing a bit of shopping. It all checks out and I don't think she'd make it up as an alibi."

"So a clone, you reckon?"

"Looks like it...Sir."

Mowgley pointedly left Quayle unthanked and passed the phone back to Melons.

"Any news?" She took it and rubbed the flip top against her jacket lapel as if to remove Mowgley's sticky fingerprints.

"No, he's still as much of a lairy tosser as ever."

"I meant about the car you tried to arrest?"

"Don't you start. Probably a clone."

"Ah. I suppose it wouldn't be too hard to find a top-of-the-range Range Rover to nick the number from."

"Yeah. I'll get Quayle on to it, but they've probably dumped it or changed the plates again by now."

Car cloning was a recent but rapidly growing problem, and Mowgley was surprised it had taken so long to catch on. It was a pretty foolproof way of disguising and selling on a stolen car, or just to get a free pass to avoid speeding and parking tickets or having to bother with insurance.

All the offender had to do was find a car of the same year, make, model and colour as the one he had stolen, take the registration number and have a set of plates made up. Legally, anyone buying a set of number plates had to produce a driver's licence, log book for the car, and a valid address. In fact, there were many ways of getting false plates. From then on, any fines or enquiries with regard to misdemeanours would be directed at the owner of the cloned car. Increasingly, organised gangs cloned cars as an extra precaution. In the days when it had been a rarer offence, Mowgley had been on an armed raid on the address of the owner of a car which had allegedly been used in a bank raid. The terrified man had been dragged out of bed at dawn and held at the local station for hours until he could prove that on the day in question he had been drilling teeth in Southampton and not wielding a shotgun in Barking. As the aggrieved dentist's solicitor had pointed out, if his client were a bank blagger, it was hardly likely he would have used his own Ford Mondeo with the distinctive registration plate of GUM 3.

* * *

Mowgley frowned. "Do you think Frog One's on to us?"

Melons leaned forward to peer through the windscreen at the French lorry. "What makes you think that?"

"Why else would he be turning off the main road and on to a country lane leading to nowhere? Did you check if the driver has a mate with him, Stephen?"

"Yes, Sir. I did and he does."

"Don't suppose you saw how young and big they were?"

"No, Sir."

Melons leaned forward as the lorry made use of all three lanes of the roundabout to gain access to the minor 'B' road. "Perhaps he's got a legitimate call to make on the way, or is doing a bit of private business. You know what international lorry drivers are like."

Mowgley frowned. "Mmmm. What do you say, Stephen, or rather, what does the manifest say? Was there more than one drop?"

"No Sir. The destination of the entire contents was logged as being the processing plant and factory in Colnbrook, just short of Slough."

"And remind me of the contents?"

"Twenty reinforced and lined composite drum containers, each filled with one hundred kilograms of a variety of specialist and standard Polish flour, Sir."

"Blimey, that's a lot of flour every week. Ain't it?"

"Not really Sir. If half of it is going in bulk to bakeries in London and beyond, that would leave only a thousand standard bags of flour for retail outlets across the country."

"Okay. That being said, if this was a legit operation it surely would make a lot more sense to bring over twice the amount every fortnight? I also don't understand why we're heading for the arse end of nowhere. Unless, as Melons says, there's an unofficial punter somewhere out here in the sticks. Where are we, exactly, Sergeant?"

Melons looked up from the road map spread across her lap. "We're on the B2145, heading from Chichester towards Sidlesham, then on to Selsey."

"And after that?"

"We fall into the sea."

"Isn't the place where we found Igor just down the road?"

"The Far Mulberry off Bracklesham Bay? About three miles from here. You think there's a connection?"

"Dunno yet, but I don't like coincidences. I never could figure out why Burgess chose to do for Mr Baysawhatsit in that exotic location."

"So what do you reckon our mate and his mate ahead are up to?"

"Let's wait and see. But they reckon the best way to hide something is to put it on show. Flour is a white powder, ain't it?"

"Eh?"

"Think about it Sergeant. Hey-up Young Stephen, is something happening?"

* * *

Despite the sound of the rain beating on the roof and windscreen, they could hear the malignant hiss of compressed air as the multiple brake lights lit up.

Approaching a sharp bend, the lorry had slowed to little more than a walking pace. With several cars queuing impatiently behind, Stephen Mundy looked at Mowgley. "He's signalling left, Sir. Shall I overtake and let the traffic clear?"

"Sod 'em. Wait until he's turned off, then dowse your lights and follow at a respectable distance."

* * *

With the moon in its fulsome third quarter, DC Mundy was able to navigate the narrow twisting lane without lights or mishap. He also found a convenient lay-by around a bend and a hundred yards from where the static lights showed that the lorry had pulled up.

"Okay chaps," said Inspector Mowgley crisply, "time to synchronise watches and send out a recce party. Stephen, you stay here and get ready to beat a hasty retreat or come and get us if we need you."

"Us? said Melons, "I don't think I like the sound of that."

"Don't worry, Sergeant, all we're going to do is take a stroll down lover's lane and have a shufti at what's occurring. If they rumble us, we just have to pretend we're a courting couple looking for a suitable place for a knee-trembler."

"I *definitely* do not like the sound of that."

"Trust me. Now, phones off and maintain radio silence. Are you tooled up as instructed, Sergeant?"

"I've got my regulation ASP expandable baton. What about you?"

"I've got my very unregulation heavy-duty Maglite, and an even more unregulation third generation Glock 17c."

Mowgley reached into his overcoat and produced a menacingly black and blunt automatic.

"My God, are you serious? Have you ever fired a pistol

before?"

"Not this one for sure. It's plastic."

"That's the point of a Glock."

"No, I mean it's *really* plastic, as in toy. It's a replica. Unlike me - and you - it can't be fired."

* * *

They reached a conveniently wide-trunked Holme oak fifty yards from where the lorry sat, its engine grumbling. Opposite was a set of tubular metal, five-barred gates, set into a high, chain- linked fence. Beyond the fence was the loom of a darkened three-storey building. As they watched, the right-hand door of the cab swung open and a figure dropped lightly to the ground.

"Well, that's a relief," said Mowgley, "if the driver's got to open the gates, he must be on his own."

Melons looked at him to see if he were joking, then said: "Not really. It's a left hand drive, remember. That's the passenger door."

"Ah, right."

Further proof of another occupant of the cab came as the engine revved and the lorry pulled forward. The man on the ground moved to the gates, unlocked and then swung them open. He raised a hand, and the lorry began to back towards the gates and then into the yard. It was heading for a loading platform which stretched across the gable end of the building. In it were set three large metal doors, each protected by roller shutters. The yard contained no more than a battered and rusting commercial waste bin, a pile of roughly stacked pallets and an elderly and equally misused forklift truck.

After seeing the lorry into the yard and to the edge of the platform, the driver's mate walked down the side of the building and disappeared.

They watched and waited, then Mowgley gave an explosive sneeze.

"For Christ's sake," Melons hissed savagely. "You're supposed to say 'bless you'," responded Mowgley mildly.

"Why have you always got to try and be funny at times like this?"

Mowgley thought about her question, and then replied.

"Because if I didn't I'd shit myself."

Melons persisted. "What if they heard?"

"What, me sneezing or you shouting at me? I don't think so over the sound of that engine revving. I don't sneeze that loud, and even you don't shout that loud."

Before Melons could answer, Mowgley pointed to the yard, where the middle of the trio of roller shutters was opening with a jerky clanking sound.

As it rose, the driver's mate was gradually revealed, and beyond him the darkened interior. The shutter raised to its full extent, the man stepped out on to the platform and signalled to the driver. The lorry moved slowly back until it was a foot from the platform, when the driver's mate held up a hand. Then came the whine of a hydraulic system at work, and the lorry's tail lift moved steadily downwards from the vertical until it was laying a few inches above the platform. The man stepped on to it and swung a long lever to release the roll-down shutter. When it had reached above head height, he stepped inside.

Mowgley shook his head and sent a spray of water flying, then ran his fingers through his hair and wiped his eyes with the back of his hand. "We should have brought a brolly. So what do you reckon? Illegal immigrants? Or worse, illegal morris dancers? Lord Lucan? Lobby Lud?"

In spite of herself, Melons asked: "Lobby Lud?"

"Sounds like a failed porn stud, don't he? It was a newspaper promotion in the 1920s. You had to spot him on the seafront and say 'You are Lobby Lud and I claim my five pounds. Of course, there was more than one Lobby. The name came from-"

Mowgley's dissertation was cut short as the driver emerged from the back of the lorry. He was pushing a sack truck, on which was loaded a cylindrical container. Mowgley estimated it was around five feet in height and perhaps a couple of feet in diameter. The sack truck landed heavily and jolted as it made the short drop from tail lift to platform. The man lowered his hands and tilted the drum back towards him to make the movement easier, then pushed the tub through the entrance and into the building.

"Hmmm," mused Mowgley. "What do you reckon?"

Before Melons could answer, the sack truck and the man reappeared. He seemed to be pushing the same cylindrical container. Reaching the edge of the platform, he turned his back to the lorry, hauled the sack truck on to the tail lift, turned again and pushed the container into the back of the lorry. Then he shut and secured the doors, pressed a button to send the tail lift on its return journey, then went back into the building to let the roller shutter down. As this was happening, the driver of the lorry revved the engine and began rolling the lorry towards the gate.

"I think the show's over." Mowgley shook his head again and discharged another spray of rainwater. "We'd better get back before young Mundy starts worrying. And we want to be ready to move quickly when the lorry gets back to the road."

"We're going to follow it, then?"

"Are we buggery. I spotted a likely-looking pub on the way here and we can catch Half Price Happy Hour if we hurry."

Thirty-one

At the bar of the Ship Leopard, Mowgley found a sausage salesman trying to escape from the landlord.

The *sausagier* (as he liked to call himself) was a short and stocky South African with an almost perfectly round face. He had come to Britain to work as a journalist, but found he preferred spending more time in pubs than even that traditionally boozy occupation allowed. He found the means to pursue his passion by making imaginatively and often improbably-flavoured sausages and selling them to licensed premises. He was a clever and witty man even in drink, and Mowgley had only realised what a drinker he was when they had met when the sausagier was sober.

Altogether, he was a perfect example of why Mowgley loved British pubs.

The Selsey Sausage King thanked Mowgley with his eyes for interrupting Two-Shits' discourse on his days as a sausage magnate, and retreated through the main doors, a string of cheese and chutney samples wrapped round his neck like a meaty scarf.

By-passing Two-Shits, Mowgley complimented Twiggy the barmaid on her top, ordered his pint, took it to his table and went to work on the *Telegraph* crossword.

"How's it going?"

Mowgley looked up to see the short, dapper figure of Dave

Hopkirk: "Hello Hoppy. I'm stuck on 6 Across, actually. 'Rubbish in a Chinese harbour'. Four letters."

Hopkirk affected a look of thoughtful contemplation, then said: "What about 'junk'?"

Mowgley pantomimed incomprehension: "What d'you mean, 'junk'? Like dope?"

"Nah. Junk is rubbish, but also a Chinese boat."

Mowgley's eyes widened. "So it is." He made as if to enter the solution, then frowned: "But that would make 7 Down a bit tricky."

"How do you mean?"

"I've got a blank, then U,N,T."

"What's the clue?"

"'Essentially female.'"

Dave Hopkirk looked perplexed, then said: "Got it! How about 'Aunt'?"

"Phew. How come I couldn't see that?" Tiring of the game without a nearby victim to entrap, Mowgley stood and shook his friend's hand.

"What you drinking, mate?"

"What's the real ale like here?"

"Like the guv'nor. Full of shit."

"Then I'll have a pint of real lager."

Mowgley made an extravagant gesture towards the heated cabinet on the bar-top. "And will you dine?"

"What's on offer?"

"There's the dish of the day, or perhaps something off the *à la carte* menu - or pasty and chips."

"And what's the dish of the day?"

"Pasty and chips."

"And if I choose from the card?"

"The range goes from pasty and chips to chips and pasty."

Dave Hopkirk stroked his cheek thoughtfully. "Okay. In that case, I do believe I'll go for the pasty and chips."

"Good choice."

* * *

The Area Drug Intelligence officer pushed his plate away, dabbed his mouth fastidiously with a paper napkin and drained his glass. "I can see why you use this place."

"What, you mean the state-of-the-art decor, eclectic customer mix, vibrant and exciting ambience and wide-ranging cuisine and wine list?"

"No. The barmaid with the really big tits."

Mowgley looked across the bar to where Twiggy was pulling a pint for King Dong. She felt their mutual regard, looked up and paused in mid-pump, smiled radiantly, then executed a perfect bunny dip.

"My God," said Dave Hopkirk as Twiggy's swelling cleavage threatened to engulf the pump handle, "you don't get many of those to the pound. Why do you call her Twiggy?"

"Obviously 'cos she ain't," said Mowgley. "Anyway, time you got the shout in. It'll give you a chance to meet Twigs." He waited till his friend was half-way to the bar, then called out: "By the way, get us a packet of salt and vinegar crisps, will you?"

Hopkirk paused. "You're not still hungry, are you?"

"No, but the salt and vinegar box is on the bottom shelf."

* * *

When DI Hopkirk returned, his eyes were still round. He put their drinks on the table and wiped imaginary sweat from his brow. "Strewth. I see what you mean."

Mowgley nodded. "Yep. They sell twice as many salt and vinegars than any other flavour when Twiggy's on duty."

"Talking of big jugs, where's your bag lady today? Are you giving her one, by the way, and if not, why not?"

Mowgley looked sharply up from his pint. "I wouldn't let her hear you say stuff like that, mater. And I ain't too keen on it, either."

"Whoah." Hopkirk waited for a sign that Mowgley was not serious, then held his hands up, palms out in a mock show of contrition. "Only asking, mate." He took a drink, looking at Mowgley over the rim of his glass to gauge the true level of his discontent. "You're a funny bloke. It's alright to get your barmaid to get her tits out, but not to mention your sergeant's."

"It's different," said Mowgley levelly, "Twiggy enjoys all that; my sergeant don't." An awkward silence followed, then Mowgley raised his glass in conciliation: "Anyway, cheers."

He took the top off his beer, then nodded at the copy of the local newspaper laying on the table between them. "I see there's been a bit of a run on your punters. Three more dead since Cottage Grove Pete."

DI Hopkirk looked at the journal and nodded: "Yeah. If you're talking about what we in the trade call 'drug related deaths', we average about two a month on my patch, so three in a row seems a bit heavy. Mind you, it could be just a spike, if you'll excuse the expression. Perhaps it'll even out by the end of the year."

"And were the other two because of an overdose?"

"Not sure yet as all this has happened in the last week. So far, what was in the needles and their arms looks as if it might have been cut by the same loony-bait that did for Pete."

"This Fentanin thingy?"

"Fentanyl. Yeah."

"And did you find any more flour bags?"

"No. No sign of any stashes or even remnants. Each place was as clean as your plate. Which is extra strange."

Mowgley looked at his plate and then paused with his glass at his lips. "Why is it strange?"

"Both were fairly active dealers as well as users."

"So what does 'fairly active' mean?"

"It means they didn't just knock out enough stuff on the side to pay for their habits. They dealt as a business."

"Right." Mowgley tapped his jaw thoughtfully, found a speck of pasty meat and moved it to his mouth. "So do you reckon it could be someone thinning out the competition, or just a coincidence?"

"As I keep saying, I'm not sure, yet." DI Hopkirk drained his glass and stood up. "Time for another, I reckon?"

Mowgley held up his free hand: "Hang on, it's not like you to buy out of turn. It's my shout."

Hopkirk smiled. "You can give me the money if you like. I just thought I'd save your poor old legs." He turned away, then looked back over his shoulder and winked. "Anyway, I fancy another packet of crisps."

* * *

"Cheers again." Mowgley reached up and relieved his friend of one of the two glasses he carried, then sighed contentedly. "This is nice. I hope you don't mind me pounding your ear about what's occurring."

"Any excuse for an early session suits me." The DI opened his third packet of crisps. "To say nothing of the view in here. Go ahead, Mad-Eye."

Mowgley smiled at the use of his school nickname. "It's just that I'm not really clued up with all this drugs stuff. I tried a bit of smoking with Pete yonks ago, and he gave me a sugar cube of green acid, which was an experience, to say the least. But I could never see the appeal of all that messy stuff with needles. I suppose you have to have an addictive personality or whatever they call it."

"I reckon so." DI Hopkirk smiled dryly as he watched his friend roll his fourth cigarette of the session before taking a deep swallow of his beer.

"So," Mowgley continued, "can you give me a sort of *Reader's Digest* about the city scene? How many and how much and that sort of thing?"

"Okay." Hopkirk put his pint on the table as if he would need to use his hands for the address. "Pay attention now, 'cos I'll be asking questions afterwards." He took an exaggerated breath. "Here we go. There's reckoned to be about a thousand regular users in Pompey. About three quarters of them will be male, and by far and away their drug of choice is heroin. They get their gear from a number of sources and dealers. The dealers range from keen local amateurs and semi- pros to more heavy types who come from London or outside Portsmouth on regular runs. Sometimes they supply the suppliers or have little teams of commission-earning salesmen."

"And is there much aggro between suppliers?"

"It comes and goes. Regular intimidation and low-level violence up to GBH and the occasional murder. They try not to knock each other off as it attracts too much attention and gets in the way of business. Sometimes when they want to make a statement, they can get quite inventive with power drills and hooking rivals up to the mains and that sort of thing. But nothing...organised."

"Why do you say 'organised'?"

DI Hopkirk shrugged and ran a finger round the rim of his glass: "Things have been happening in the last year."

"What sort of things?"

"For a start, the price at street level has been dropping sharply."

"Why would that be?"

"Competition, mostly, I reckon. It's as if someone is flooding the market. To be fair, though, the price of H' has been dropping steadily for the past fifteen years or so. In 1985, an average street price would be around £50 a gram. Now you can get a half- gram bag for a tenner."

Mowgley sat back and looked at the smoke rising from the ashtray. "So it could be some sort of big team moving in like an out-of-town supermarket and doing the competition in with special opening offers...and the odd bit of homicide to discourage them."

DI Hopkirk shook his head and smiled at the allegory. "Don't know if I'd put it that way, but yes, I suppose so. Why don't you ask your lady friend?"

It was Mowgley's turn to look round-eyed: "What, the new Super?"

"No. Madame Stanton. People do talk, you know."

"Ah. So what do you reckon to her? And I don't just mean the size of her tits."

Hopkirk moved his shoulders in a don't-really-know gesture: "I've only met her once. I was briefed By BCU that she was coming down a month ago, and we met for a drink when she arrived, but that was it. Her bag carrier calls from London every day to ask for any updates, and I report any unusual movements or events. But that's all. If anything, she seems to want to keep me at a distance."

"You didn't get on when you met, then?"

"Not so much that. It was just like she wasn't really interested in the local scene and didn't want me getting involved in her little project. That's not unusual in this game, as you know better than most. I gave her a couple of my contacts, but as far as I know she didn't use them."

"What about Dave Burgess?"

Hopkirk looked puzzled: "Who?"

Mowgley echoed his friend's expression: "Didn't you give him to her?"

"Not guilty mate. Never heard of the bloke."

Hopkirk finished his pint and looked at his watch: "Blimey.

It's been fun, old pal, but unless there's any more business I'd better get on."

"Can't think of anything else, I'm afraid." Mowgley drained his glass and they stood and shook hands. The Ferry King began struggling into his overcoat, which, he noted, seemed to have shrunk in recent times.

On the other side of the table, DI Hopkirk methodically buttoned his Crombie from the top down, smoothed it and his hair and looked across to where Twiggy was serving Bob the Builder. "I might make this my local. By the way, when are you seeing not-so-plain Jane Stanton again?"

Mowgley finally connected the single button with a hole, then said: "Later today. Why?"

His friend shrugged. "Why don't you ask her about this Burgess bloke and let me know what she says? I'd like to know where she got him from if he's local. And I forgot to say, at our meeting, Milady seemed more interested in you and your lot than my little operation and team."

"Oh? Why's that, d'you reckon?"

DI Hopkirk looked thoughtful, then said. "Well, when you think about it, as an SPU body, she's more interested in wholesale than retail. Where the stuffs coming from and who's bringing it in. Big fish and all that. And as you're the bloke allegedly in charge at the ferry port, it's only natural that she should be more interested in you than me. Or perhaps it's just that she'd heard about your boyish good looks, sense of style and deep level of sophistication and charm. Or perhaps not."

Thirty-two

He found her standing in the shelter of the ancient cloisters, looking up at the spire.

"I bet this is the first time you've been in church for a good while."

She turned, saw him and smiled. "Only weddings and funerals. What about you?"

"Ditto."

"Do you realise this is also the first time we've not met in a pub?"

"Blimey. Why does that make me feel anxious?"

She shook her head and smiled affectionately, "Don't panic, we're going to one now."

As they walked across the green, she linked her arm with his. It was a natural movement, but made him feel somehow uneasy.

She stopped, then cupped an ear: "Listen. It's funny how peaceful it seems in here although the traffic's just yards away."

He nodded "It's the same with graveyards. I never could work that out. Places like this seem to take you to another time, if that makes sense."

She smiled tolerantly. "It makes sense because they are of another time, you dimbo. This old building has been here in one shape or another for the best part of a thousand years.

And it's a cathedral not a church, so a bit special. There was a church here in 1066. Nowadays it's known throughout Britain for its regular displays of modern art."

"I'm impressed. I wondered what that metal elephant was doing over there. I didn't know you took an interest in ancient places of worship?"

"I don't normally, and that elephant is supposed to be a horse. I just had a look at the brochure while I was waiting for you. But I do like old things."

"Is that why you like me?"

"She punched his arm playfully. "Who said I like you, you silly boy?"

* * *

It had stopped raining, and they drove away from Chichester with the roof of the Porsche down. As he cringed in his seat, he saw that Jane Stanton's face was animated with the sheer pleasure of driving fast and aggressively badly. In less than a mile she jumped lights, cut corners and tail-gated and enraged other drivers by changing lanes at the last moment.

Having navigated the out-of-town road system and beaten the descending arm on a level crossing by seconds, their progress was eventually halted by a set of road works.

When he felt able to speak, Mowgley said weakly: "I don't suppose you could think about taking it a bit easier?"

She laughed. "What, do you want to live forever?"

"Brian Blessed as Prince Vultan in *Flash Gordon*. 1980, I think..."

"Eh?"

"Just a game me and my sergeant play. That was his best line."

"She don't like me much, does she?"

"Who?"

"Your bag lady, Mizz. McCarthy."

"That's the second time someone's called her that today. I don't think she dislikes you. So, where are we going?"

"Wait and see."

Leaving a string of drivers in various levels of outrage in its wake, the sports car quit the main coastal trunk route and turned into the old A27 road. As they passed through a small village, Mowgley pointed at a roadside restaurant. It was an 18th-century thatched house, and a freshly re-painted railway carriage sat incongruously in the grounds. Over the entrance was a large sign inviting visitors to come onboard and enjoy the Pullman Dining Experience.

"Once upon a time," Mowgley said, "that was Bert's Caff."

"What, the train?"

"No, the flash restaurant."

She turned and looked at him quizzically. "How utterly fascinating."

He ignored her exaggerated yawn and continued: "Bert was my grandfather. He bought this place for sixpence when he left the Navy. He loved growing his own veg and keeping a few chickens, and he was the local part-time postman as well."

"So you could have been a carrot cruncher instead of a big-city boy. What happened? Why don't you still own it? You'd be rich."

Mowgley shrugged. "My gran hated the countryside. She made him sell up and take a pub in Pompey. Funny how things turn out, ain't it?"

She turned to look at him, the slipstream causing her hair to mask one side of her face. "Sure is. Is that why you have a problem with women? Because your granny sold your birthright?"

"I don't have a problem with women. Well, only if they have a problem with me."

"Fair enough. I'm the same with blokes." She brushed the hair from her eyes and waved graciously to the purple-faced driver of an oncoming lorry as she accelerated past a tractor and returned to their side of the road with all of three seconds to spare.

* * *

Mowgley tottered from the car, took a deep breath and, when stabilised, looked approvingly at the old inn. It was satisfyingly decrepit and unbranded by the dread hand of pub-chain ownership, and stood at the end of a long and winding dead-end lane. Starting directly beyond the garden were miles of mud flats, creeks and narrow channels leading to the open sea.

Jane Stanton followed his gaze and said. "Don't tell me you wouldn't like to spend the winter of your days here."

"As long as I was on the right side of the counter. I know too many bitter former coppers who thought that taking a boozer would be the same as being a customer but getting paid for it." He put his shoulders back and inhaled noisily. "Funny how mud smells quite nice when it's part of the sea, isn't it?" Pointing beyond the pub and across the smoothly shining acres to a distant spire, he said: "They reckon Harold sailed from around here, and may be buried at Bosham church."

Jane Stanton combed her hair with her fingers, then pressed a button on her key fob to restore the roof of the Porsche. "Harold who? Steptoe?"

"Duh. King Harold, dopey. You know, the one who got the arrow in the eye. Allegedly."

"Do you know better?"

Mowgley shrugged. "No, but a lot of people disagree with the story. I reckon it's hard enough sorting out the truth about things that happened last week, let alone hundreds of years ago."

"You're not wrong. By the way, I forgot to ask how you got to our meet. Someone give you a lift?"

"No," Mowgley lied, "believe it or not, I caught a bus."

"I don't believe it. Why?"

"You said to come alone and not to tell anyone, and it made a nice change to sit on the top deck and look in people's gardens. I used to do that when I was a kid, and pretend I was driving the bus."

"You liked being in control even then, then?"

"Doesn't everyone? Especially if someone is taking them for a ride."

* * *

Mowgley stretched contentedly and began to roll a cigarette.

"So is it my turn to ask some questions?"

"If you like. But which ones and why?"

"That's a question, and you said it was my turn."

They were sitting on a raised decking area which ran parallel with the muddy foreshore. Sailing boats and motor cruisers which would have cost more than the price of a modest home in Portsmouth bobbed at deep water moorings or slumped on mud berths closer to shore. Big houses which would be priced at more than a terrace of former Pompey workers' cottages sat in their own grounds, looking smug at the knowledge of their worth and desirability. Mowgley put aside thoughts of envy and reached for his lighter.

"So why did you want to meet me at Chichester? What were you doing there? And why did you say to come alone? Bit dramatic was it not?"

"Not really. I had a bit of business with a friend, and I wanted you all to myself afterwards."

"Was your mate male or female?"

She bridled theatrically. "You're not the only man in my life, you know."

"I didn't know I was in your life."

She blew out a cloud of smoke. "Oh, you are, mate. Very much and for all sorts of reasons. Any other questions, or can we just enjoy the moment?"

"A few more. For instance, why are we here and why are you being so nice to me?"

Her eyes narrowed as she smiled. "Does it show?"

He made no reply, and they drank and smoked and watched a line of sailing dinghies moving slowly along a creek towards the yacht club next to the pub. Then she said: "To be honest, I'm being nice to you because we might not be seeing each other for a while."

"Does that mean you've done what you came down for?"

She shook her head and combed her hair again with her fingers. "No, not yet. But I need to go away for a while."

"To pursue your enquiries?"

"Sort of. Anyway," she reached forward and stubbed out her cigarette in a businesslike manner, "aren't you going to get me up to speed with your enquiries? I hear you've been talking to the local DIO."

"Dave The Drug Hopkirk? We're old mates from school."

"Yeah, so I heard. Mods and Rockers and all that ancient stuff.

No need to ask which of you was what." She paused, then added: "I also heard you've been out and about a bit with your funny little team."

"Funny little team? Do you mind? My team is hand-picked."

"So are vegetables. So let me have it, sweetheart. Go ahead and spill the beans."

When he had winced and commented on her rubbish Bogart impression, Mowgley did what she asked.

After detailing their discovery of the flour bags and DC Mundy's research on the Polish flour mill and the French haulage company and their tailing of the lorry, he fetched another round of drinks.

When he returned, he saw that she was using her mobile phone. She closed it as he approached and reached up for her drink. He slid on to the bench seat opposite her, and raised his glass. "Cheers. So who was that? Another man friend?"

"Not really. It was my guv'nor back at HQ."

"Ah. Is he or she pleased with your progress?"

"I think so. Hard to tell with him, really."

"I had a boss like that. So what do you reckon to my theory?"

"About the Russians bringing in heroin in flour tubs?" She nodded in approval. "It sort of fits. Like you said, hiding a few kilos of white H amongst tons of white flour seems a good idea. But it's a lot to lose in one hit if their truck gets bingoed."

Mowgley nodded. To be bingoed was an ironic term amongst the intercontinental lorry driving fraternity for being randomly selected and searched at the quayside by Customs. Most smuggled shipments of class 'A' drugs were of a modest size not only because they were easier to secrete in small amounts, but the loss would not be disastrous if they were discovered.

"Having said that," said Jane Stanton, "It could be that they only had a kilo or two in that container they offloaded. It didn't have to be all heroin. If it was in plastic wrap and in the middle of the flour in an airtight, foil-lined drum, it would make it awkward for the dogs. And you know what shit people talk about how good dogs are."

Mowgley nodded agreement. "So what sort of money could we be talking about if they are setting up a regular system?"

She widened her eyes, shrugged, then said: "Pay attention. As a very rough yardstick, heroin goes for thirty times the price of gold. That's not because, like gold, it's in short supply, but because it's illegal. Because of all the cutting and messing around with the product, it's very hard to come up with proper figures, but the best guestimate is that the worldwide trade in illegal cocaine, heroin and synthetic drugs is worth anywhere around a couple of hundred billion dollars. To put it in perspective, that's more than double the worth of the combined global tea and coffee market."

She took a pull on her cigarette, then continued. "As I'm sure you know, opium comes from the poppy, and is processed into heroin. The ratio is about ten to one, so a kilo of opium from Afghanistan or elsewhere will make a hundred grams of diamorphine, or pure H. The farm gate price is relative peanuts, but that shoots up with each process and handler. But, for all sorts of reasons, the price of heroin has slumped in recent years."

"Even so, if the Russians are controlling everything from import to sales, it'll be very big numbers."

Jane Stanton nodded. "It certainly will be. Well worth knocking off the small fry and setting up a major supply route through a southern port."

"And they just happened to choose mine," observed Mowgley glumly.

"Cheer up, if they hadn't I wouldn't be here and we would never have met, would we? I hope that's some consolation."

"True. So what's next?"

"In the short term, buy me another drink, then you can show me the place where the tub was dropped off."

"Are you sure?"

"Sure I'm sure. Why not? I just want to see the lie of the land and get a feel for the place. No harm in having a look from the outside before I risk making myself look a right wally again. If the place looks right, I can set up an official tail for next time."

Mowgley emptied his glass and rose from the table. As if speaking to himself, he said: "How did I know this was going to happen?"

She handed him her glass. "How what was going to happen?"

"A return to the scene of the crime."

"Don't worry, we'll do no more than weigh the place up. Anyway, as I said, do you want to live forever?"

Walking to the car, he looked across the mud flats at the setting sun. "No, but another few decades would be nice."

Thirty-three

Compared with her previous performance, Jane Stanton drove almost sensibly through the narrow lanes and long, dark tunnels of skeletal trees.

Mowgley lit and passed her a cigarette from a packet in the glove box and watched as she put it to her lips. The light from the dashboard cast her face in planes of light and shadow, and he thought how serene yet excited she looked.

She felt his eyes upon her and asked: "What are you looking at?"

"I was just thinking how much you like all this."

"All what?"

"This."

She exhaled a plume of smoke and smiled reflectively. "Yes, I reckon I do."

"Did you always want to be in the job?"

"Sort of. It was either the police or the army, but I didn't fancy wearing a uniform, taking orders and being regularly propositioned by some hairy dike."

"So why did you choose the police?"

"Hah hah. What about you? Did you think you could serve the community and help bring law and order to the mean streets?"

"Not really. Why do we do anything? I liked watching *Z Cars* when I was a kid, then I got to know some CID blokes who used my local. I liked the way they'd seen it all but hadn't let it get to them. And some of them did actually want to make their bit of the world a better place."

"Oh yeah? A bit different from the Met, then. And has it all lived up or down to your expectations so far?"

"Yes and no. Mostly no, if I'm honest."

They drove on in silence for a while, then she asked: "Is it far now?"

"No, about a mile."

She lowered the window and the sudden rush of air made the end of her cigarette flare. She took a last drag, then threw it into the dark and re-closed the window. "So tell me about this place. Is it a working factory or a warehouse or just a drop-off point or what, do you reckon?"

"According to my DC's enquiries, it's a rubber factory. Or was."

"I feel a joke coming."

"No, it really was. Hampshire Rubber Mouldings specialised in providing industry with custom-designed grommets and blow mouldings, whatever they are. And they did so for the past forty years."

"So what happened?"

"The factory changed hands last October when the owner retired and his sons didn't fancy a life of grommeting. A holding company bought it, and my DC is trying to find out who holds the holding company."

"But you reckon our Russian friends might be behind the firm? If so, it looks like they're really going into things big time and want to own the means of distribution and perhaps even production."

Mowgley nodded. "The old factory would be a good depot and cutting shop. Just up the road from the ferry port, not too far from the Smoke. Isolated but not too isolated and a good excuse to have lots of machinery and strong smells. They could be cutting and bagging for distribution to London and the south-east until they grow the operation."

"Or the delivery you saw could just be because a lot of Poles work there and fancy a regular and direct delivery of knocked-off home-grown flour."

He gave an exaggerated shrug. "Maybe, baby."

* * *

Inspector Mowgley looked across at Jane Stanton to see if she had noticed what he had noticed. It was not until she had slowed down and braked that he had realised he hadn't told her yet that the turning was after the next bend.

"It's the next on the right," he said.

"Ah."

She snatched a look at him and then said: "From what you said, I thought it would be around the bend."

The Porsche turned into the lane and Mowgley pointed out the lay-by Mundy had used the day before.

She turned the engine off and the lights died, leaving them in darkness.

He looked across at her; "Are you sure you want to do this?"

She did not reply immediately, but continued to look straight ahead. Then she gave a little shrug and turned towards him. "What do you think?"

"Like you said, we could just take a look from the outside."

"Yes. That's true." She continued to look at him for a moment, then took the keys from the ignition and opened the driver's door.

* * *

The premises of Hampshire Rubber Mouldings were in darkness. The low gates were closed and secured with a chain and heavy- duty padlock, and in the yard Mowgley could see that the fork lift and pallets were in the same location as the day before. "Nobody at home, by the look of it."

She nodded and stepped out from the cover of the oak tree. "I reckon you're right."

He turned back towards the car and asked a question to which he already knew the answer. "Shall we beat it, then?"

She frowned. "Seems silly not to have a look round while nobody's here, don't it?"

* * *

They climbed over the five-bar gate without difficulty, her

taking off her high heels and hoisting her skirt, and he assisting.

After replacing her shoes and smoothing her skirt, Jane Stanton led the way past the loading bay and down the side of the main building. They had passed a couple of serious-looking sheet metal doors before she stopped and softly swore.

Mowgley looked around sharply. "What's up?"

"I forgot my phone. We might need it and I need to be contactable. It's in my bag in the car."

He held out his hand. "Give me the keys and I'll get it. Save you doing all that performance with your shoes again."

"Better not, you'll only set the alarm off. I'll only be a tick." Her teeth shone white in the evening gloom. "Just don't wander off and walk into a load of dustbins or whatever."

"I'm going nowhere Ma'am. Trust me."

She turned and walked swiftly away, then he called after her and she stopped and looked back. "What's up?"

"You're not going to get that bloody flame thrower, are you?" She shook her head. "What for?"

Then she was gone and he stood and thought about rolling a fag. He heard a faint rattle and his heart rate soared until he realised it was Jane Stanton climbing over the gate.

After looking around, he walked across to the high chain-link fence running parallel with the side of the building, then sat on a low stack of broken pallets.

He had made himself comfortable and had got his baccy tin out when the dusk burst into an intense, flaring brightness that caused him to shut his eyes and throw up a protective hand.

When he opened his eyes and they had become used to the glare, he saw that its source was a security light above one of the steel doors, and standing in the pool of light was the cause of its illumination. The fox was smaller than the one he had caught in the headlights after leaving the dog track, and perhaps a vixen. Of whatever gender, it was obviously much less well-fed. Being a country fox, it was also much less used to encounters with humans, and quickly loped from the light and into the surrounding darkness. He watched the white tip of its brush until it disappeared, and was leaning over to pick up his tobacco tin when there was a rasping, creaking sound as the door below the security light began to open.

Mowgley left the tobacco tin where it lay and had time to get to his feet and take a few steps away and towards the yard before the door opened fully. Although he could not understand the words, the shout was obviously an instruction to stop.

He turned back towards the light, then slowly raised his hands, palms out, to the level of his shoulders. As well as being an automatic placatory gesture, he did so because the man facing him was holding a gun.

* * *

Although not an expert in automatic weaponry, Mowgley had seen enough action movies to know the man was cradling an AK-47 assault rifle from the distinctive curved magazine and stubby pistol grip. Most importantly, the good news was that it was not yet pointing at him.

The man standing unconcernedly in the full glare of the security light was as tall as Mowgley and much younger. Apart from having a deadly weapon at his disposal, the heavily-muscled arms cradling the rifle indicated he was also in better shape than the detective.

As they stood looking at each other, Mowgley saw that the man was wearing camouflage-patterned combat trousers above heavy boots. Above the belt he wore a blue tee-shirt on which was the Superman logo, and on his head was a ball cap with Mickey Mouse ears. On his face was the sort of mask affected by asbestos workers and Japanese tube travellers during an avian 'flu scare.

With the rest of his features obscured, the only clue to the wearer's mood or intentions were his eyes. They were too far away for Mowgley to make an assessment, but as the man was bringing the muzzle of the automatic rifle to bear on him, he thought it a good idea to raise his hands higher and try to look as least confrontational as possible.

* * *

The tableau held for what seemed a long time.

Then the man spoke, clearly asking a question. Mowgley's experience of Russia and its language being limited to a package tour to St Petersburg with his former wife, he smiled inanely and said 'Thank you' and 'Goodbye' in what he hoped was understandable Russian and an ingratiating tone.

The man grunted with what could have been amusement or irritation, then took a step forward. He also turned slightly, then moved the gun's muzzle round to point directly at the detective. Whether this action was preparatory to the man ushering him through the door or shooting him. Mowgley was never to discover.

As he raised his hands higher and smiled even more inanely, he and the man's attention were taken by a shout from the direction of the yard. After fleetingly registering that her Russian seemed as good as that of the man with the gun, Mowgley spun round to where Jane Stanton stood. Somewhat irrationally given his situation, he felt a burst of relief as he saw that she was holding a hand gun and not the dragon's breath shotgun.

Even more irrationally, her appearance made Mowgley feel empowered to drop his arms and start to walk towards his rescuer.

He had taken almost two steps before the bullet ripped into his body and he lost all sense of who and where he was.

Epilogue

Detective Sergeant Catherine McCarthy and DC Stephen Mundy walked together from the cemetery gates.

"It was quite a turnout," said Melons as they reached her car, "I didn't realise so many people would want to see him off."

"No," agreed Mundy. "I think he would have been pleased."

"Yes. And a lot of the people he worked with would be retired now, but they still made the effort." She pressed the key fob to unlock the car and patted him gently on the shoulder. "At least it was sudden and he didn't suffer."

Mundy nodded. "The doctor said the stroke happened in his sleep. Dad just went to bed and never woke up."

Melons smiled sadly and gestured to the car. "Well, I suppose we'd better go and see if old misery guts has caused a nationwide NHS strike yet..."

* * *

"Why have they put you in here?"

Melons looked round the ward and took in the rows of cubicles containing a profusion of elderly and confused men.

Mowgley scowled and struggled to sit up. "It's revenge by that Scotch cow."

"Its Scots or Scottish, and I don't think calling her Angus or even Doctor Angus is likely to win her over. But why the geriatric ward?"

"She said it's full of grumpy old men who sleep all day and then cause ructions all night, so tailor-made for me. Bloody cheek."

"Never mind." Melons pulled up a seat at the bedside and motioned Stephen Mundy to do the same. "So how are you feeling today? The ward nurse says you're making good progress."

"Then why can't I have a fag?" He adopted a wheedling tone: "Did you bring me some baccy? At least give me a couple of yours so I can have one in the bogs."

Melons shook her head. "You know you're not allowed to smoke until your chest wound gets better. And anyway, Dr McLaughlin disapproves of smoking."

"She disapproves of anything that gives pleasure. And she's got a typical woman's logic. I've explained to her that sports-related injuries cost the NHS five times as much as treating allegedly smoking-related problems. And it's a fact that taxes on fags bring in more than the entire cost of the NHS. *And* smokers die earlier than non-smokers and save the state millions."

"So?"

"So, instead of trying to stop us smoking, the government should encourage people to take it up. The health warnings should be on tennis rackets, not fag packets."

Having worked himself up into a glow of indignation, Mowgley relapsed into a coughing fit.

When he had got his breath back and Melons had again refused to give him a cigarette, Mowgley asked if she knew where DCI Stanton was.

"She's on extended leave at the moment. The word is that she's gone to the South of France. Her secretary at SPU says she needs to recover from the trauma."

"The trauma? The bloody trauma?" Mowgley started coughing again, but waved away the glass of water Melons offered him. "Let me get this straight. She shoots me and gets extended leave to get over the shock?"

Melons opened her handbag and took out a cigarette packet, then remembered where she was and put it back.

"Well, to be fair, she didn't mean to shoot you. Or that's

what her report said. And so far, IU seems to think she did the right thing."

As Melons had told the patient when he was first well enough to receive visitors, there would be a full-scale investigation into events leading up to the shooting. According to a contact in the Investigation Unit, DCI Stanton's initial report said she had returned from her car and heard raised voices from where she had left Inspector Mowgley on watch. She had, as per relevant operational procedure, drawn her sidearm and approached the scene. Seeing the situation and that a fellow officer was in mortal danger, she had made a split-second assessment and decided it was too late for her to attempt to negotiate with the gunman.

Consequently, she had shouted to her colleague to get down, and fired a single shot at the man with the AK47. Unfortunately, Inspector Mowgley had stepped into her line of fire and the bullet had struck him in the upper right chest, causing him to fall to the ground. She had then released three more shots, hitting the man with the automatic weapon and eliminating further threat.

"Did the right thing?" Mowgley rolled his eyes and made a sound deep in his throat. It sounded to Melons like a bad impression of a famous cartoon dog. She leaned forward. "Beg pardon?"

Mowgley made the strange noise again. "I said harrumph. It's what people say in books when they're expressing a mixture of anger and disbelief at something someone has just said."

"And what is it you don't agree with?"

"Most of it." He did not add that, as he remembered it, Jane Stanton had not shouted in English for him to get down, but something in what sounded like Russian. Nor would he be telling IU that, when he briefly came to, he seemed to remember her walking across and standing over him after she had checked that the man with the AK47 was dead. He also had a picture in his mind of her looking down at him. The Glock could have been dangling from her hand, but it seemed to him to be pointing at his head. After a moment, she had put the gun away and taken out her phone. Before he re-entered the darkness, he watched her making the call for assistance, and then dialling another number.

Melons patted him reassuringly on the upper arm. "Ah. Well, you'll be able to give your version of events before IU makes up its mind."

"My version of events? You make it sound like contesting claims about a road traffic accident."

"Sorry. Anyway, do you want the other bit of news about DCI Stanton?"

"Depends on what it is."

Melons looked across the bed at Stephen Mundy, then said. "It's not official, but there's talk that DCI Stanton is going to be recommended for an award."

Mowgley tried to sit up, failed and fell back on the pillows. "An award? An *award*?"

"Yes. Do you know you sounded just like Dame Edith Evans as Lady Bracknell saying 'A *handbag*' then?"

"Bollocks. What sort of award?"

"Erm, the Queen's Award for Gallantry."

For once, Mowgley was speechless. He buried his head in the pillow and closed his eyes, groaning softly.

Melons looked at him for a moment, then reopened her handbag, took a cigarette from the packet, lit it, took a drag and blew the smoke in his face.

Mowgley inhaled deeply, opened one eye and reached out for the cigarette. After a long, almost sensual draw, he slumped back.

Melons signalled to Mundy and as they both stood she said: "Well, we'd better let you get some rest, "Do you need anything before we go?"

Inspector Mowgley took another luxuriant draw on the cigarette. "How about some good news? Am I going to be given an award? Has Cressida double-barrel run off with the bird with the big tits at her office?"

"No, none of that. But there is some really good news."

"So what is it?"

His sergeant held out a hand. "Guy has asked me to marry him."

Mowgley looked at the large and very sparkly ring. "And is that supposed to be good news for me?"

"Of course. For a start, he wants you to be best man. As long as you promise not to try and make a speech at the reception."

CASE SUMMARY

CASE No: O357 (coll. 'The Cabin Trunk Murder')

DATE of REPORT: 28.2.2000. AUTHOR: DC S Mundy

OIC: DI J Mowgley

OOI: DS C McCarthy/ DS D Quayle

OAO: DCI Jane Stanton

SUMMARY POINTS

1. The origins of the two arms in the Hermes handbag found at Sandy Point, Hayling Island remain unknown. The arms are being kept at the mortuary department of the COP Path Lab. The money and substance/s in the bag remain in evidence dockets at CBU.

2. No connection was established between the contents of the Hermes bag and the yacht found run aground at the entrance to the Chichester Channel. The body of the yacht's owner was discovered by a dog walker on the southern tip of Thorney Island four days after the grounding of the yacht. It was established that he had recently bought the vessel and was sailing it single-handed from Ryde on the Isle of Wight. The deceased was a retired Medina Council official and it was his first solo voyage. Investigations revealed he had no links with illicit class 'A' drug operations in the region.

3. The identity of the body found in the Gauguin Suite of the French owned car ferry boat Pont Aven has not been established. Anecdotal evidence suggests that it was the remains of a would-be illegal immigrant, approached by Messrs Burgess and Basayav (see 'Deceased') with an offer to give him passage to the United Kingdom via Portsmouth Continental Ferry Port. He was killed during the overnight crossing and dismembered. The torso was left in the Gauguin Suite; the head, arms and legs have not been recovered. Both

his killers are themselves dead, and there is no evidence of involvement by any other parties.

4. The identity of the male shot by DCI Stanton at the Hampshire Rubber Mouldings site at 1930 hrs on 21.2.2000 was established through the good offices of Europol as being that of Danil Aleksey Bessonov (37). He was a known associate of a branch of a Russian criminal association known as The Brotherhood. In the incident, he suffered one gunshot wound to the chest from a distance of approx. eight metres, followed by two shots to the head at closer range. He was pronounced dead at the scene by the leader of the emergency medical unit summoned by DCI Stanton for DI Mowgley, who was accidently wounded in the incident.

Summary and proposed action/s

After the shooting incident, concerted, co-ordinated and ongoing action by officers of The Metropolitan Special Projects Unit, Hampshire Serious Crimes Investigation Team, Europol and the appropriate divisions of the French and Polish Drug Enforcement Agencies has been under way. Arrests of a number of the principals and operatives of the French haulage company (Livraison Express) and the Polish flour mills (Polskie Factos Maka) have, at time of writing, led to no charges being laid as yet. After a series of targeted (intelligence-led) and an upscale of random searches at the ferry port, no evidence has been found to indicate that the importation of significant amounts of Diamorphine continues. Similarly, no evidence has been produced to confirm that the shipments have ceased. The investigation continues.

Glossary

For reasons discussed at the beginning of this book, Portsmouth has over the centuries developed its own language. As with all such words and expression, the origins of those listed here will depend on whose claim you choose to believe. By definition, street-talk can have no conclusive provenance. The entries are in alphabetical order and I have included some which do not occur in the book. For obvious reasons, I have spelled these non-words phonetically.

Bok:
From the Romany language and simply meaning 'luck', but used in Portsmouth in a negative form to mean the act of bringing bad luck or the person who brings it. My dad claimed my sailor uncle was a bok for Portsmouth FC as they always lost when he was in port and went to Fratton Park.

Brahma:
There are various spellings but only one pronunciation for this word, which can be used as a noun or adjective. Broadly, it means something or someone of outstanding quality, as in 'What a brahma Ruby' (see below) or 'She's a right little brahma.' Unlikely, I would have thought, but it may have some connection to the impressive bull of that name. One of the three major deities in the Hindu pantheon bears this name, which may also have some bearing on the matter.

Cushdy:
Another Romany expression, broadly meaning 'good'. You might make a cushdy bargain, or say that someone has had a cushdy result. Sometimes the word is used on its own in reaction to hearing of someone's good fortune, as in 'Did you hear about Baggy? He's moved in with that brahma-lookin' nympho widow who owns a pub.' An appropriate response would be: 'Yeah? Cushdy...'

Dinlow:

Fool, idiot. Often used in the short form of 'din', and can also be used as an adjective as in 'You dinny tosser.' I am told this is yet another Romany word with common currency in Portsmouth.

Iron:

A gay man. One half of the rhyming slang 'Iron hoof' for 'poof'. Other and seemingly limitless non-pc allusions include shirt-lifter and turd burglar. Lesbians may be referred to as muff-divers or minge-munchers. There is a well-loved if apocryphal tale that, in the 1970s, an anonymous wag took a small ad in the For Sale section of Portsmouth's daily newspaper. The clearly naive young lady who took the call duly typed it up and it appeared next day as follows: *For Sale: One muff-diver's helmet. Only slightly used.* The lovely thing was that her bosses could not reprimand the staff member who took the call for *not* knowing such an improper expression.

Lairy:

This is a very common way of describing an irritating general attitude, as in 'he's a lairy bastard.' Alleged to originate from mid-19th century cockney 'leery', and said to be common to south of England, particularly coastal areas.

Laitz:

A state of absolute rage, as in 'he went absoloootly laitz, didn't 'e?' NB. Another London-esque linguistic custom in Portsmouth is to end statements with a question, as in 'I've gone down the road to see the mush, 'aven't I?' and 'he's only done a runner, 'asn't 'e?' Origin unknown.

Muller:

To murder, but used mostly in a benevolent setting as in 'I could muller a pint'. Allegedly, the expression derives from the name of one Franz Muller, who committed the first murder on a British train when he killed and robbed Mr Thomas Briggs, a banker, on the Brighton Railway in 1864. Muller was hanged later the same year in one of the last public executions at

Newgate prison in front of a mostly drunken crowd said to number 50,000. The murder resulted in the introduction of corridors to link railways carriages and the establishment of emergency communication cords. Again, the expression is said to be common to the South coast.

Mush (pron. 'moosh'):
An address to any male friend, stranger or enemy, to be used as in 'Alright, mush?' to a mate, or 'What you looking at, mush?' to someone you would quite like to hit. Again said to come from Romany, and is now somewhat dated and generally being replaced with greetings to friends and strangers by 'mate'. 'Mater' may be used with a particularly close friend. 'Matey' has more or less disappeared, but was for hundreds of years reserved for people who worked in the Naval Base, as in 'Dockyard matey.'

Oppo:
A naval term for a close friend. According to the most likely source, it is short for 'opposite number' and referred to the man on board who did the same job as you during another watch. It paid to become friends for all sorts of reasons.

Pawnee:
Rain. Corruption of Romany *parni* for 'water' and *pani* for 'rain'. Allegedly also from the old Gujarati word for water, picked up then corrupted by British troops in the early days of the Raj.

Puckah:
Real, genuine or the 'proper job'. For example, Mowgley might say appreciatively: 'Now, that's a real puckah pasty'. Origin, like so many of our slang expressions, is in our days of Empire. In Hindi and Urdu it means 'ripe' or 'fully formed'.

Ruby:
Fairly modern and universally popular rhyming slang for 'curry'. Derived from Ruby Murray (1935-96), a husky-voiced Belfast-born songstress at the peak of her fame in the late 1950s.

Schtum:
To keep 'schtum' merely means to hold your tongue, especially when speaking could cause you trouble. Origin probably from the German 'stumm' meaning 'silent'.

Schtoomer:
An obstacle, block or problem. Yiddish origin.

Scran:
Food. Credited generally to the RN via Liverpool or Newcastle, but also said to derive from Romany.

Shant:
As with skimmish (see below), a noun or verb referring to ale or beer. Some Scots claim it as their own, others attribute it to the Royal Navy.

Shoist:
Free, gratis. As in 'How much was your car?' 'Shoist, mater - I nicked it.'

Skate:
Any Royal Naval rating. The term allegedly comes from the 18th century practice of nailing a fish of that name to the mainmast on long voyages for use by the crew in the absence of any obliging females on board (The genitals of the skatefish are said to be very similar to those of the female human).

Skimmish:
Alcoholic drink, but usually confined to beer. Apparently peculiar to Portsmouth, but origin unknown.

Spare:
Apart from the obvious, this word has two main uses. A 'bit of spare' is an available single female. To 'go spare' is to lose one's temper in an explosive manner.

Sprawntzy:
Smart, well turned-out and confident-looking. Origin not known, but 'sprawny' is Polish for efficient of self-assured.

Squinny:
Once again, a word which can be used as a noun or a verb or adjective. You can squinny or *be* a squinny. Basically it means whinge or whine about something in particular, or to generally be a moaner. According to academic sources it is a derivative of the word 'squint' and came into common use in the Middle Ages, but I am not convinced.

Wheee:
According to decades of research (by me) this word/expression is absolutely unique to Portsmouth. As 'Well I never' might be employed in more refined circles, 'wheee' is brought in to play as a reaction to any piece of information or gossip from the mildly surprising to the truly shocking. Thus it would be used in the same way but with a different level of emphasis if someone said their bus was late that morning, or the next-door neighbour had formed a satanic circle and taken to keeping goats in the back garden for sacrificial and other purposes. I have asked people from all across the county, Britain and the world to try it out, but they can never replicate the depth, subtlety and variety of meaning conveyed by a true Pompeyite saying 'Wheee...'

Yonks:
A long time. Like so many other examples, apparently imported into Pompey *lingua franca* by the RN. Some respected etymologists claim it comes from 'donkey's years', but I think that's a load of cack...

Printed in Great Britain
by Amazon

61420102R00153